This Scot of Mine

Clara could not have made the invitation any clearer.

She didn't know where such boldness came from within her. She had never forayed into intimacy like this. She didn't know she had it in her. She supposed it had something to do with the way he made her feel . . . something to do with the fire in her blood.

He said her name again. "Clara." In that husky brogue of his she felt herself melting, sliding deeper into a puddle of desire.

They hadn't even kissed. Not a true romantic kiss. She did not count the chaste peck the morning of her wedding.

And heavens, she wanted him to kiss her.

She wanted his mouth on hers. She wanted to taste him with an ache that went bone-deep. Despite his gruffness, his mouth looked beautiful. There was a tenderness in the well-carved shape that she wanted to explore.

By Sophie Jordan

The Rogue Files Series
THIS SCOT OF MINE
THE DUKE BUYS A BRIDE
THE SCANDAL OF IT ALL
WHILE THE DUKE WAS SLEEPING

The Devil's Rock Series
BEAUTIFUL SINNER
BEAUTIFUL LAWMAN
FURY ON FIRE
HELL BREAKS LOOSE
ALL CHAINED UP

Historical Romances
ALL THE WAYS TO RUIN A ROGUE
A GOOD DEBUTANTE'S GUIDE TO RUIN
HOW TO LOSE A BRIDE IN ONE NIGHT
LESSONS FROM A SCANDALOUS BRIDE
WICKED IN YOUR ARMS
WICKED NIGHTS WITH A LOVER
IN SCANDAL THEY WED
SINS OF A WICKED DUKE
SURRENDER TO ME
ONE NIGHT WITH YOU
TOO WICKED TO TAME
ONCE UPON A WEDDING NIGHT

Sophie Jordan

THIS SCOT OF MINE

The Rogue Files

AVONBOOKS

An Imprint of HarperCollinsPublishers

THIS SCOT OF MINE. Copyright © 2019 by Sharie Kohler. All rights reserved. Printed in the United States of America. No part of this book may be used or reproduced in any manner whatsoever without written permission except in the case of brief quotations embodied in critical articles and reviews. For information, address Harper-Collins Publishers, 195 Broadway, New York, NY 10007.

First Avon Books mass market printing: April 2019

Print Edition ISBN: 978-0-06-246366-1
Digital Edition ISBN: 978-0-06-246367-8

Cover design by Patricia Barrow
Cover illustrations by Jon Paul Ferrera
Cover photography by Media Photo/Michel Legrou
Chapter opener art by Claudia Pylinskaya / Shutterstock, Inc

Avon, Avon & logo, and Avon Books & logo are registered trademarks of HarperCollins Publishers in the United States of America and in other countries.

HarperCollins is a registered trademark of HarperCollins Publishers in the United States of America and other countries.

FIRST EDITION

19 20 21 22 23 QGM 10 9 8 7 6 5 4 3 2 1

For Rosanne, pumpkin bread–maker extraordinaire . . .
and so much more.
You're the best.

The Curse

*O*nce upon a time, a beautiful peasant girl fell in love with the laird of the castle. The young and handsome laird took the maid's love and gave her his in return—but not enough. For when she told him she was with child, he spurned her, too ashamed to wed someone so beneath him. Heavy with the laird's child, the heartbroken lass was turned out into the cold where she and the babe perished to the Highland winter . . . but not before she invoked this curse:

May all future lairds of Clan MacLarin live out their days knowing they are marked to love, but not to live. Until a laird of the MacLarin line lives to see his firstborn draw breath, this curse shall never be broken.

Chapter 1

*L*ady Clara Autenberry was ruined.

She knew it just as she knew the color of her eyes—a rather dull shade of brown.

Indeed. Her eyes were like mud . . . and so was her reputation. Two unchangeable facts. As invariable as the stars. With every passing mile that carried her farther and farther from London, the reality of her new circumstances became all the more tangible to her.

She was gone from London. Gone from Society. Gone from any life she had thought to have for herself.

Gone. Gone. Gone.

The bricks at her feet and on her lap had long since turned cold. She burrowed into the many blankets occupying the carriage for warmth. The musty pelts prickled her face.

Mama had made certain they packed plenty of furs and blankets for the journey. Between tearful farewells, Mama had warned of the frightful cold. Not that her mother had ever ventured so far north. Mama was warm-blooded and London was cold enough for her. She could scarcely wrap her mind around her children living in such a frigid clime—or being so far away. But away Clara must go.

"I will visit. We all will," Mama had promised with fortifying breath. "In the summer months."

Nodding, Clara had fought back tears. "Of course." She'd donned a smile and tried to be brave as she hugged the rest of her family goodbye. All stood on the stoop, waving as they sent her off to her banishment.

Shivering inside those blankets she now clutched up to her chin, she wondered how much longer it would be until they reached Kilmarkie House and whether she would be frozen to the core before that happened. Almost immediately she squashed the peevish thought.

She didn't deserve comfort. Especially not on this journey. This journey was her penance. As would be the rest of her days. She was a foolish, rash girl and she might as well grow accustomed to the consequences of her behavior.

Guilt was not a misplaced sentiment. After all, Clara was not the only one to bear the weight of her actions. Her entire family was affected. Mama and her stepfather. Her little brother and sister. The twins were but children yet. They did not deserve to suffer the stigma of her actions. Even Enid could suffer as a result of her behavior. Her half sister was presently being courted by the second son of a viscount. Hopefully that budding relationship did not fail because of Clara.

It had become clear to her the moment Rolland broke their engagement and denounced her that she had to go. At once. She must flee.

Before her family became as lost as Clara. She'd known what needed to be done. She was taking herself far away. Removing herself entirely until she was but a foggy memory to all those in Town.

It would be as though she were dead. A dismal thought, but true nonetheless.

It had been her suggestion to travel to Scotland to her brother's home. Scandal would not touch him all the way to the Black Isle where he lived and kept very little Society. Apparently, from his letters, he and his wife enjoyed life there quite well. Clara hoped she would, too.

At least she hoped she would find some contentment, for now it was to be her home.

Her life was forever changed. She would never again be that much-sought heiress, invited to all the most coveted parties, her name included on every hostess's guest list. No more.

Ruined. What a wretched word. As though she were some soured piece of fruit rotted to the point of inedibility.

"You could not have fallen to disgrace when the weather was more temperate?" Marian complained, grabbing the loop swinging above the door as the carriage gave a sudden lurch.

"I didn't *plan* my disgrace," Clara grumbled, gripping the edge of the seat and readjusting her position.

"No?" Marian asked archly, skepticism ripe in the single word.

Clara winced, but didn't object further. There was nothing Marian did not know of her situation. No sense pretending. She knew all of Clara's secrets and could be trusted to keep them.

The carriage hit another rough spot in the road.

"Heavens," Marian moaned, pressing a hand to her stomach. "Will the agony never end?"

"The roads are wretched," Clara agreed.

Soon, however, the agony did come to an end. The carriage pulled to a stop. A scrabbling sounded from the driver's perch as the groom hopped down, followed soon after by the coach-

man. Her stepfather had insisted they take an
armed groom in addition to their driver. Marian
claimed it was because Scotland was full of dangerous men.

Clara did not think there could be too much
danger, however. Her brother would not choose
to live here otherwise. Especially not with his
expanding family.

The armed groom opened the door for them.
They descended with assistance from the groom
and the aid of a block.

"Ohhh." Marian released a long breath. "How
good to be on solid unmoving earth again." Her
lovely round face bore a green hue. Her skin had
been that unfortunate shade for most of the journey north.

"The earth never moved. *We* were the ones
moving," Clara reminded drolly.

"It's like the North Pole here," Marian complained with a shiver, her breath escaping in
cloudy pants.

"Been to the North Pole, have you?" Clara inquired.

"I've never been north of Cheshire before. But
it's a reasonable guess." Marian lifted her skirts,
mindful of the muddy yard, and moved ahead.

Clara assessed the white stone building with
its thatched roof. Warm light glowed from its
windows, a much welcome sight.

"Come, you. Let's get out of the cold," Marian called back to her.

Nodding, Clara followed.

As soon as they entered the dim interior of the inn, the buzz of conversation wrapped around them. A fortnight ago, she would have been wide-eyed entering such an establishment. Even under escort and accompanied by Marian, she would not have dared crossed the threshold. She was a duke's daughter, after all.

The voices were heavy and thick as syrup, masculine brogues that warmed one from the inside . . . similar to the Spanish Madeira Mama liked to sip after dinner. Mama never minded if Clara joined her in an occasional glass. In Spain, her family had been served the drink with every meal, after all. It had been mother's milk to Mama. Moving to England from Spain had been an adjustment for her to be certain. Ladies rarely, if ever, imbibed. One of many differences she had to endure when she became the Duchess of Autenberry.

Clara shifted her shoes on the rough wood planks. The place was dim and musty. She could smell years of smoke in the bones of the building. Cobwebs hung from the high beams. A faded old tapestry depicting warriors armed with swords and pikes, running Roman soldiers into the sea, hung on one wall.

Marian wrinkled her nose as she looked around, looking decidedly unimpressed.

Clara rather liked it. It felt . . . medieval. Almost as though she had stepped through time. She did love reading of knights and ladies. *The Canterbury Tales. Beowulf. Sir Gawain and the Green Knight*. She might look exactly like her mother with her olive complexion and coal-dark hair, but she possessed a keen interest in the literature and history of her father's country.

She shook back her hood, letting the rich velvet fall to her shoulders. A quick pat to her head assured herself that the thick mass of hair was still in place.

It took Marian a long time every morning to restrain the waves for Clara, and even then her hair never felt very secure. One of the housemaids back home typically dressed her hair every morning. Arranging ladies' hair wasn't Marian's forte. She was a governess by training, not a lady's maid.

Hopefully there was someone in her brother's household who could tackle the chore with some success. Otherwise, Clara was going to cut the mass into something more manageable. Whack it off just above her shoulders. The idea was bold. Young debutantes did not wear their hair short. She winced. But then she was no debutante anymore. The reminder produced both relief and a pang of loss. Bewildering, to be sure.

Clara no longer had to concern herself with propriety. She had seen to that. She would live out her days a spinster. But she was free from Rolland at least. That was all that mattered. It was reason enough for her to embrace a life of solitude.

She inhaled the tempting aroma of something savory and delicious that lapped over the musty odor of the inn. Her stomach rumbled, reminding her that she had not eaten a full meal since breakfast.

"Good day, ma'am." An older man, presumably the innkeeper, bobbed his head several times and performed a sloppy bow before Marian.

All of this after giving Clara a quick cursory assessment and dismissal.

Clara gave a resigned sigh. It was something she was accustomed to. Marian with her golden beauty was the quintessential English rose. People were awestruck by her appearance. It happened all the time. Back home and apparently in the wilds of Scotland, too.

Marian's fair curls and sea blue eyes and porcelain complexion were the subjects of sonnets. Usually very bad sonnets, but sonnets, no less.

Clara inspired no poets.

Marian never gloried in the attention. Clara knew it made her uncomfortable. Especially when gentlemen callers would spend more time gawking at Marian, sitting dutifully nearby and embroidering quietly, as they paid call to Clara.

The innkeeper looked to Marian expectantly. "Shall I escort ye tae a table?"

Marian motioned one hand toward Clara, the action quick, her ducked gaze almost embarrassed. "Yes. My mistress and I would like that very much."

She was always quick to correct any misapprehension.

The innkeeper gave a slight start, his eyes shooting to Clara. He looked her over with a small amount of astonishment, as though seeing her for the first time. "Madam?"

Nodding brusquely, Clara addressed the proprietor. "Please tell me there is a very large fire nearby, kind sir."

"Indeed," Marian seconded, chafing her gloved hands together and then pressing them to her cheeks for added warmth. "And refreshments?"

Clara nodded in agreement.

"Aye." The innkeeper motioned vaguely to a closed door on the left. "The parlor is private and where I would typically place such proper ladies as ye, but it is verra drafty, I fear, and ye both appear tae be unaccustomed tae the cold."

"Noticed that, have you?" Marian muttered under her breath as she continued to warm her cheeks with her gloved hands. "Isn't it supposed to be spring soon?" she asked to no one in particular.

Clara cut her a chiding look. "The public room will be fine for us to wait while our horses are refreshed," she reassured him.

Marian glanced toward the door. Boisterous sounds carried from within the room. "In there? You're certain?"

"Of course. Don't be squeamish."

"Och, course ye be welcome tae warm yer bones in there if ye dinna mind sharing the space wi' others." He stepped ahead of them. "I'll show ye tae a table by the fire."

Marian looked at her, shrugged and then trailed after him, the lure of a fire apparently too great a temptation.

Clara followed them through the door into the crowded space.

The room was rowdy and their arrival did not go unnoticed—not in a room largely populated by men. Several stopped and stared, elbowing each other and nodding in their direction.

None of these Scotsmen were shiny-armored knights as portrayed on the tapestry in the entrance hall, but they did look like something from another century in their tartan.

Several boasted beards and hair that flowed past their shoulders. One man picked at his teeth with a dirty-looking dagger, watching them keenly as they were led closer to the fire.

"I can smell them from here," Marian whispered over her shoulder at Clara, her gloved fingers cupping her nose.

"How can that be?" Clara whispered back. "They're not *that* close in proximity."

"Oh, it can be." Marian nodded and tapped her nose. "This never lies."

"Dinna mind the laddies," the innkeeper spoke loudly, casting a warning glare over the room. "They're an uncouth lot, but they ken better than tae bother any of my patrons."

One of the Scotsmen lifted his tankard of ale in salute. "I take 'ception wi' that. We be proper gents! No' an uncouth lad among us."

Marian snorted at that dubious assertion. The innkeeper pulled out their chairs for them while shooting a quelling look to the man.

Marian wrinkled her nose and dusted off her chair before sinking into it. Mama had often laughed that Marian possessed more airs than a queen. It wasn't *un*true. Certainly her manners were more polished than Clara's. Marian was circumspect, never rushing into ill-advised situations and warning Clara against doing so. It was usually Marian's steady advice that tempered her actions.

Except Clara had rushed headlong into her betrothal with Rolland. Even Marian had not been able to save her from that.

Sinking down into her seat in this inn in the middle of nowhere, she felt a hot rush of regret.

Marian had advised her against accepting the Earl of Rolland's suit from the start—but his charm had blinded her. And other factors, too.

Factors she was actually ashamed to acknowledge now.

Every matchmaking mama in Town was eager for him to pay call to *her* daughter and he had chosen Clara. It had felt nice—*good*—to be chosen.

It had felt even better to watch all those mamas and daughters who had treated her so unkindly over the years turn green with envy. So yes. There had been that. Her ego had been a contributing factor to her blindness when it came to Rolland's character. Ashamedly, she could admit that to herself now.

Mama had liked him, too. She had seemed proud that her daughter won his favor above all other debutantes. She wanted the best for Clara and she had mistakenly thought the earl was the best.

Marian had not been so blinded. Not so gullible as Clara or her mother. Servants always talked, and Marian might work abovestairs, but she was still privy to the servants' gossip below and she had warned Clara that Rolland was ill favored by his staff.

Clara had discovered the truth of what manner of man he was on her own. The hard way—and then it had been too late. The banns had already been read. With only a fortnight until their wedding she had felt desperate, trapped like a cornered animal. Desperate enough to do something rash.

"I'll be back wi' some of those refreshments, ladies." The innkeeper bobbed his head and backed away.

The nearby fire succeeded in warming them. They both sighed in mutual satisfaction. Marian finally lowered her hands from her face.

Clara looked around the room as they waited for their refreshments.

Several of the men played cards. Bottles of whisky littered their tables. One man spoke loudly, his brogue slurred, evidence that he was well into his cups. In fact, based on the movements of several of the men, she suspected a great many of them were well into their cups.

"More whisky," one shouted, banging the empty bottle on the top of the table.

A harried-looking serving girl with wisps of hair sticking to her sweating cheeks hurried forward with a fresh bottle. Clara watched with bemusement, making certain not to be too bold in her staring. The last thing she wanted to do was attract further interest.

The same girl who brought the men their whisky soon returned with a tray for Clara and Marian. She set it down and poured steaming tea into cups. Marian wasted no time selecting a buttery biscuit from the tray and biting into it. "Hmm." She nodded in approval and reached for another one while still chewing. "Ambrosia." She patted her stomach. "I fear I've lost a stone since we started this journey."

Clara rolled her eyes at the slight exaggeration. True, some of the inns they had frequented did not boast appetizing menus. Shortly after crossing the Scottish border, they had stopped at an inn that served them a stew more resembling something that would be fed to the hogs.

"You'll soon reap the benefit of my brother's kitchens. I'm told he has an excellent chef."

"We cannot reach there soon enough," Marian murmured around a mouthful. "Aside of this"— she held a biscuit aloft—"I've scarcely eaten anything edible this entire journey."

Clara smiled indulgently at the exaggeration and reached for a biscuit, her hand stalling midair. She shivered as a fresh draft blew through the public room. She leaned instinctively closer to the fire and canted her head to the side thoughtfully. "Did it just become colder in here?" She rubbed at her arms beneath her cloak and glanced about to see if a window had been opened to explain the draft.

Marian shrugged, her concentration fastened on the tea and food before them. "Hmm. Not that I noticed."

The chill did not go away, however.

Goose bumps broke out over her flesh, and she wondered if it was something other than the cold. She glanced around uneasily. She wasn't inclined to superstition, but she remembered when she was little and her mother's aunt had come to visit. She'd been widowed for the majority of her life and wore black bombazine like armor, garbed from head to toe in the stiff fabric. A rosary hung from Aunt Gustava's waist. She constantly clutched and lifted the beads to her lips any time she felt *espíritus* pass.

"What is an *espíritu*?" Clara had asked.

Aunt Gustava had fluttered her old gnarled fingers in the air. "The ones that came before us. They're dead now, but some wander. Lost. You can feel them when they're near. The air grows cold and your flesh feels like ants swarming beneath the surface."

Clara knew it was fanciful, but she found herself wondering if there were *espíritus* lurking about right now. If that could explain her sudden cold . . . her shivering skin, her sense that something had changed.

Her gaze darted about the room, searching for anything amiss.

Everything seemed normal. Nothing had changed since she and Marian first walked in the room. The great fire still crackled feet away. The beleaguered serving girl circuited the room. The boisterous Scots still drank and talked and played cards.

The door to the room swung open and a band of Scotsmen stepped inside, their boots thudding solemnly on the floor.

A sudden hush fell over the room at the arrival of these newcomers, and she knew. Clarity swept over her.

She knew that whatever she felt, whatever she sensed . . . had arrived.

Chapter 2

They were an intimidating lot. Big. Tall and broad-shouldered. Their unsmiling faces set into grim lines. The man at the front of the group stepped forward a pace. Her stomach dipped. Clara would have noticed him even if he stood to the back of the group. He was not to be hidden. He was the tallest, his shoulders the broadest, but he was also the youngest. Not a streak of gray in his gleaming brown hair. Even though several of the new arrivals boasted beards, he did not. She had a clear, unfettered view of his face.

And it was a spectacular face.

Marian noticed, too. "Oh, my . . ."

Clara did not need to look at her friend to ask the meaning of that remark. It was perfectly understandable. Any female with eyes would react to the sight of this man. She certainly was because she was gawking at him. At his ridiculous square jaw. At the lovely lips, even if unsmiling. The deep-set eyes so icy a blue that she could even detect their stunning color across a dimly lit room.

In the sudden hush, tension swelled on the air. She looked back and forth between the two groups of men, sensing the words, the challenge, even if unspoken, passing between them.

Trepidation joined with the anxiety pumping through her blood.

Self-preservation bade her to gather Marian and go. Leave at once as any proper, safety-minded ladies of good breeding would do.

And yet she stayed put.

The new arrivals were all attired in tartan like the others already here except they wore different colors. She knew that meant they were from a different clan. Rivals perhaps. She'd read that these Highland clans frequently harbored long-standing rivalries.

"MacLarin!" one of the inebriated Scots shouted. "Fancy seeing ye 'ere!"

The man with the spectacular face had a name. Of course he had a name. *MacLarin.* She whispered it in her mind, committing it to memory for those long spinster nights ahead.

MacLarin. MacLarin. MacLarin.

Too bad she didn't know his Christian name. That would feel much more intimate for all future fantasizing.

MacLarin stepped deeper into the room, which cast more light on him from the nearby fireplace and lanterns. "Is it?"

Her breath strangled in her throat. Even his voice was mesmerizing.

No doubt he could feel her stare. She couldn't stop it. Couldn't look away. Couldn't force it into something casual instead of what it was—a manifestation of her most ardent admiration.

He was like something in an oil painting. She could imagine him depicted on canvas—a wild Viking launching himself from a boat, sword in hand, ready to raid. Or perhaps a magnificent steely-eyed god, casting thunderbolts down from the sky upon hapless mortals.

"I believe you're in the wrong place," MacLarin charged, his brogue velvet deep.

He was not yelling and yet the weight of his words dropped with no less force. She wondered what that was like, to have that kind of power, to possess such ability to influence with mere voice.

All her life people had made a point to make her feel less, believing they had the right because she was undeserving, the daughter of an upstart who did not deserve to be the Duchess of Autenberry.

When Rolland proposed, Clara had thought things would be different.

She had thought she had finally *arrived*.

She had thought she was finally accepted among the *ton*.

The reminder of her naivete stung, and she told herself not to be dazzled by this man's handsomeness. He was merely a man at the end of the day. Two legs and eyes like all the rest of them. Rolland had dazzled her and look how toxic he had turned out to be.

"Nay. I'm no' in the wrong place." The man seated at the table adopted a thoughtful expression and leaned back in his chair idly. The legs creaked under the pressure. "I felt like celebrating and preferred tae do it 'ere. So close to yer home."

One of the men beside MacLarin lunged forward, his face red and blustering, "Ye bastard!"

MacLarin caught him, a strong, well-shaped arm stretching out to stop him. "Easy there now, Graham."

Clara's gaze traveled the length of MacLarin's arm. His forearm was covered in some manner of leather bracer. The kind of thing a warrior would wear into battle. She sat a little higher and craned her neck, attempting to better see what she could of him within his cloak—and yes.

There, at his side, a sword was strapped. He was a flesh-and-blood warrior directly from the pages of a story book.

"What is happening?" Marian hissed across the table.

"Shh." Clara waved her silent, watching avidly, not risking looking away for fear that she might miss something in this encounter.

It was simply too diverting. Better than a novel because this was real.

Graham spat on the ground and growled in a brogue so thick she could scarcely understand him. "Ye would no' be celebrating because ye came in possession of a fine bull, would ye?"

"A bull?" The man at the table blinked and looked with mock innocence at each of his companions. "Och, ye lost yer prize bull, did ye? I think I 'eard tale of that." He tsked and shook his head. "Terrible news that! Fine beast ye 'ad there. Ye canna trust anyone these days."

"My bull is no' lost," MacLarin inserted calmly, resolutely.

"Nay?" The man seated was clearly enjoying himself. "Is it no' lost tae ye then, MacLarin? Certain of that, eh?"

"*You* took my bull and you damn well ken it, Bannessy." Again, he spoke with quiet menace, and the gooseflesh on her arms prickled anew. "I'll be having it back."

Then he smiled—MacLarin—and she realized with some awe that he was enjoying himself, too. They all were. The air was thick with tension and these men were reveling in it.

"Och, MacLarin. Ye think *I* took yer beast?" Bannessy pressed a hand over his chest, dropping back down on all four legs of his chair. "That's a 'arsh allegation." His mirth faded as he stared at MacLarin standing across from him. "Prove it."

Long moments stretched whilst neither spoke. A bit of wood cracked and crumbled in the hearth, sparks popping in the silence. She dared not blink for fear of missing something. She adjusted in her seat, her hand gripping the back of her chair.

It was quite the most extraordinary scene. Something one might see enacted on a stage, although of course it wouldn't be nearly so realistic as this.

"Clara," Marian whispered loudly, "we should leave."

MacLarin heard her. He looked in their direction.

Clara's grip on the back of her chair tightened and she straightened her spine, her unblinking eyes watching him.

His gaze touched on her first and then Marian before looking away, dismissing them.

Clearly they were of no interest. Clara released a huffy breath, unaccountably offended.

Then, unexpectedly, his stare flew back to her. As though she had called him to look again at her. His glittering gaze settled on her. She couldn't breathe. He stared at her. *Her.*

Not beautiful Marian.

Not the Duke of Autenberry's ruined sister.

Not the Earl of Rolland's rejected betrothed.

He was seeing *her.* Clara. Her heart squeezed.

Squaring her shoulders, she stared back, suffering the arctic bite of his eyes.

She knew she looked out of place in this setting. She and Marian were the only pops of color in the room—she in her rose-colored dress and Marian in sunny yellow. In fact, aside of the serving girl, they were the only apparent females in this establishment. He was probably wondering how two seemingly proper ladies ended up here.

Their stare-down couldn't have lasted very long, but his gaze left its mark, inscrutable as it was. It singed her skin. She would think about it long past when she left this place. Which was the height of wrongness. She knew better. She had learned not to let one's pretty wrapping addle her head.

Wrong choices were a thing of the past. She had vowed that there would only be solid, sensible decisions in the future. She would be making no more life-altering mistakes. No more poor judgment. She'd learned her lesson.

"Clara, he's staring at you," Marian hissed.

One of MacLarin's friends nudged his arm and whispered something, clearly prompting the man to end his rude staring.

With a decisive nod, MacLarin strode forward to the table. She jerked in her seat when he grabbed Bannessy and hauled him to his feet, dragging him over the table in one ruthless move.

Mayhem erupted.

It was as though a torch had been lit. MacLarin's men dove for the other men. The Scotsmen met and clashed, knocking over tables and chairs and crockery.

Marian screamed and jumped to her feet. Clara followed suit—minus the scream. She gaped in silence, her gaze following MacLarin as he rushed through the fray.

She'd never witnessed a fight. She did not realize it could happen with such . . . ease—or such ferocity.

MacLarin was beating the feathers out of his opponent.

She knew she shouldn't find it diverting. Or stimulating. This was a taproom brawl. Hardly dignified. It was boorish behavior. Savage.

Yet she was enthralled . . . and standing much too close to it all.

"Clara! Back!" Marian tugged determinedly on her arm, trying to pull her to the wall where she pressed herself.

Clara couldn't oblige. This was as close as she ever got to real life. Unfettered. Honest. In Town everyone wore masks. They presented one face and then stuck the dagger in your back when you turned. This was real. This was true.

The din was blaring, but that didn't stop the innkeeper's voice from carrying over the melee. "Stop this! MacLarin! Bannessy! Yer ruining m'place!"

MacLarin dealt a swift blow to Bannessy's chin, lifting him off his feet and propelling him backward—laughing all the while.

Laughing. The man actually laughed with all the irreverent joy of a boy at play.

The proprietor wagged a finger in his direction. "I 'spect payment fer the damages, MacLarin!"

Bannessy stumbled back to his feet, tossed his long hair from his face and charged MacLarin, catching him in the middle and launching them both onto a table alarmingly close to where she stood.

MacLarin managed to twist himself atop Bannessy, delivering several grinding punches to his opponent's ribs.

Clara winced. She had never seen such violence . . . and yet the men appeared to be enjoying the brawl—delighting in it even. It was as though they found life in the act of destruction.

It was insanity and yet she could not look away

from the primal scene. *He* was primal. Laughing, growling, fist-swinging . . . she did not know men like him existed.

"Clara! Wake up, would you? Cease your ogling." Marian seized her arm and started pulling her through the fracas. "Let's go."

It was no easy task. They dodged bodies and fists and flying objects.

A whisky bottle spun through the air and Clara jumped back a step, narrowly avoiding being struck in the head. She didn't escape the spray of alcohol, however. The front of her dress was soaked with the pungent drink.

"Clara!" Marian called from several feet away. Her companion stood free of the rabble, closer to the door. The space between them quickly filled up with tussling bodies. Clara stood on her tiptoes, trying to keep sight of her friend. Marian hopped, her head appearing and disappearing amid bodies.

An opening appeared through a crack in bodies and she darted for it. She was almost there, almost to Marian when a person collided into her. She cried out as she flew into one of the only tables still standing.

The air left her in a rush as they crashed to the floor, the table broken to jagged bits beneath them.

She wasn't alone on the floor.

A man was wrapped around her. His body bigger, harder. Solid. He draped over her like a heavy blanket, his breath warm on her cheek.

His chest mashed to her chest, his heartbeat a strong thud against her breasts.

Hard arms came around to circle her—almost as though he was attempting to save her from being crushed. Except she didn't feel very saved. She felt well and thoroughly caught. *Pinned.*

"Oww," she moaned, coming awake to the discomfort of a man who outweighed her by roughly four stones suffocating her. "Can't. Breathe."

Or move.

Or see much of anything save the spots and stars flashing in her vision.

She managed to punch weakly at his shoulder. "Get off me, you great lummox!"

"Are you daft, lass?" The MacLarin brute lifted up off her and she expelled a great gust of air.

"Me?" she managed to get out, still recovering her breath. She scrambled up into a sitting position, pressing a hand to her bodice and wincing at the soaked fabric beneath her fingers. "I'm not the one engaging in fisticuffs and injuring innocent bystanders . . . you, you . . . Highland savage!"

His eyes widened and she realized a bit belatedly that she should not have perhaps insulted the man.

"Beggin' your pardon," he sneered. "It's a rare thing for *innocent* bystanders tae cast themselves in the midst of matters that dinna concern them." He spit out *innocent* like it was something he doubted existed. Something he doubted *she* was.

"Oh!" She gathered up her considerable skirts—slapping his hand away when he extended it to assist her. He was clearly *not* a gentleman. He did not need to pretend otherwise.

Standing, she looked down her nose in the precise manner she had seen her haughty half sister do many times. Enid had perfected the art of disdain. "Perhaps you and the rest of these *gentlemen* should take a reprieve from pummeling each other to death over a . . . bull, was it?" She squeaked and jumped closer to him as a chair flew through the air and crashed into the wall above her head.

His nostrils flared but he didn't so much as flinch. No, he did not even cast the remnants of the chair a glance. He stared. Unflinching. At her. Acting as though chairs were thrown near his head all the time. Perhaps they were. This man reeked of danger. He probably was accustomed to a life riddled with chaos and disputes.

"It's a *prize* bull. No' so easily replaced."

She snorted. "He's a . . . cow."

"A bull is no' a cow," he said with disgust.

She rolled her eyes and waved a hand around

them. "You're squabbling like children and should be ashamed of yourselves."

He made a show of sniffing in her direction. "You should mind your drink, lass. It might save you from being so clumsy and verra nearly getting yourself maimed."

"I haven't been drinking! One of you splashed whisky all over me and now I smell like a distillery!"

His gaze crawled over her, stalling on her already hot face . . . and she felt her face grow only hotter under his scrutiny. Even the murkiness of the room couldn't hide how red her face must be.

Her once elegant coiffure felt lopsided. A lock of ink-dark hair fell in her face. She blew at it and when that didn't work she tried to shake it back off her face in an attempt to appear dignified. The attempt fell woefully short.

He watched her keenly, one corner of his mouth lifting up in a mocking smile. Oh, the beast. He was laughing at her.

Suddenly his hand came up and he touched that lock of hair, seizing it between two fingers and tucking it back into her messy coiffure.

Everything around her blurred and faded to the background. The brawl still raged around them, but she couldn't focus on anything but the man in front of her—his face, his brilliant gaze, the lips that were so close, moving now as he spoke in that low, guttural brogue, "Aye, lass. This be no place for the likes of you."

"This is a public establishment." She pushed at his chest and tried not to notice the breadth and firmness under her fingers. He was like stone. He failed to budge. "I have every right to be here." Blast. Why did her voice sound so small and trembling? Her eyes betrayed her, drifting to his much-too-near lips in consideration. They looked . . . soft. He was all hardness except there.

Goodness, where had all the air gone?

It was like he had reached inside her and yanked out her very breath. Her lungs felt tight and compressed. She desperately fought to suck in oxygen.

She had permitted Rolland to kiss her. A simple and chaste kiss. *Before* she learned what manner of man he really was. Before she learned of his depraved practices. No female in his household was safe from him. She shuddered, imagining what her life would have been once she belonged to him. Once she lived beneath his roof.

That kiss, thankfully, had been brief.

Standing here like this—chest to chest—the sensation of his fingers on her hair felt much more intimate than that perfunctory kiss of a lifetime ago.

Fighting off the dizzying effect he had on her, she continued, "Shame on you for turning this place into a madhouse . . . unfit for civilized people."

He chuckled and she felt that sound right in the pit of her stomach. "Mayhap a civilized and delicate Sassenach such as you should no' have ventured so far into the Highlands."

"I'm not delicate." She was many things, but not that. "This is chaos for anyone anywhere at *any* time."

He chuckled, studying her as though she were some specimen he had never seen before. She well understood the sentiment. "You're a feisty lass."

Marian was suddenly at her side, crouching low and panting, her eyes darting wildly as though she feared attack. "Come. We're leaving."

"Aye." The Scot nodded with a grin that didn't match his solemn eyes. "Run along now. This is no place for tender ladies." He addressed them both, but his gaze stayed fixed on Clara.

She bristled.

He was right, of course. She should leave, but she didn't appreciate being ordered about by anyone. It brought forth a slew of uncomfortable memories.

Rolland had commanded her. When she first hinted at ending their betrothal, he had revealed his true nature. The ugliness inside him had come out in full glory.

You're mine and I'll never release you. Understand that, Clara? Now whatever notion lurks in that dim brain of yours, forget it. You will do as I say like a good little cow and show up at the church or I'll drag you there myself.

Of course he had changed his mind.

She had seen to that—even if it had resulted in her present circumstances. She harbored no regret. It was the only way. It had been the only way for him to release her from the betrothal.

"Clara!" Marian pleaded as a pair of scuffling men slid near their feet, forcing them to dance sideways lest they get dragged into the fray.

MacLarin smirked. He knew the outcome. Knew they would leave—flee with their skirts hiked around their ankles.

Even though she wished to thwart him, wished to wipe the knowing glint from his blue eyes, she permitted Marian to pull her away. It was the sensible thing to do, after all.

They fled the inn to the safety of their carriage. To their very cold carriage—the perfect metaphor for her future existence.

Cold. Safe. Where nothing would ever happen to her.

Chapter 3

"Ye feeling out of sorts?" Graham plopped down across from Hunt, setting a fresh bottle of whisky on top of the table with a decided clack.

Hunt shrugged and glanced around.

The room had mostly been set to rights, the broken furniture and glass cleared away. Hunt and Bannessy had already paid the innkeeper for this day's deeds. The innkeeper was mollified for the time being. Until the next time. And there would be a next time. There always was.

Graham shook back the long auburn strands from his face, showcasing the nasty bruise forming around his eye.

Hunt reached across the table and dragged the bottle of whisky toward him until he was practically hugging it to his chest. "I'm fine. Why do you ask?" He gripped the particularly stubborn cork top and tugged it free with a pop.

"Yer always more cheerful after a brawl."

Hunt dipped his head in acknowledgment of that truth. Nothing cheered him more than knocking skulls. It was a distraction. It was a release from the constant hunger prowling inside him, however fleeting.

This time had been different, however. There had been no release. No. Instead there had been *her*. A definite distraction. Only not the kind he needed.

With an exasperated sigh, Graham reached across the table and snatched back the whisky bottle. "Give me that if ye dinna intend to pour. What's ailing ye?" He poured himself a generous glass, liquid splashing all over the table. "Yer no' the one whose face feels like a horse trod all over it."

"Still without my prize bull," he grumbled as if that were the source of his ill temper.

"Och, we'll get 'im back. Ye 'ave more friends than Bannessy does. People like ye more. Someone will give up the location of that bull. The bastard canna 'ide him from us forever. No' as big as 'e is." He winced and worked his jaw. "Think my tooth might be loose."

Hunt reached across the table and tapped a

finger against his friend's ravaged cheek. "Looks like raw meat."

"Och! Stop. It 'urts!" He swatted at Hunt's hand and downed his glass, immediately pouring himself another.

Hunt's gaze swung toward the doorway. Even though she had long since passed through it, he still stared at the spot he had last seen her. "Did you see the lass?" He couldn't help asking.

"The bonny fair-haired lass? Aye, I'll be seeing her in my dreams."

"Nay, the other one. With the dark hair." The fair-haired lass was beautiful, but nothing like her friend. Her friend had been extraordinary—even if she possessed the temperament of a viper. He scowled. "She looked at me like I was something unsavory . . . a bit of dung beneath her boot."

"What do ye expect? She's a Sassenach. And a grand one from the looks of her fancy togs. They've probably come tae tour castles and trod all over the graves of fine Highlanders simply tae relieve their bored little lives." He slammed back another glass and poured a third.

His words did nothing to alleviate the uncomfortable sensation in his chest. Sassenach with a bored little life or not, the memory of the lass nagged at him. She was different. Sultry-eyed. Shiny hair darker than the deepest loch.

He snorted. The thought was far too poetic for

him. He did not think about women in such terms. Or rather he did not permit himself to think about them. Not like that. Not in any manner that might lead to true and carnal interest. He was far too careful for that.

When the need for female company struck him, there was Catriona. Safe, beautiful Catriona. Their arrangement was simple and it satisfied both of them. He didn't have to live his life like a monk. A very good thing indeed.

Up until now, Catriona had always been enough. When he had an itch to scratch, she had satisfied it. He'd never longed for anyone else. That way led to ruin. But a few minutes with a dark-haired lass and suddenly his skin felt too tight for his body . . . his thoughts spinning and going places they had never dared tread before.

The lass had sparked something inside him. Something he couldn't shake. He knew the sensation for what it was, even if he had never felt it before. *Yearning.* But he would cast it out. She was gone. Vanished into the air like smoke. There was no risk of seeing her again.

He reached for an empty glass. "Damn it all," he mumbled.

He would never see her again. There was no harm in letting himself think about her a little longer. Staring into the flickering flames of the fire, he remembered those almost feline eyes of hers . . . the brown like an aged cognac. Her mouth looked like a Renaissance painter had brushed it on—full and dusky pink and like something out of a dream. And her voice. She had a voice throatier than most females. Refined and cultured, but with a husky gravel that made his skin prickle with heat. *Had* made his skin prickle. No more.

He took a long gulp of whisky and poured himself another glass, noting how closely the color matched her eyes.

Suddenly, he cursed. Permitting himself to think about her was an exercise in stupidity. It only made him want what he could never have and he had given up on wanting things he couldn't have years ago. He knew better. He'd always known his limitations.

Living under the cloud of his curse had taught him that he could never forget. Never want. Never love.

KILMARKIE HOUSE ROSE up through the misty Scottish fog. Clara's shoulders sagged and she exhaled with some relief as she peered out the window of the carriage at her brother's home. They were finally here. She was glad for that. It was her future home after all. The relief rushing through her soured somewhat at the reminder.

She could never go back.

She let that fact roll around in her head like an aimless marble. Mama and Colin and the rest of her family were very far away. They had not forced her to leave Town, but she knew it was for the best. They'd insisted she could stay, but she couldn't do that to them. She was a damaged creature. She would not inflict any of her shame on them.

She would only see them occasionally. No. Not occasionally. *Rarely*. Her throat tightened. There would be no theater. No shopping on Bond Street. No riding through the park with Marian. No museums or ices at Gunter's.

She shook away the dismal thoughts and vowed to make the best of it.

Kilmarkie House looked lovely. Something out of one of the storybooks her mother had read to her as a child. Alyse had written to her of the dolphins visible from the shoreline. She said it was only a short walk from the house. Clara couldn't wait to see for herself. After the upheaval of the last couple months, she looked forward to peaceful days. Strolls along the shore. An exploration of the grounds. She was certain she could count on her brother to have an extensive library.

"At last!" Marian scooted eagerly to the edge of the seat as though she would launch herself from the carriage the moment the door opened. "A proper meal and a proper bed." She nodded enthusiastically, the golden ringlets framing her face bouncing charmingly. "I cannot wait." The rigors of travel had not even dented her loveliness.

Clara exhaled. "Nor can I. First I will stand in front of a fire and thaw myself." Later, she would take herself to see the dolphins. Perhaps tomorrow. Once she'd had a good night's sleep. Once her bones unfroze and she had reunited with her family.

She winced and braced herself, undeniably nervous of the forthcoming reunion. There would be some awkwardness. How could there not be? She was coming to them in a state of disgrace. Her brother no doubt would want an explanation. He deserved that.

As they stepped down from their carriage, they arrived to a warm welcome. Apparently the explanation would wait.

Marcus and a trio of dogs barreled toward them. The dogs were the size of small ponies in varying shades of brown and gray. The beasts ran ahead of Marcus. Tall and handsome as always, her brother looked exceptionally fit, attired in riding clothes and looking rather windblown with his cheeks ruddy and his dark hair tousled around his head.

He swept her up in a hug, her feet skimming the ground. She gave a small squeak of delight, patting his shoulders. "We weren't expecting you for another few days. You made excellent time."

She nodded as he set her back down on her feet, not bothering to disagree even though the journey had not felt brief in the least.

The massive front door to the house opened. Some members of the staff emerged, preceding Alyse, Marcus's wife. Her sister-in-law advanced at a waddle, her belly protruding several inches in front of her.

"Hello, there," she greeted, embracing Clara. "We're so delighted to have you here with us."

"And I'm so looking forward to being here . . . and being a proper aunt." Her gaze cut to Alyse's stomach. "Soon from the looks of it?"

"Aye, soon." Alyse smiled up at Marcus as he slid an arm around her generous middle and pulled her close. It had been almost two years since Clara had last seen Marcus and Alyse and they looked quite well. Alyse's skin was luminescent, her eyes bright and her lovely light brown hair shiny as a penny.

"Now, Clara, I hope you'll forgive us." Alyse reached out and settled a hand on Clara's arm in a conciliatory manner. "We thought you wouldn't be here for a few more days. We've dinner guests this evening." She bit her lip, watching Clara hopefully.

"Oh." Her chest deflated a bit. She had been anticipating some time to acclimate with Marcus and Alyse. She had not counted on guests—

strangers. From everything she had heard, there was not much in the way of Society in these parts. That had been a contributing factor for her to relocate here. She was not aware Marcus and Alyse were given to much entertaining, isolated as they were.

And yet staring at Alyse's hopeful face, she knew she could not object.

Alyse rushed on, "There should be time enough for you to catch a quick nap so that you can be refreshed before the dinner hour. Cook is making her famous chipolata sausages. They're these wonderful decadent things. You will love them."

"They sound marvelous," Clara managed to get out.

They were taking her in . . . damaged as she was. She did not want to be inflexible. She did not wish to be difficult. She needed to be as bright and merry as possible. *Grateful.*

"Of course." She forced a smile that felt brittle as glass on her face. Her brother watched her closely so she fought to keep the smile in place. "That sounds lovely. I'd love to meet any friends of yours."

Alyse looped arms with her. "Of course. They shall become your friends, too." Her fingers gave a comforting squeeze. "This is your home now, after all. All our friends will be yours."

Chapter 4

Clara woke foggy-headed to a mostly dark room. Someone had lit a lamp on the dresser and she blinked in the near darkness, lifting her head from the pillow as her eyes adjusted to the gloom.

Night peeked between the curtains and she knew she had slept well past dusk. She was still tired. Exhausted. She stretched with a moan. The rigors of the journey had finally caught up with her and she felt as though she could sleep well into tomorrow. Indeed, next week. Alyse was wrong. The brief nap had not been enough. She hardly felt refreshed.

"Wake up. It's time for dinner. Let's get you dressed, my lady."

It was the maid who had helped her settle into her chamber earlier. Clara groaned in discontent and scratched her head, her fingers catching in the snarl of her tangles. It would be a chore to tame the mass.

Marian was likely sleeping in a comfortable bed nearby, happy that someone else would take over the task of Clara's hair for a change.

It would be strange not dining with her after so many nights of each other's exclusive company. Clara had invited her to dine with them tonight, but her friend had declined.

"I intend to sleep until well into tomorrow," Marian had said. "And I think it best if you spend the evening with your brother and his wife and their guests without the hindrance of me."

The maid tugged Clara from bed. Biting back a grumpy reply, Clara obliged and pushed herself to her feet. She longed to sleep more, but she wanted to eat, too. Her stomach growled as though to confirm this. She was certain it would be as excellent a meal as Alyse promised. And after the meal, after their guests departed, she would sit her brother down for a much-needed conversation. She dreaded it, but it needed to be done.

Certainly once he knew the full truth the worry would fade from his eyes—at least in part. Because the reality would create a new set of concerns for him.

Her reputation was in tatters. Just not in the manner he thought.

The situation was not what he thought. It wasn't what *anyone* thought, but he deserved the truth and she would not be able to keep it from him for long even if she wanted to.

She would get it over with tonight.

The maid helped her dress into a ruby gown fringed in gold piping. Mama had never dressed her in the pastel colors that so many other debutantes wore. With their similar coloring, Mama knew what best suited her. She insisted Clara needed bold colors to complement her olive complexion.

Once Clara was dressed, the girl skillfully arranged her hair into plaits and artful loops atop her head. Looking at herself in front of the mirror, she almost felt like the girl she used to be—back in Town.

She descended the stairs to join her family for dinner, feeling decidedly more confident in her elegant dress and arranged hair. Armored.

She felt ready. Prepared for anything. Even the revelations to come that would be uncomfortable and more than likely incite her brother's wrath. He'd warned her that the Earl of Rolland was not a good match.

A valet opened the doors to the dining room for her.

"I'm sorry I am late." Her gaze swept the dining room, lighting on her brother and Alyse . . . and a third person. He rose to his feet slowly, his eyes widening as his gaze settled on her.

She stopped and swallowed thickly.

Oh. No. Not him. She was ready for anything except him.

"You," she breathed.

She wasn't supposed to ever see him again. Her hands opened and closed at her sides as though she needed something to grip . . . something to hold on to amid the sudden storm of her thoughts.

What was *he* doing here? Had he followed her? It seemed too incredible to believe. How had her brother permitted him in the house?

Her gaze rolled over him. He was attired somewhat better in a jacket, even though he still wore his tartan kilt. A large strip of the same fabric wrapped around his torso and up over his shoulder, pinned in place with an ornate clasp. His hair was groomed tidily and didn't fall around his face like he'd just dashed over wind-swept crags.

Then it dawned on her. He was their guest. To quote Alyse . . . their *friend*.

It was inconceivable, but glaringly evident. Her brother was friendly with a savage Scot that destroyed establishments . . . over a cow.

"Aye," he acknowledged with a nod of his

head, his eyes resuming their normal size. "It is I."

Marcus and Alyse both looked back and forth between them in bewilderment. "You two have . . . met?"

Clara nodded, her face overly warm. "Yes. On the way here we stopped to freshen the horses. This man was . . ."

How did one explain it?

Involved in a brawl? Destroying the inn over the matter of stolen livestock? Crushing me with his bigger body and brushing the hair from my face far too intimately?

"I was there as well," the Scot offered in that deep, shivers-inducing brogue.

Nothing more than that. Nothing about the brawl or how inappropriate their encounter. Nothing about how their bodies had been plastered together.

It was just as well.

The memory made her face burn fire.

He, however, looked quite unaffected. Indeed there was no hint of that past exchange between them at all. No mention of that history between them in his speech or manner, but there was an awareness gleaming from his eyes. He well remembered their sparring banter. One corner of his mouth curled. And he knew she remembered, too.

"We were not formally introduced," she said.

"Ah. Of course." Her brother seemed satisfied enough with that explanation. "Laird MacLarin is our closest neighbor, Clara. He has become a true friend to me and Alyse."

A laird. Blast it all. So he was no *ordinary* Scot stirring up trouble at the local inn then. No local riffraff, it seemed, but a man of position and property. His arrogance made a bit more sense now, but it was still inexcusable. She was quite done with boorish men.

Immediately she felt self-conscious, the balance between them suddenly shifted. By all accounts, in her current status, her own family could have cast her out and Society would not frown on them for it. No longer deemed fit company for those of quality, *she* was not *his* equal and that fact rubbed at her ego. All the little raw and vulnerable places inside her stung from that knowledge.

Like it or not, with her reputation in tatters, *he* was *her* better.

He was a man of position and accustomed to deference and able to get away with doing whatever he wanted. Just like Rolland. An image of a whip flashing through the air made her cringe. Rolland's hand had held that whip, had wielded it with such gleeful brutality. She shoved down the memory and roamed her gaze over the Scotsman again, pausing on the signet ring he wore.

She had not noticed it on their first encounter. Perhaps he had not worn it. Even from where she stood she could see the large ring depicted some manner of crest. The Clan MacLarin?

"Lady Clara." The Scot moved to bow over her hand. She tried not to tremble as he gripped her gloved fingers. She also tried not to notice the way he smelled of wind and leather. She stopped herself mid-inhale. No. She would not breathe him in. She would not let herself be dazzled by a man.

Still holding her breath, she stared down at the bent head of the man she had thought to never see again.

The gold-shot brown hair needed cutting. It fell past his collar and her palms tingled as she wondered whether the strands felt as soft as they looked.

Bad thought. Bad, bad thought.

She tugged her hand back and rubbed her fingertips against her side as though she could rid herself of his touch, but the sensation still lingered. There was no wiping it off. No ridding of it.

He watched her, his eyes narrowing where her hand wiped at her dress.

His lips thinned. He said nothing, but she knew he'd taken offense. Good. Let him think he repulsed her. Maybe that would deflate some of his unmitigated cheek. She'd marked that about him from the moment she spotted him. Aside of his ridiculous good looks, he was far too sure of himself. That had been spectacularly obvious when he commanded her to run along like some pesky hound.

"Shall we dine?" Alyse asked.

They all took their seats, settling in amid an awkward hush of silence.

Clara took pains to avoid looking at him during the first course. A herculean task since she could *feel* him staring at her. He was probably as shocked as she to find them thrust together again.

Her brother soon filled the silence with conversation. He had years of practice as a nobleman moving in all of the highest circles. He was charismatic and could make conversation in the most stilted of circumstances.

"This is a treat." Her brother gave her one of those worry-laced smiles, as though he were trying to persuade her of the fact. "We don't have much in the way of Society here, so having you and MacLarin both joining us is a delight."

"Indeed," Alyse agreed. "Not that we don't enjoy it here with just ourselves." Her hand drifted to rest on the rounded mound of her belly. "Of course, our numbers are growing. It shall never be only the two of us again."

Marcus winked at her, lifting his glass in a

toast. "And now our beloved sister is here with us. Soon we will have quite the merry tableau."

Marcus and Alyse shared a rather secret smile that hinted at the intimacy and love between them.

Clara recognized the sentiment. However rare it might be witnessed about Town, she had seen it between Mama and her stepfather daily. Foolishly, she had thought she would have that with Rolland. Even though Mama and Marcus had found that, she now knew it was something not so easily acquired. Something rare. She, for one, would never have it. She blinked suddenly burning eyes at the reminder that such a thing was lost to her forever.

She smiled wobbly as her brother and sister-in-law shared another loving look.

She tried to suppress a stab of envy. Jealousy was an ugly emotion. She knew that, but she had not considered what it might *feel* like to be in the constant presence of two people so thoroughly enamored with each other—what it might feel like to watch their family grow over the years whilst she stood at the fringes. She herself staying the same. Never changing. Nothing exciting ever happening to her.

Well, except she would get older. She would age and slide closer and closer to the end of her life with so little to show for it.

She reached for her drink and took a long gulp

at the dismal thought, wishing it was something stronger than sherry.

She was freshly jilted with her reputation in shreds.

Of course she would have such grim reflections.

She was happy for her brother. Truly. How could she not be? When he left London all those years ago, he had been rather angry. Selfish. Then he met Alyse and now he was a better person for it.

And yet . . . here Clara sat, her burdens all the more acute in the face of such glowing happiness.

The sensation of being watched forced her head back up. She found the Scottish laird studying her with those piercing eyes of his. She flushed. This dinner was endless. She tried not to squirm. His blue eyes were far too probing. He couldn't possibly know her thoughts, but she felt he could see directly into her soul. It was an unnerving sensation. Rolland had never looked at her with such intensity or ever with such astuteness, as though he were seeing beneath all her layers.

"Sorry your grandmother could not join us, MacLarin. We always enjoy her company," Marcus commented as they now worked their way through the evening's second course.

"Her aching bones make it so it is no longer easy for her tae ride or sit in a carriage for such a duration." Even as he spoke he was still staring at her. He lifted his glass to his lips and drank, one of those blue eyes daring to wink at her over the rim.

Oh! The nerve. Face burning, her gaze shot back to the pheasant and sausages on her plate. She began cutting vigorously.

"Tell me, MacLarin," Marcus began, wiping at his mouth with a linen—but not before looking her way. It seemed he had noticed MacLarin's staring. He leaned back in his chair, idly holding his glass. "How is that prize bull of yours?"

Ah. The bull again. Apparently the beast was renowned if even her brother was inquiring. She watched on with interest as she swallowed a bit of roasted parsnip.

MacLarin's nostrils flared ever so slightly. "He's . . . misplaced. Temporarily."

Marcus leaned back in his chair with a huff of laughter. "Don't tell me. One of your fellow Scotsmen has relieved you of him."

MacLarin scowled and she couldn't help noticing that the expression on him did nothing to mar his beauty. Unfortunate, that. "Simply borrowed."

"Borrowed?" Marcus shook his head, still laughing. "In England we call that theft."

"Well, you're in Scotland now," MacLarin reminded rather gruffly.

"Indeed."

"My bull will soon be home where he belongs."

At his belligerent tone, she couldn't hold back a short laugh. Regrettably, his eyes shot back to her at the sound.

She arched an eyebrow at him, obliged to speak. "Come now, sir. You do realize you're getting your feathers ruffled over a cow?"

"I told you." His eyes glinted. "A bull is no' a cow."

She shrugged as if it were no account . . . knowing the gesture would only exasperate him. For some reason irking him made her feel better. It was diverting at least.

Marcus shook his head with a smile, motioning for more wine as he leaned back in his seat. "I always enjoy these visits, MacLarin, where you educate me on Scottish customs."

"Someone has tae," MacLarin replied with easy arrogance. "How else will you raise your brood up tae be proper Highlanders?"

Clara snorted.

Very presumptuous of him. He was speaking to the Duke of Autenberry. Her brother might reside here, but he was as English as they came, as would be his offspring. Undoubtedly one day he would rightfully claim his seat in the House of Lords.

The laird's eyes narrowed at the sound and he canted his head slightly, leveling her with his undivided attention. "Do *you* plan tae stay long,

Lady Clara?" The way he said *Lady Clara* was faintly mocking. At least to her ears. She was certain no one else in the room detected the undertone, but she did.

"Clara is going to live with us," Alyse eagerly supplied. "And we are so very excited to have her here."

Because that's what happens when you've been banished from your life.

She took another long sip of sherry and tried not to reveal that her move here was anything less than pleasing.

"Ah." His eyes remained fixed on her and yet they were unreadable. "Then she will be wanting tae learn our customs as well."

"My skills of observation are keen. I'm sure I will learn everything I need to know in short order," she proclaimed over the soft clink of cutlery on plates.

He smirked, his gaze skimming her with a bemused air that set her teeth on edge. "Things are no' always learned quickly, Clara."

She flinched at the intimate use of her name. For some reason, it embarrassed her, implying a familiarity that should not exist between them. She could not bring herself to look at either Marcus or Alyse to note their reaction. They likely thought nothing of it, accustomed to their friend's ill-mannered ways.

She was certain he was referring somehow to her behavior at the inn where he had so sneeringly called her a Sassenach. *Mayhap a civilized and delicate Sassenach such as you should no' have ventured so far into the Highlands.*

They were served a fragrant medley of seafood that her brother exclaimed over in delight. "Clara, we have only the freshest fish here."

While Alyse and Marcus turned the discussion to the merits of mussels versus scallops, she leaned sideways so that she could hiss under her breath at MacLarin.

"How dare you address me so informally?"

"Why does it bother you so much?" Clearly, he understood her meaning.

"It's impolite."

"Forgive me, I was no' schooled in proper etiquette. 'Tis all one can expect from a *Highland savage.*"

She stifled her wince to have her words flung back at her so aptly. "Indeed," she snapped and stabbed her fork at a chunk of fish on her plate.

Her gaze stalled on his hands as he used his knife and fork. They were large. The wrists thick and broad, lightly peppered with hair. So many gentlemen in Town possessed hands not much larger than hers. When she clasped hands with them to dance, their hands had felt as delicate as a bird's. Sometimes she felt as though she should lead.

MacLarin's entire hand could cover a great deal of space. She had a sudden flash of his hand on her body, on her bare skin. The rougher pads of his palms against her tender flesh.

A strange tremor ran through her and her belly contracted, the muscles tightening and fluttering in a way that made her reach for her glass of sherry with shaking fingers. She could definitely use a more fortifying libation.

She sucked in a sharp breath. Blast her wayward imagination. It was galling to know this man had roused such a reaction in her. She had no business entertaining such thoughts. Not of Laird MacLarin. He was too *big*, too *coarse*, too *wild*. Not that it would be acceptable if he was the opposite of those things. She had no business entertaining such thoughts of her with *any* man. She forced her gaze straight ahead, determined not to look at him or his attractive hands for any length of time again.

"Once the weather warms up a bit we can take a boat ride out in the firth," Alyse's voice startled her.

Clara's breath fell a little faster as she turned to stare at her sister-in-law, feeling unreasonably caught, her pulse like a hammer at her throat. There's no way Alyse could know her thoughts. "Lovely," she murmured.

Alyse smiled, appearing blithely unaware of the tension coursing through Clara as she cracked a crab, laughing and ducking as it sprayed out juice. "The dolphins race right alongside the boat. It's exhilarating."

MacLarin, however, didn't glance in her sister-in-law's direction. The crab could have jumped from the plate and latched on to Alyse's nose. He was not the least interested. Indeed not. His gaze remained locked on Clara. For some reason his gaze seemed very bright and very focused on her right then. She shifted in her seat.

"That sounds delightful, Alyse," she responded for lack of anything else to say. Oh, when would this night end? She longed to return to her room where she could bury her head in a pillow. She thought she wouldn't have to see anyone once she arrived here. Mama had said she would be in seclusion. This hardly felt like seclusion right now.

Clearly she was not the only one at the table who noticed the Scot's penchant for staring. Marcus looked from MacLarin to her and back again, his expression turning thoughtful as he traced the rim of his glass.

"MacLarin?" Marcus prompted, watching with interest as their guest did not turn at his name. "MacLarin?"

"Hmm?" The laird finally turned.

"I was asking if you've had any more problems

lately with your neighbor to the east? Bannessy? The last time we spoke, you mentioned he made off with your cook?"

"Aye. Bannessy is no' tae be trusted." MacLarin shrugged as if this was to be predicted. "Strife is expected betwixt our clans. I would fret if we were no' in some manner of dispute."

The servers arrived to take away the last of the dishes. The meal was finished and not soon enough as far as she was concerned.

Marcus rounded the table to his wife.

Clara gained her feet and MacLarin fell into step at her side, offering her his arm. She scowled down on it, supposing she had little choice but to accept. With a grunt, she placed her fingers on his sleeve, barely touching.

"Surprised tae see me again, lass?" he queried softly.

Lass. She bristled. She didn't care for that address either. It was even worse than when he called her Clara. He probably spoke to every female so informally. She was not *any* female though. She was *Lady* Clara. She winced at the arrogant thought—especially considering she was not entitled to such high regard anymore.

"Indeed," she agreed. "I am quite surprised to see you, *lad*." She smirked.

The corner of his mouth kicked upward. "I've no' been called a lad in years."

From the size of him, she was not surprised. "Well, I can assure you I have never been called 'lass' by anyone *ever*."

"Oh, I am certain of that, *Lady* Clara." No doubt about it. He was mocking her. His blue eyes glinted. "I'm honored tae hold the distinction of being your first."

Her head whipped to stare at him with a sharp breath, convinced there was innuendo in the remark. Innuendo of the most vulgar variety. His curling lips only served as testament to that. Oh, he was a wicked man!

He continued, "We dinna stand on ceremony here. You may have tae release some of your haughty ways if you wish tae acclimate."

"Haughty?" She stopped and stared at him in affront. She could not count the number of times Mama had reprimanded her to be more circumspect, *more* haughty like Enid. It was almost laughable. Mama would be proud of her in her dealings with this Scot. The nerve of this man to criticize her. "You do not know me at all, Laird MacLarin."

He turned to face her, her brother and Alyse forgotten somewhere ahead of them. They stood close. Not as close as when they had been on the floor at the inn when he had been crushing her with his bigger body, but close enough for her to smell his scent. Wind and leather swirled in her nose.

"Right you are." He nodded.

She nodded back. "We are strangers."

And they always would be strangers. Contrary to what she told Alyse, she would never be friends with this man. He roused her temper in a way that barred friendship. It was simply not possible.

They started toward the drawing room. Alyse was already settled on a sofa inside, knitting on her lap. She smiled at Clara and patted the seat next to her.

"MacLarin?" Marcus stood in the threshold. He inclined his head in the direction of his study. "Care for a whisky?"

MacLarin's gaze flickered to her before looking back at her brother and nodding.

With a grateful sigh, she slid her hand from his arm and stepped inside the drawing room, eager to be free of him. She would be spared those penetrating eyes.

He'd likely spend the rest of the evening with her brother and do whatever it was men did when they sequestered themselves in the study.

She would soon be able to excuse herself. When she woke in the morning he would be gone.

Then her new life here would truly begin.

Chapter 5

*H*unt gazed at the closed doors of the drawing room even as Autenberry described the recent renovations he had begun on the crofters' cottages.

He murmured appropriate comments in the lulls of conversation, all the while wondering when they would rejoin the ladies. When they would rejoin *her*.

It was beyond stupid of him to fixate on her. She was a lady. English. A duke's sister. And there was the curse. Always the curse standing in the way.

He knew that, but he could not seem to stop himself. She was so very different from any female he had ever met. For God's sake, she smelled of bergamot and oranges.

"MacLarin? Are you paying attention?"

"Hmm?" He snapped his gaze from the door and back to the man he had somehow remarkably befriended over the last few years. Never would he have imagined he had anything in common with an English peer, but then he supposed the Duke of Autenberry had proven himself to be quite different than the notions Hunt had ever harbored of noblemen.

Autenberry angled his head and looked at him curiously. "You're quite . . . distracted tonight."

"Am I?" He shrugged, hopefully looking unmoved. Autenberry did not ease his staring and after some moments Hunt heard himself filling the silence with the inquiry: "Your sister . . . she will be here for some time then?"

The moment he asked, he regretted it. It made him appear interested, affected, and he could be none of those things. He certainly did not need to give her brother a differing impression.

"She is here to stay."

"Stay?" he said slowly, as though the word was beyond his comprehension.

Autenberry took a deep drink, gazing over the rim at Hunt. Instead of confirming, he said, "You like her. My sister."

Not a question. A statement.

Hunt opened his mouth several times, ready to deny the charge, but one look at Autenberry's face and it was pointless. The man had already made up his mind. He watched Hunt with a bemused expression, daring him to deny it.

And deny it he could. *Like* was an oversimplification of his feelings toward Lady Clara. She roused all manner of emotions, but he couldn't claim to *like* her. No, he felt nothing as tepid as that.

"My sister is a pretty girl." Autenberry lowered his elbow to rest on the side arm of his chair.

Hunt grudgingly acknowledged that with a nod. "She will no' find much Society here unfortunately."

As an unattached female, she would definitely not attract a husband in the Black Isle. Not a suitable husband of her rank, at least. She'd likely head south before the last of the snow thawed, where a lass such as herself could find proper appreciation. He'd wager on it.

"That's for the best," Autenberry said after a few moments. He tossed back the rest of his drink in one swallow and sighed.

"She has no use of Society?" Hunt gave a derisive snort and shook his head, discounting that possibility. He had never heard such a ridiculous thing, and he didn't believe it for one moment. What marriageable female of good breeding didn't want a husband? Maneuvering polite Society was the only way to achieve a match. He might not move in their lofty circles, but he knew that. He knew where Lady Clara belonged, and it was not here.

Autenberry turned to stare into the fire, his expression brooding. "Rather Society has no use for her. Unless it's to condemn and scorn her for their amusement."

He processed that, trying to make sense of Autenberry's meaning and not succeeding. "I'm sorry tae hear that," he said, unsure what else to say, and unaccountably bothered at the notion of anyone treating her shabbily.

Autenberry reached for the bottle and poured himself another glass. He drank long and deep. When he next lifted his gaze, Autenberry's eyes latched on to him, sharp and glassy.

"She's ruined."

Hunt frowned. "Beggin' your pardon?"

"It won't be secret for long." He grimaced. "I fear most of London already knows. My sister is ruined. That's why she has come all this way to live with us."

Hunt stared, lips moving. No sound forthcoming. The announcement robbed him of speech. He shook his head, struggling to wrap his mind around the revelation. It didn't seem quite possible that such a proud female could ever have taken a misstep that led to the complete loss of her reputation.

"Your . . . sister?" He pointed toward the drawing room doors.

"She made a mistake," Autenberry amended with a wince. "A grave mistake. One that will be evident soon enough."

Hunt sucked in a breath. Comprehension eddied through him. She was with child. Out of wedlock and with child.

Silence fell between them. What could he say? He understood about grave mistakes. He'd lived his life with a dark cloud hanging over him, the gravest of mistakes always so close, ready for him to stumble and fall. Ready to take him and pull him under. Consume him at his very first lapse.

"Perhaps there is a silver lining?" Autenberry gestured vaguely with his fingers. "They say everything happens for a reason."

"Who says that?"

"I don't know." Autenberry shrugged miserably. "People do." He continued speaking. Hunt listened with only half an ear, his thoughts churning at this unexpected revelation. She was with child. She carried another man's child.

He snapped back to attention at the duke's words. ". . . I mean, there are still benefits for someone to marry Clara. She's not lost. There could be—"

"I'll marry her." Hunt hadn't planned to say

the words, but the moment they escaped him, the moment they were out there on the air, he did not regret them.

Autenberry blinked. "I beg your pardon?"

Hunt rose to his feet. "I said, I'll take her for my wife."

Autenberry, a man never before at a loss for words, stammered, "Y-you will? Just like that? After everything I told you?"

"Yes." He nodded. He would marry her . . . *because* of everything Autenberry had told him.

"WHAT DO YOU mean he has offered for me?" An uneasy tickle started at the base of her spine. Clara sank down in the chair, not trusting her legs to support her anymore.

She narrowed her eyes on her brother and that sensation in the small of her back only intensified at the look in her brother's eyes. It was a look of pure triumph. As though her brother had unraveled some wickedly tangled knot.

Clearly there was some mistake. Or he was jesting with her. Although her brother had never been the type to pull pranks. He was much too mature for that.

"It is just as I said. He has offered for you." Marcus nodded as though this were a splendid thing—something she should be as thrilled about as he evidently was. "Of course, you don't have to marry him. You don't have to marry anyone . . . but you might wish to consider his suit."

"This doesn't make any sense." She pressed a hand against her forehead, wondering if she were caught in some kind of dream—or nightmare rather.

It was cruel. Impossible. She could not entertain the notion of marriage.

"I think she requires a bit more explanation, Marcus," Alyse supplied with a wry twist of her lips. Her gaze seemed to convey that she would appreciate an explanation, too.

"Why must such a thing be met with confusion?" Marcus looked genuinely perplexed. "You're lovely and clever. You're the sister of a duke with a significant dowry. Any man would be—"

She made a sound of disgust. "Is that it then? He's in need of money?" Why did her voice suddenly rise an octave and why did she feel such a stab of disappointment? It was a valid motivation for marriage. It should not offend her so very much. Marriages among members of the *ton* happened all the time for that very reason.

"No. To my knowledge, MacLarin is quite comfortable."

"Then it is position he's after? Clearly you have

not explained to him that marriage to me will gain him no increase in status. In fact, he will most likely be banned from every polite circle in Town—"

"The man doesn't give a damn about the *ton* and what, or rather *whom*, they deem acceptable."

She ignored her brother's language and dropped her hand from her forehead, looking him steadily in the eyes. "You told him?" It was less a question and more a statement of fact. Her stomach experienced a sinking sensation.

Marcus shifted uncomfortably. As though the subject of her ruin was too uncomfortable a topic for him and something that must be skirted.

"It was mentioned. Of course. I would not trick him into marrying you without full knowledge of circumstance."

Without full knowledge.

That meant only one thing. Her brother told him everything as he knew it. Soiled goods. Tainted. Marked. Broken. All words that could be applied to her now. All words that this world believed her to be.

They were all the things MacLarin thought of her now. And yet he still wanted to marry her.

"Then this makes even less sense. Why should he want to marry me as I am? I just met the man!"

If there was a voice that whispered through her

mind that he weighed on her thoughts too much for a man she had only just met, she ignored it.

"I think it obvious," Marcus replied.

She stared at him blankly.

He continued, "Clearly he is smitten with you."

"Smitten?" After a pause, she laughed. "He most certainly is *not* smitten with me."

Marcus frowned. "I fear you do not see yourself in the same flattering light I do."

That was most definite. Her brother had always doted on her. When she came along, he was practically a man already, but he had always made time for her. He'd treated her with such warmth and affection and delighted in all her antics.

"He did stare at you at length. It was quite bold," Alyse offered, looking almost apologetic to agree on the point.

"Indeed!" Marcus nodded. "The fellow could not take his eyes off you."

"And that is reason enough to offer marriage?" She stopped and glared at her brother. "You suggested it, didn't you? Admit it."

Her brother dropped his gaze and it was confirmation enough. Her stomach sank.

"Heaven help me, you did! You asked him if he would marry me! I didn't know I was so unwanted that you would throw me at the first unmarried man to walk through the doors. I have not even been here a full twenty-four hours, Marcus!"

Marcus wagged a finger at her. "Now see here, it wasn't like that at all. I wouldn't have even entertained the offer and be speaking with you on the matter if I did not know him to be a good man, Clara. We've become well acquainted with MacLarin since moving here. I would not permit just any man to court you. Believe me in that."

She shook her head, not listening. "You should have sent me away to the Continent or America where I wouldn't burden you."

"Clara, it's not like that. MacLarin is quite charming. Bold and clever. You should get to know him better." Alyse tried to reach for her arm, but Clara surged up from her chair, suddenly desperate to be gone from this room, this place and the outrageous things she was hearing. "Your brother only wants the best for you, Clara."

"And your neighbor is the best apparently?" She snorted. "More accurately, he's all that is left. You see him as my last chance."

Alyse clucked her tongue and shook her head whilst her brother snapped, "And what if he is? MacLarin comes from an old, venerable clan. He's a powerful man in these Highlands. He will take good care of you. He would treat you well."

"Is that all that matters?"

Strained silence fell. Her chest rose on a labored breath.

Oh, this wretched world that viewed a woman as chattel to be judged and manipulated and used . . . that limited her choices to the match that afforded the least abuse.

"There are worse things than being unwed and alone," she whispered.

She'd already faced that truth when she weighed the consequences of going through with her marriage to Rolland.

Marcus exhaled, his shoulders slumping slightly. "Of course, that is true, Clara, but he is a good man. I wouldn't give my sister to just anyone. You deserve a good husband . . . a good life."

And he was so confident she would have that with this Laird MacLarin?

"You needn't give me to anyone," she muttered.

"I am only thinking of you and—" He stopped himself, but she knew what he meant to say. His gaze dropped to her midsection. His implication was clear. He was referring to that matter that he could not yet speak of directly.

He was thinking of her unborn child. Of course.

The child who did not exist.

The lie she had fabricated.

A myth woven to escape an inevitably bleak future with Rolland.

She closed her eyes, squeezing them in a long-suffering blink. Now. Now was the time to tell him. She could not wait another moment. With a decisive nod, she opened her mouth.

A sudden knock at the door silenced her, however.

No one bade enter before the door opened and in walked the man her brother had asked to marry her. It was galling. Heat fired her face.

It was as though the room suddenly shrank with the addition of him. He looked grim, his mouth set in a flat line. Hardly the visage of a man in the happy throes of proposing.

A wash of emotions flooded her. Humiliation, shame, anger . . . and a sharp sense of inferiority. She hated that last thing the most. She had always been confident. Her mother had showered her with love. She had never doubted her worth before now.

You're not broken.

She squared her shoulders and reminded herself that she had made all the decisions in her life up to this moment and that wouldn't change now. She was fortunate to have a family that respected her voice and didn't oppose her independence.

If this man thought she would drop to her knees in gratitude at his proposal, he best think again.

MacLarin settled his gaze on her.

She stared back at him obstinately.

"May I have a word wi' your sister?"

The words were spoken to her brother, but he never took his eyes off her.

Marcus hesitated, glancing to her, waiting for her decision. He would not abandon her alone with MacLarin without her agreement.

She hesitated as well. Eventually curiosity won her over. She had an overwhelming compulsion to hear him out—to find out what could possibly motivate him into offering for her hand.

She nodded at her brother. "I'll speak with him."

Marcus flew into motion. With one hand on his wife's arm, he escorted her from the room. Alyse cast her an encouraging look as she went.

Clara stared after them, hardening her resolve. She could do this. She was not a wilting flower. Her brother may have gotten her into this infernal situation, but she could handle matters.

The door clicked shut and she wasted no time. "My apologies for whatever has compelled you to seek this audience with me, sirrah. You needn't feel pressured to do anything foolish, no matter how nicely my brother asked it of you."

He considered her for a moment in which she attempted not to fidget beneath his regard. "He did no' ask me tae do anything, foolish or otherwise."

She processed that with a small dose of bewilderment. Her brother had admitted as much. "No?"

"I volunteered."

"Why would you do that?"

"Do you no' need a husband?" He ambled slowly closer.

"So this is a magnanimous gesture then? Wed the poor ruined girl so that—"

"You're no' poor." His gaze flicked up and down over her, taking in her gown and the jewels at her throat. "You're no' an ordinary lass at all. Even without all your finery, anyone can see that."

The words sank in, bringing a warm bloom of pleasure. Blast it.

She pushed away what felt dangerously like praise. She would not permit him to turn her head with his fine words. "Oh, so it is my dowry then that compels you?"

"Is that what you think of me? That I'm the sort of man tae propose tae a woman for mere coin?"

She bristled. "I assure you there is nothing *mere* about my dowry."

He shrugged with a snort. "Do you no' think you're temptation enough, lass?"

She shivered at his words delivered in that

rumbling brogue. Temptation enough? Her? No, she did not believe so.

"I'm quite the scandalous creature. My brother told you that." Her chin went up a notch. Let him think the worst of her. The sooner he realized that, the sooner he would leave her alone and be on his way.

"You think tae scare me away, lass?" His eyes trailed hotly down the column of her throat to her cleavage. She resisted lifting a hand there to cover her flesh. A scandalous creature would not bother. "Scandalous creatures are my favorite."

Oh! He was depraved.

She gave a shaky laugh, attempting to mask how much his words affected her.

"Any sane man would head for the hills," she whispered in a furious rush, feeling confused and conflicted all of a sudden.

His gaze roamed over her again and heat spread to other parts of her body—not just her face. Parts of her body that she'd scarcely ever acknowledged herself. Suddenly she felt a pulse in those places. A longing pull.

"So only an insane man would wed you?" His lips twitched and, oh, there was danger in that seductive curl of his mouth. He might be an uncivilized Scot, but the ladies he could seduce in

Town would be legion. "I'm no' certain who you think more poorly of . . . me or yourself."

"It's not an insult to either one of us. I'm a realist, Mr. MacLarin."

Now she was. Recent events had taught her to be. She had shelved the dreams of her girlhood.

"Hunt," he went on to say.

"I beg your pardon?"

"You may call me MacLarin or Hunt."

"That would not be seemly."

"We are discussing the matter of our marriage." Again his eyes swept over her and it was like he was saying something else, some other word than *marriage*. A word that should not exist in any lady's vocabulary, but it existed in hers.

She'd read things she should not have. Texts, books on eroticism and fornication she had found hidden in their vast library back home. She was indeed a scandalous creature. That much was true. Perhaps if other girls her age had liked her . . . if they had bothered to befriend her, she would not have had so much time at her disposal and developed a curiosity for things best left to ignorance. However, she could feel no regret at knowing such things. Knowledge was power.

The knowledge she had gleaned from those pages burned through her mind now and she had a sudden flash of this man, the Laird MacLarin, with his large hands sliding over her body, doing the very things she had seen illustrated so boldly on those pages.

He continued, "I think it more than appropriate for you tae call me Hunt."

Dear God. If he only knew her thoughts and what a depraved wicked female she was . . .

"We are not marrying. You should not depart this day under that misapprehension."

It was all she could think to say, all she could cling to as she tried to cast the fever-inducing images from her mind.

His mouth twitched anew. "Oh, I'm no' leaving yet. The ride home is tae long. I'm staying the night."

Her stomach fluttered. He was staying the night. The words pounded through her like the rush of stampeding hooves. They would sleep under the same roof. Why did that make her so very uneasy? Just because the man had offered marriage did not bind her to him in any fashion.

She shrugged, adopting an air of nonchalance. She had perfected the art of behaving unaffected when so many of the other debutantes snubbed her. "So long as you're not laboring under any misapprehensions about you and me whilst you remain here."

He nodded, looking so relaxed and so very sure of himself right then that she wanted to hit something—mostly *him*. "You might change your mind, however. In time. I'm only a day's ride away from here."

"I'm not fond of your arrogance."

"It's no' arrogance. It's confidence." He drew a few steps closer and she had the vague sense of a predator closing in. "And you do care for it. You liked it back at the inn." His blue eyes glinted knowingly and she feared he might in fact have an idea at the wicked bent to her thoughts. Heavens help her.

"I did not!" Drawing a breath, she circled around a wingback chair, feeling more comfortable with it between them.

His smile turned smug. "Come. You liked me then."

Clara huffed, hating he thought that . . . and hating that there was truth to it.

She had been drawn to him. When she didn't know his name. When he was simply a Highland ruffian with bold manners. When he couldn't possibly be a man who existed in *her* world. When he could not possibly be her husband.

And he still couldn't be. That had not changed.

His thick brogue went on to say, "You like me *now*." Oh, the arrogance of the man knew no bounds! "Dinna fash yourself. I like you back, lass. I would no' be here now unless I did."

Oh, that growling voice made her skin shiver.

He liked her? What did that even mean? She

was afraid to ask . . . afraid that it might make a difference and she couldn't allow that.

She stormed around her chair, heading straight for the door. "You're mad if you think I'm to believe tender feelings can be developed in so short a time. 'Tis more likely you want to find yourself wed to a duke's sister, be she ruined or not—"

He seized her hand and she gasped at the contact, stopping in her tracks. Her head whipped around to face him again.

He didn't yank at her hand, but the sensation of his warm grip, the callused fingertips abrading her skin, was enough to render her motionless. She looked down the length of her arm to their linked hands and back up to his face, her heart beating like a wild bird in her chest.

"You're the mad one if you think I'm here because of yer brother. I don't give a damn who he is."

That would be a first. Rolland had cared greatly. Every gentleman to ever call on her had cared a great deal who her brother happened to be. It was likely all they cared about. They would not have paid suit otherwise.

"It is not an insult," she whispered. "It is how things are done. Even here, I am sure. Betrothals are made because of who someone's brother is . . . or someone's father. Family connections are everything."

"Then suffice tae say, I'm no' like any man you ken because such things mean nothing tae me."

His eyes glittered, and she, perhaps stupidly, believed him. There was more to him. She read it in his eyes, something lurked there that set him apart.

"Position," he added, "matters no' at all. A lass who can stir my blood? That's something that matters, though."

She sucked in a breath. What was he saying? She affected him? She *stirred* him?

She tugged her hand free, and he let her go. Oddly, she felt compelled to linger now, to unravel the mystery of him.

"It is fair to say . . . I don't know you at all." She rubbed at her hand where the phantom of his touch remained.

He stepped closer. "Would you no' like tae? Aren't you just a wee bit curious of this thing between us?" He waved two fingers between them. "Would you no' like to explore it further?"

Curious? Yes. Curious enough to bind herself to him for the rest of her life . . . that seemed unwise.

"Or are you scared?"

"I'm not scared," she shot back and realized too late that she had played into his hands. She should have denied that there was anything between them, but her words implied agreement that something existed between them.

He chuckled. "You want tae ken why I want tae marry you, lass?" She could only nod once, her voice lost. Her mouth was suddenly too dry for her to speak. "Because the notion does no' terrify me, and before you, marriage to any female made my blood run cold."

She gave an uneasy laugh, assuming he was jesting, but his eyes were utterly serious.

He was being sincere.

It seemed ridiculous that marriage should terrify him. She resisted asking for clarification. If she were seriously going to entertain his proposal, it would matter. As she wasn't, it didn't matter. She didn't care. His matrimonial choices, or lack thereof, made no difference to her. Really.

He moved away toward the door. "I'll leave you tae consider my offer." At the door he stopped again and looked back at her. "It may also be worth mentioning. I'll be a good father tae your bairn."

The air left her lungs in a whoosh. She felt his words to the very marrow of her bones. He was acknowledging she carried another man's child.

He stared at her very directly. Unwavering. Unblinking. There was no skirting the subject for him. No mincing words. It was more than her family could do. They loved her too much. They couldn't utter the shameful words. Her brother had not been able to confront the topic, too embarrassed. Even Mama had spoken only in generalities.

"Why? Why would you do that?"

He smiled slowly. "I like you, Clara. I like children." He shrugged as though it were as simple as that. "A child should have a father and you a husband. I can be that man for you both."

"Why?" she pressed.

He exhaled. "Because I *am no' able.*"

"You are not able . . . to what?"

"I am no' able tae have children," he clarified, holding her gaze.

"Oh." It all clicked.

As his confession sank in, so did comprehension. He didn't like her. Not really. He liked that she came with a ready-made family for him. At least he believed that to be the case. "I am s-sorry that you are unable . . ." Her voice faded away. How did one give voice to such a thing? It was indelicate.

"You needn't be. You need only marry me. Think on it." Still smiling faintly, he departed the room.

She thought about his offer. Long after he left her, his words played in her mind. Long after she retired to her own bedchamber. He had no difficulty offering his name to a child not of his issue.

What manner of man was he?

It was as he said. He was unlike any man she knew and blast it if that didn't intrigue her.

Chapter 6

*W*hat do you mean he proposed?" Marian demanded, sinking down on the edge of Clara's bed, pulling her head back as though she had just tasted something foul and sought to reject it.

"Oh, it's all Marcus's doing." She almost regretted waking Marian and telling her everything. Of course, Marian would want to know every detail—like a dog with a tasty soup bone. She would be relentless, and Clara's head was currently spinning far too much to make much sense of anything. A detailed retelling really was beyond her at this moment. She needed to be alone. She needed time to think.

"Your brother?" Marian shook her head. "What does he have to do with this?"

"Well, he told Laird MacLarin about me—"

Marian's eyes rounded. "Your brother told him . . . about you . . . about everything?"

Clara nodded. "Everything as Marcus knows it." Which was a far cry from everything. She winced.

Marian looked at her sharply. "He still does not know then? When do you plan to explain the situation to your brother and Alyse?" She motioned to Clara with a wave of her hand. "This is the type of thing one *will* notice."

She blew out a breath. "Yes, of course. I'll tell them soon. Very soon." The need for that conversation had been made abundantly clear this night. Her brother was tossing her at the head of the first eligible man to come along, thinking he was doing what was best for her. She had not foreseen this at all. She had just escaped one poor match. She had not anticipated getting entangled in another one.

Marian rolled her eyes. "That will go down splendidly. Your brother will likely ride back to London to challenge Rolland to a duel."

"He will not. That will only make matters worse. He wouldn't wish that for the family."

Marian waved a hand. "So let me understand this. Your brother told him you're ruined with another man's child and the man *proposed*?"

She sighed and shook her head. "Confounding, isn't it?"

Marian nodded. "He's mad!"

"That's what I told Marcus." Shaking her head, Clara faced the dressing table mirror again and resumed brushing her hair, feeling satisfaction at the crackling sound as she pulled the bristles through the long length.

"So you said no?"

"Of course."

Several moments of silence passed before Marian asked, "Are you certain about that?"

She halted mid-brushstroke and flicked her gaze to Marian's reflection in the mirror. "What are you suggesting?"

Marian shrugged awkwardly. "Well. It's not as though you will get another opportunity. And truly, Clara, all jesting aside . . . he must be a genuinely *good* man to propose believing you're in a delicate condition."

"So he's either a *good* man or a *mad* one?" She laughed lightly but stopped when she read Marian's earnest expression.

"It seems more than likely he's a good man."

"Does it?"

Marian stared at her solemnly in response to her question.

"You're serious," Clara announced.

Marian rose from the bed and strolled over to where Clara sat. She placed her hands on Clara's shoulders and gently squeezed. "Your reputation is in tatters, Clara. It doesn't matter that you won't have a child in the near future. You allowed everyone to think that. They will simply assume you lost the babe. Your good name is gone . . . but this man has offered you his name. His protection. And you would live close to your brother. You would have family nearby. That is tempting, is it not?"

She could say nothing. Marian wasn't wrong. She made valid points, and Clara had always respected her opinion so very much.

Marian had been with her since she was sixteen when Clara's governess had taken ill and retired to the country to live with family. Mama had hired Marian to fill the role. She was only two years Clara's senior, having just completed school herself. Even when Clara outgrew the need for a governess, Mama had kept Marian on as a lady's companion since the two of them had become so close. It was Clara's greatest regret that she had not listened to Marian's evaluation of Rolland from the start.

Even now, with all her newfound respect for Marian's advice, it was so very untenable to Clara . . . the notion of marrying a man she only just met was unimaginable, especially after the last disaster.

Marian continued, "He's quite attractive. I know you think so, too."

She shook her head. "What if he's like Rolland—?"

Marian snorted. "He is not. The earl didn't possess an honorable bone in his body. The man was a monster whilst MacLarin has offered for you despite your tarnished status."

It was true. By his own words and deeds, he had already proven he was nothing like her former betrothed. He liked her. He liked children, and he could not have any of his own. For some reason she did not share that tidbit with Marian. It may round out this story and fill all the holes, but it felt too personal to share with Marian. It wasn't her truth. It was his, and she would not bandy it about, not even with a trusted friend.

"I will think on it," Clara agreed, the words coming slowly. She expected them to feel wrong on her tongue.

But they didn't.

They actually felt right, and it was that which she thought about long into the night.

HE WAS MAD. Stark mad. Just as she had accused him.

He paced his bedchamber, whisky glass in hand. He downed the last of it and approached the bottle, cursing to find it empty.

Of course she had said no. She didn't want to

marry him. She didn't even know him. She was likely brokenhearted for the father of her unborn child.

And that fact filled him with a maelstrom of feelings.

Relief and jealousy warred within him. Which was the height of absurdity. Her condition was what even made it possible for him to marry her. *To have her.*

She had a past. She was no dewy-eyed untarnished maid. And yet he had wanted her since he first saw her at the inn. The fact that there was another man in her very near past was unfortunate . . . and fortunate. It was the only thing that made her a viable bride. He'd have to overcome those flashes of jealousy if he was to have her.

And he wanted to have her.

When Autenberry had explained the situation, he'd jumped at the prospect, scarcely giving it any thought. It had seemed too good to be true. He could be married and raise a child and avoid the curse that had haunted the men in his family for generations. He could have what he had always thought himself denied.

He snorted. He was acting as though she had agreed to marry him. She had not. Nor did she appear inclined to change her mind.

It *was* apparently too good to be true . . . because

she had no desire to marry him. Legitimizing her child evidently did not matter enough for her to consent to be his wife. It was a bit wounding. He had always believed himself to be a handsome man. Lasses flirted with him. He had many friends and was generally thought to be good company. It went without saying that he was an influential man in these parts. He'd even gone as far as to tell her he could not have a child. It was essentially the truth. As close as he could get without telling her about the curse.

A knock sounded at his door.

He hesitated a moment before moving toward it.

He pulled open the door and the air expelled from him in a rush. Of all people he expected to see at his door at this late hour, he never counted on her.

She was covered up to her neck in a robe that hid her nightgown, but even so, it twisted his insides having her so close and without a corset on—just free-flowing lawn trimmed in silk ribbon and her bare body beneath. One tug of the ribbon at the center of her chest and her dressing gown would part open to reveal the nightgown beneath. He swallowed the lump in his throat.

"Lady Clara," he greeted as though young ladies appearing at his bedchamber door in the middle of the night were commonplace. Far from it. There was only Catriona.

In his youth he had foolishly risked a few trysts before the full ramifications of how short-lived his future would be had settled on him—at least how short-lived it would be if he continued down a path of illicit dalliances.

His palms grew damp just looking at her.

He motioned inside his room. "Would you like tae—?"

"That's not a good idea," she said, her manner efficient.

Of course. He nodded, his gaze drifting to the long plait of hair draped over her shoulder. The hair was as thick as his wrist and dark as night. He couldn't help imagining it loose and spread out over his pillow. He wanted to bury his nose in it. Bury himself in *her*.

"I need only a moment to say what I've come to say." She laced her fingers together very properly before her.

He gave an encouraging nod.

She moistened her lips. "Thank you for the honor of your proposal." She bit her lip in the most fetching manner. He wanted to pull that lip free and soothe the tender skin with his own lips. He shoved down the inappropriate impulse. He had more self-control than that. "I should have perhaps said that at the first." She exhaled a breathy semblance of nervous laughter. "Thank you." Pause. "And . . . I will consider your proposal, Laird MacLarin."

He digested that a moment before replying, "You will?"

She blinked up at him. "Yes. It's the sensible thing to do." Her chin went up. "You had to know I would reach that decision."

"Actually, I was no' so certain." Mostly because he was accustomed to disappointment . . . to going without when it came to women.

"Oh." She looked vaguely uncomfortable, a frown forming on her lovely mouth. "Did you change your mind then?"

His earliest memories were of sadness and disappointment—listening to his mother weep from inside her chamber. She scarcely looked at him when she emerged from her bedchamber, but when she did it was only to remind him that he was cursed.

That his life must be about denial or he would end up as miserable as her.

Never make the mistake yer da did. Never forget the curse. It is real and it will hunt ye like a bloodhound. There be no escape.

And yet here was this lass, her lovely face upturned, her tempting lips promising him a chance. A future different from the one he'd always assumed to be his destiny.

Perhaps he could beat the curse, after all, and have a semblance of a marriage. For months, at least, he could have her in his bed. Then, when that ended, he'd still have something left. Something worthwhile. He'd be a father.

"I did no' change my mind," he finally answered her. "I meant it." However rash it seemed even now, he would marry her if she would have him. He would take this girl and her child and claim them both as his own. "Should ye agree, we should act quickly. Given your condition . . . as soon as possible." He glanced to her stomach. She was not yet noticeably increasing, but time would affect that change soon enough.

Her face reddened and she nodded jerkily. "Once I've made up my mind on the matter, you will be the first to know."

"I await your pleasure." He inclined his head, a thrill coursing through him. He tried to tamp it down. She had not accepted definitively. Until she did, he should be temperate. Patient. He should be the man he always was, expecting nothing when it came to women and matters of the heart.

She studied him a moment longer, distrust lingering in her gaze. It appeared as though she would say more, but then she held silent, pressing her lips together in a mutinous line. There was more to this lass. A great deal more and he was keenly interested to know everything there was to know about her.

"I will inform my brother that I'm *considering* your suit and you will be staying a little longer." She gave an efficient nod.

Before he could say anything else or peel back a layer for a deeper glimpse of her, she spun around and fled down the corridor.

Chapter 7

Clara's heart pounded a hard tempo as she closed her hand around the latch of her bedchamber door and pushed it open, ready to flee inside. Her words chased after her, though, nipping at her heels, echoing inside her head as if someone else had uttered them.

I will inform my brother that I'm considering your suit and you will be staying a little longer.

Unbelievably the words had originated from her.

"Clara!"

She jumped at the unquiet whisper and whirled around to face her friend in the dimly lit corridor. The wall sconces cast flickering shadows over Marian's lovely face.

"Marian!" Clara sighed, pressing a hand to

her heart. "You gave me a fright." With a quick glance up and down the corridor, she pulled her friend inside her chamber.

"Nothing compared to the fright you gave me when I spotted you slipping out of MacLarin's room!" Marian's voice dipped to a hush at the mention of his name.

"I did not go *inside* his chamber." The distinction mattered. "I merely wanted a word with him—"

"A word?" Marian canted her head. "About what?"

Clara sighed. "I wanted him to know that I have decided to give his proposal proper consideration."

Marian smiled widely. "Ah. Then it begins."

An uneasy trickle started down Clara's spine. "What begins?"

"The courtship, of course. And this time will be different. Last time I stayed out of it, but no more. You need me." With a decisive nod, Marian clasped Clara's hands and gave them a tight squeeze. "This time we will be certain before you agree to marry him."

Clara eyed her friend warily. "We?" She snorted. "And how do *we* go about acquiring such certainty?" After all that had transpired over the last few months, she doubted she would ever feel certain of any man . . . much less ever certain of her judgment when it came to them.

She would, in fact, value her friend's opinion on the matter.

"With your secret weapon, of course." A martial look entered Marian's eyes.

"What secret weapon?"

"Me."

"You?"

Marian bobbed her head. "It's time for me to infiltrate the staff."

IT TOOK MARIAN less than twenty-four hours for her self-proclaimed infiltration of the staff. In point of fact, before breakfast. She stormed into Clara's bedchamber and brusquely ushered the maid out of the room as she was putting the finishing touches on Clara's hair.

"I've solved it! I know why he wants to marry you!" she declared once she had rid the room of the girl.

"You do?" Clara could not help the skepticism from creeping into her voice. MacLarin did not strike her as the sort of man to share his inner thoughts—especially not with members of the staff who were wont to gossip.

"I do. John, one of the upstairs footmen, is quite enamored of me. I permitted him certain liberties—"

"Marian! You didn't!"

Marian waved a hand. "Pah. 'Tis not what you think. Don't look so horrified. He merely smelled my hair."

"Smelled . . . your hair?" Clara shook her head in bewilderment.

"Yes. Well, he wanted other things as well, but that was the only liberty I permitted."

"Why?"

"For information, of course, and it was worth it." Marian's eyes gleamed in satisfaction.

Clara leaned forward on the edge of her bench. "Well, then. Tell me. What information have you gathered?"

"He is cursed."

"Cursed?" she echoed. She did not know what she had been expecting to hear, but definitely not that. The word felt foreign on her tongue, something nonsensical. "What does that even mean?" Certainly Marian did not mean cursed in the sense of one who was hexed.

Marian leaned forward and whispered as though foretelling a grave prophecy. "His family, the men of his line, all die once they've fathered a child. For the past five generations not a one of them has lived past the birth of their firstborn."

Clara stared at her friend, waiting for her to confess this was some grand jest.

Marian simply gazed back at her, sober as a vicar at a funeral.

Clara let out a puff of nervous laughter. "You jest."

Marian shook her head. "No."

"Come, you're having me on. There is no such thing as a curse."

Marian lifted one shoulder in a shrug. "You know that and I know that, but apparently Laird MacLarin does *not*. In fact, I think most everyone around here thinks the curse exists. After John, I questioned one of the stable hands. Even he knew of it. The curse is common knowledge in these parts."

"You mean they believe in the lore of it? The fairy tale. They cannot believe it is anything more than rubbish."

"As God's truth, they believe it to be real. MacLarin's father died a few weeks before his birth . . . and his own grandfather died, I'm told, in a fall from his horse when he was riding back to the castle upon news that his wife had gone into labor. Broke his neck, he did! Apparently it is customary for all the MacLarin men to die before the birth of their firstborn." She winced. "Rather, their *only*born."

Clara released a breath and leaned back on the bench until the edge of the vanity table dug into her back, absorbing everything Marian just revealed.

Not a one of them has lived past the birth of their firstborn.

She shook her head, rejecting that possibility. "Unfortunate accidents. No more."

Marian looked at her grimly. "You cannot persuade any of these locals to that effect."

She remembered his words then. He said he could not have a child, that he was not able. This was what he meant then? Not that he wasn't *capable* of fathering a child, but that he could not— he *should* not.

"He thinks marrying me shall spare him this curse," she said slowly, full understanding dawning.

"More than that." Marian nodded. "He believes you will be giving him another man's child, but one he can claim as his own . . . effectively cheating the curse."

She digested that, comprehending how it might seem that way to someone who believed himself the subject of such a curse.

"Only I won't be giving him another man's child." Indeed, that was quite impossible.

"No, you won't." Marian inclined her head in agreement. "But if he knows that particular truth, he won't wish to wed you."

It was a strange reality in which virtue and her maidenly status nullified her eligibility as his wife.

"No," she murmured. "He would not wish to wed me in that case."

Marian snorted. "Ironic, is it not?"

"Indeed." Clara nodded brusquely. "That decides it then."

"What is decided?"

"Well. Clearly he wants a certain type of wife, which I am not. It *should* lead me to refusing his suit."

"It would seem so, yes."

She inhaled. Rationally, she knew she should refuse his proposal. He was not offering marriage out of any altruistic motivations or because he was besotted with her as her brother seemed to think. He wanted the lie. He wanted the Clara she was pretending to be. Not the real Clara.

The real Clara would send him running.

She should decline his offer and remain as she was—soiled goods without prospects. No offers of marriage ever forthcoming. A lifelong burden to her family.

Marian watched her face closely, as though she could read Clara's thoughts. "You know there are no such things as curses or spells."

Clara nodded in agreement. "Of course."

Marian went on, "So why not go ahead and marry the fool man and show him just how wrong he is?"

Clara felt her eyes widen in her face at what Marian was suggesting. "You're mad," she muttered.

Marian shrugged. "Now we know his motivation. Mad as it is, it's harmless. He's not an evil man. By all accounts, he treats his staff well. Your brother likes him, recommends him . . . and that lovely face of his is no hardship to look at."

Clara fell quiet for some time, turning everything over in her mind. "So . . . I . . . I'd be doing him a favor of a sort? Saving him from his own superstition. Once we're wed and our marriage takes its natural course . . ." Her voice faded, and she shook her head. "I don't think so. He wants a child. Not me. He can find someone else to give him that."

"When you end up increasing with his child, he shall thank you," Marian finished confidently.

Her lips twisted wryly. "I suppose that would be one way for him to realize there is no curse." Clara shook her head.

If she agreed. If she embraced a union with MacLarin. If she went ahead and married him.

If she allowed herself to trust a man again.

Her friend was overlooking that she'd have to marry him first. Live with him. Welcome him into her bed, her body—all before telling him the truth.

That was terrifying.

She smoothed her palms down the front of her dressing robe, fortifying herself. She had earlier decided to consider MacLarin's proposal . . . now she wasn't sure.

"I need to talk to my brother." It was past time

she told him the truth. She was eager to get that over with. Then she would decide what to do about the Laird MacLarin . . . and the rest of her life.

"And what will you tell your brother?"

She took a restorative breath. "Everything."

Chapter 8

*Y*ou should marry him."

Clara gazed at her brother. He stared back at her solemnly.

"Did you not hear anything I just told you?"

"I heard everything, and you should marry him, Clara," he repeated, each word falling heavily on the air. "Of course, you can live out your days here with us . . . *or* you can seize a chance at respectability. A chance at a family and home of your own. I won't force you to wed him, but you should consider it."

She'd heard him, but it was difficult to accept.

It was too incredible that he thought she should still move forward and marry MacLarin even after she told him the truth of what happened in London. She had expected Marcus to put an end to that notion once she made her confession. She had expected him to tell her the idea of marriage to MacLarin was ludicrous.

None of that happened.

He stood before the fireplace, one hand propped on the ornate mantel, his expression grim. His body was as rigid as a slat of wood, but he looked away from her—almost as though he could not look at her because he was *that* disappointed in her.

It hurt.

She had very little memory of her father. Life had always been Mama, Marcus and Enid. Growing up, Marcus had been larger than life. A father figure. Eleven years her senior, he had always taken the time to dote on her, spend time with her. Even if that meant playing dolls. He never minded.

Oh, she knew Marcus had been a bit of a rake. Women, drinking, gaming. Even as a girl, the tales had reached her ears.

But he'd always had time for her. Her handsome older brother would sweep her up into his arms and throw her in the air like she weighed a feather. He'd never treated her like a *half* sibling. She was always his precious baby sister in every sense.

Except right now.

Right now she felt as though she had failed him. Failed him in the worst sense . . . and that crushed her.

She had known it was going to be difficult confessing the truth to her brother, but nothing could have prepared her for this. When he thought she was pregnant, she had felt pity from him. Seen it mingling with the sadness in his eyes.

Now there was only anger and frustration in his face, in every tense line of his body, in the slight flaring of his nostrils. She had the vague impression that he wished to throttle her, and that was a wholly new sensation. She had always amused him. His patience with her had been boundless.

Clara turned her gaze from him. She could not bear it. She wanted him to look at her as he used to, not like this.

Alyse sat on a settee nearby, her knitting forgotten on her lap. She was in the process of fashioning a baby's bonnet. At least she had been, before Clara's intrusion and shocking revelations.

"How can you say that, Marcus?" Alyse asked. "After everything she just revealed? She needn't feel so very compelled to marry now. She's *not* ruined. Not at all! It was all a misunderstanding—"

"The need still remains. I wish it did not, but it does." He released a heavy sigh and rubbed at the center of his forehead. "Rolland saw to that. The damage is done. No one will believe she didn't cuckold the bastard. Her good name is forever lost. That will never change. Nothing has changed." He looked at Clara rather bleakly and she felt wretched.

At these words, she wavered in her determination not to wed MacLarin.

She wondered if there was not something she could have done differently, and the only thing she could think of was never meeting the earl— never attending that afternoon lawn party or any of the other fetes where Rolland had been present. Once she met him, her course had been charted.

"Hasn't it, though?" Alyse asked. "Clara is not compromised. She is not increasing—"

"But sullied just the same, thanks to that black-guard." Marcus's hand on the mantel tightened into a fist. "I've half a mind to ride to London and call the bastard out."

Evidently Clara wasn't the only one he wanted to throttle. At least there was that.

Alyse's face paled at his declaration.

"Put that nonsense out of your head directly," Clara admonished with a wave at her sister-in-law. "You've Alyse to consider and your child soon arriving. See how your words have affected her." She tsked in disapproval.

With one glance at Alyse's face, Marcus moved to sit at her side and gather her into his arms. "I'm speaking rashly. Forgive me. I would never do such a fool thing, of course. It will benefit no one." His gaze met Clara's over his wife's head. "This matter with Clara will be resolved to all our satisfaction."

Clara tried not to look so surprised. "Is that so?"

"You have an offer from Laird MacLarin. He comes from a fine old family with extensive property and a prodigious amount of respect in this area. A simple glower from him will quell any rumors, should there be any this far north. These Highlanders do not put a great deal of stock in what occurs to the south of the River Tweed anyway."

"Yes. About MacLarin . . ." Something in her voice must have alerted him that she wasn't finished with confessions this day. She cleared her throat. She had not yet told them about the curse.

He looked at her sharply. "What about him?"

"My visage alone did not prompt him to propose. The man is not some lovesick swain, contrary to your suggestion that I have snared his ardor."

"Then tell me . . . why does he want to marry you?"

"He believes himself cursed." Heavens. That

sounded even more ridiculous uttered out loud than it did in her head.

"Cursed?" Alyse echoed.

Clara made short work explaining everything Marian had learned to them.

Alyse gave an airy laugh. "Hunt cannot be that superstitious. He's much too reasonable."

"He believes in this curse," Clara insisted.

"Well, then what? He'll *never* marry? Never father a child? Absurd!" Alyse looked bewildered. "He will let this superstition rule him? I cannot believe it."

"That would appear to be the situation. Well, that is until *I* arrived and he thought he found the perfect bride." She snorted. "One already begotten with child."

Throughout the entire conversation, Marcus stared down into the flickering fire as though mesmerized by its fiery dance. She knew he was listening, but she had no notion of his thoughts until he at last said, "Marry him."

Silence descended. The fire popped and a bit of charred wood crumbled in the hearth.

"I beg your pardon?" She leaned closer, her dress rustling against the brocade upholstery.

Marcus lifted his head, his eyes flat. "Marry him."

"Marcus?" Alyse's voice rang with reproof.

"He only wants to marry her because he thinks she will deliver him another man's child. He is convinced he will die if he goes about matrimony in the natural way of things. It's utterly mad!"

"Indeed. Entirely ridiculous. He wants a child. Eventually, he shall have one and see the error of his thinking."

Had her brother been speaking with Marian? They both used the same logic.

Marcus continued, "Once he's married and sees what a splendid wife our Clara is, once she's given him a son of his own, he will drop to his knees and thank her."

"*Thank* her?" Alyse echoed, shaking her head doubtfully.

"That's quite a great amount of supposition, brother. Although I should thank you for assuming I shall be a splendid wife." And fertile. Who was to say she would give him a child?

Alyse looked affronted. "Of course, you would be a splendid wife, Clara. You're wonderful."

Marcus swiftly pressed on. "Tell me, Clara, do you believe there is the slightest veracity to this . . . curse?" He moved from the mantel and approached her. "Do you believe it even remotely possible?"

She made a sharp sound of derision. "Of course not. There are no such things as curses."

"There you have it then. Marry him. It will

benefit you both." He dropped down into the wingback chair across from her.

"You think I should marry him under pretense."

"If you tell him, he won't go through with it." Marcus's eyes held hers. "So for yourself. For *him*. Yes, I do think you should marry him under pretense."

She shook her head, still terribly conflicted. "I've lied enough and made my share of mistakes lately. I'm trying very much to do the right thing now." She rose to her feet. The right thing didn't present itself in any clear or obvious path, however.

She moved toward the door.

"Clara," her sister-in-law called after her. "Where are you going? What will you do?"

She glanced over her shoulder. She didn't know what she was going to do. Or worse.

She *did* know and she was afraid it would only be another mistake.

GOSSIP IN THE Fife was not that different from gossip in a town or city. As soon as anything of interest was released into the ear of even one soul, it spread like wildfire from castle to village to crofter's cottage to peddler's cart. For that reason alone, Hunt knew he had to visit Catriona.

If Clara accepted his proposal, that juicy bit of gossip would travel on the wind. He needed to be the first one to tell Catriona he might be marrying. She deserved to learn that news from him.

They had been friends without expectations of anything else, anything more. And yet the intimate nature of their relationship compelled him to give her an explanation. She deserved that simple courtesy.

Hunt woke early to set about his task. Not that he had slept much the night before. He was up before dawn and ready to ride.

After Clara knocked on his door the night before and announced she would accept his suit and give his proposal consideration, he had stared into the dark, contemplating his potential future as husband and father. He had not realized how much he wanted either of those things before. Life was full of surprises. One moment he was busy about reclaiming his bull, and the next he was seized with the need to marry the Duke of Autenberry's sister.

For years, he'd believed no woman was safe. No woman allowable into his life except Catriona, and now there was this lass. Clara with her soulful eyes and hair like midnight. Someone so different from all of his experiences.

He wondered at the identity of the man who dallied with her and then abandoned her. He assumed that was the situation. What other reason could she be here, unwed and in the family way?

Then he realized it didn't matter.

He didn't care about the man in her past because he was just that—in her past. If she would have Hunt, he would be the man in her present. Her present and future.

Eagerness hummed along his nerves. He looked forward to that. Looked forward to bedding her. Looked forward to raising a child and being a father. Certainly after the child was born, he'd stay out of her bed. It was the wisest course of action. He would not take a chance. He would not risk the curse. But they could enjoy each other for several months. Certainly that would be long enough to satiate his desire. More than enough time for him to have his fill.

Catriona lived halfway between Kilmarkie House and MacLarin lands. Convenient. Whenever he visited Autenberry he'd stop and stay overnight with the widow.

She was always happy to see him and it was no different today. She was carrying a bucket of beetroot toward her cottage when he rode into the yard. He dismounted, tethered his mount and relieved the bucket from her.

She flashed him a bright smile. Catriona was a few years his senior at eight and twenty. Widowed three times, she professed herself done with marriage. She'd been a young lass when she first married. Soon after she lost her first babe. It was a brutal experience that very nearly took her life. The midwife declared her lucky to be alive in the same breath she pronounced Catriona barren.

It would seem the midwife's prognosis held true. In the ten years since, Catriona had buried three husbands and never found herself with child again.

She lost her first husband to cholera; her second drank himself dead, falling in a nearby stream as he stopped to relieve himself and drowning. The last died of an infection. None gave her a child. Her unfortunate history made her the ideal lover for Hunt.

She, like everyone else, knew of the MacLarin curse. She'd called upon him after her third husband expired, making the trip herself, bold as you please.

I'm no' hunting fer husband number four, but I'm no' inclined tae live the rest of my days as a nun. I dinna suppose ye are fond of living as a monk, Laird MacLarin.

They'd wasted little time divesting themselves of their garments right there in his office. It had been quite a satisfactory arrangement these last four years. It served them both well. He'd thought it enough. More than enough.

He'd thought he could live his life quite contented with occasional visits to Catriona. But now that had changed.

It was no longer enough.

She pressed a kiss to his cheek in greeting. "Come in out of the chill."

He followed her inside and set the bucket on her worktable.

She hung her coat on a peg near the door while keeping her heavy tartan cowl on. "Can I make ye some tea?"

He nodded. "That would be verra nice, aye."

Still smiling, she set the pot to fire.

He studied her as she moved about her cottage. She was still an attractive woman. The tiny lines around her hazel eyes marked her as a female given to pleasure. Despite the grief that too often afflicted her, she was given to merriment. She would have no trouble attracting another lover.

"I dinna expect tae see ye. Assumed ye would be scouring the countryside searching fer yer prized bull."

He winced. His quest for his missing bull suddenly felt a lifetime ago. How quickly his interests had deviated. "Heard of that, did ye?"

"Indeed, it is all the titter through the Fife."

"Aye, well, I've gotten a little sidetracked from that chore."

"Enacting revenge on Bannessy?" She chuckled. "Reclaiming yer property? Upholding the MacLarin clan honor? I dinna think anything more important to ye than those things."

As annoying as the observation, it did have a ring of truth. Not that he would admit to such a thing. "I do concern myself with other matters."

"Do ye? Such as?"

She poured their tea. He watched her a moment, appreciating her work-roughened hands as she prepared him a cup. She was accustomed to hard labor, and he had always respected that about her.

"I've decided tae marry," he announced.

Her gaze shot to his. She set down the teapot with a sharp clack. "Ye jest."

He continued, "You deserved tae hear it from me. It is no' for certain yet, but I have proposed tae a lass."

She shook her head. "'Tis suicide."

"Circumstances make it feasible." He did not need to air all of his and Clara's personal affairs.

"Who is she?" She slid his cup toward him, tea sloshing over its sides.

"The Duke of Autenberry's sister."

"Och! A fine lady then." She laughed with a touch of bitterness. "Does that have anything tae do wi' yer sudden change of heart?"

"You ken me better than that."

"I thought I did. Now I'm no' so certain. I never ken ye tae be a fool."

He opened his mouth and then closed it. He wouldn't argue the matter with her. He didn't come here to persuade her into believing as he did. He came her to apprise her of his potential change in status. "I'm verra sorry if I've hurt you, Catriona."

"Hurt me? I've buried a baby and three husbands. I'm barren. Ye havena hurt me, Hunt. Ye dinna possess such power." She leveled him a look that conveyed he was silly to even consider such a thing. She gave a disgusted shake of her head. "If ye want tae kill yerself over a lass, then go on wi' ye. I wish ye all the best."

He sat for several moments before pushing back his chair and standing. Taking tea now felt pointless. A pretense. He'd done what he had come here to do. He turned for the door when her voice stopped him in his tracks and had him looking over his shoulder.

"Am I tae assume this puts an end tae us then?"

He nodded. "If she accepts my proposal, I shall hold tae my vows."

She canted her head, her lips twisting wryly. "So ye will be that manner of husband. I should no' be so surprised."

"What manner?"

"Loyal."

He shrugged. "She has no' even accepted. It may no' come tae pass."

"Oh, she will." She leaned back and sipped from her cup. "Look in the mirror. Lasses swoon over that bonny face of yers. She will no' be able tae resist." She nodded vigorously, sending her auburn plait bouncing over her shoulder. "She will be counting herself the most fortunate of lasses on yer wedding night."

He sighed wearily. "Catriona."

Her hazel eyes sparked. "Wot? I ken what it's like tae share yer bed. I shall mourn the loss of yer fine body."

He opened the door, holding on to the latch for a moment. "Take care of yourself. I hope you find happiness." A rather sentimental thought, but he meant it.

She lifted her teacup in a salute. "Enjoy yer marriage, Laird MacLarin, however short-lived it be."

As he left her cottage behind and walked into the chilled air, he pushed her words aside, telling himself she was wrong. She did not understand.

He was doing the right thing.

Chapter 9

*H*unt did not arrive back at Kilmarkie House until after dinner.

He found the duke and duchess in the drawing room, and after a few minutes of forced niceties, Autenberry took pity on him.

"Well, MacLarin, I can tell from the look of you that you're anxious to see her. Clara is in the music room."

He found her there, tapping idly at the keys of a pianoforte. Her profile was lovely, her skin like heavily creamed tea. His mother had taken her tea that way. Almost more milk than tea. And a good dollop of whisky in it, too. He frowned a bit at the memory of his mother. Whisky had been her crutch. She could not make it a day without the stuff. Correction. She could not make it hours without imbibing.

Shaking off such thoughts, he inquired, "You play?"

Clara turned on the bench, startled at his entrance. "I'm a gently bred lady." This she said with some sarcasm. "Of course I play. My mother saw to that."

"I suppose I will have tae obtain a pianoforte for you."

"Oh?" She looked at him with an unreadable expression. "So certain I shall be living under your roof then, are you?"

He forced a smile. This wooing a woman was new to him. Understandably, it was not one of his best skills. He'd lived his life avoiding any deeper engagement with the fairer sex. "Will you no' be?" For some reason his chest tightened, as though a great deal depended on her answer— and he supposed a great deal did. His entire future, in fact.

She stared at him a moment with those deep brown eyes and then looked down at the keys again, stroking them idly with slim, elegant fingers. The tightening in his chest increased to a twisting discomfort. He wanted that hand to pet him in such a way . . . in long, stroking brushes of her fingertips.

"Where were you today?" she finally asked.

He shifted, the question unexpected. Not only was wooing a new experience, but having to answer for his whereabouts was new, too. "I had an errand."

"An errand." She smiled as though amused, still not looking his way. "Is that what you call her?"

"Her?"

"Yes." She looked up, her gaze unflinching. "Your friend. The widow. Your lover?" She arched a fine eyebrow at him and lifted one shoulder in a half shrug. "The staff talks. They knew at once where you went. Apparently you visit her often."

His life had always been a point of interest in the Fife. There were wagers on whether or not he would reach his thirtieth year, after all. In five generations, no man of his line had succeeded in living to such a ripe age. He was the subject of much attention. Just as everyone knew his story, they knew Catriona's, too. They knew why the cursed MacLarin dallied with Catriona. She was cursed in her own way, thereby making them a suitable match.

"I did visit a friend . . . tae tell her that I've proposed marriage."

"Indeed? A little premature, don't you think? I haven't said yes."

From her stiff posture and evading gaze, he feared he had her answer now and it wasn't a yes.

She stepped forward abruptly, moving past him, as though she could not be gone from him soon enough. "I was already once engaged to a man whose suit I should never have accepted," she tossed over her shoulder. "I've learned much from that mistake. I won't repeat it. If I were ever to agree to marry again, I must be absolutely certain of the gentleman." Turning, she faced him fully, her dark gaze sweeping over him in distaste. "I am most assuredly *not* certain of you, Laird MacLarin."

He released a huff of frustration. "There is nothing in this life you can be absolutely certain of."

"That is a cynical view."

"It is truth. Something I doubt the father of your child ever gave you."

She flinched.

"Life is risk," he added, gentling his tone. He did not wish to hurt her. Obviously that would not help win her.

"*You* are not a risk I wish to take."

He seized her hand, stopping her from going. "Is that it then? We are done."

"Did we ever begin?"

"You said you were considering my proposal."

"And I did."

"It has not even been a full day. You made up your mind so quickly against me?" He lowered his voice, hoping it affected her because touching her affected him. It got to him—*she* got to him—tightening his gut and sending a delicious thrill along his spine.

His thumb brushed her pulse point at her wrist and her breathing hitched, grew raspy and came noticeably faster. Damn it.

Sensation traveled from his hand to his arm and shot to every part of his body. How did she affect him with such lack of effort? Was he really that weak? That susceptible to her allure?

The answer was glaring. YES. Yes, he was.

"My rejection of your suit comes as a shock?" she asked with a toss of her head and lift of her chin. "We've only known each other for a short amount of time."

"Strangers marry all the time," he countered reasonably. "Arranged marriages are no' so uncommon. Not where you're from . . . not here either."

"But this is not that scenario. We both have a choice here. *I* have a choice. Why should I choose this? Why should I choose you?"

"I've always been a man tae ken his own mind, and I have my mind set on you, Clara."

"Do you now?" Mockery laced her voice. "Well, that is your problem. It has nothing to do with me."

"We would be well suited."

"Because I can give you a child?" she countered, her voice twisting into something bitter, as though she resented this as his reason for wanting to wed her.

"In part."

She hesitated at that admission. "Only in part? What else could possibly motivate you? What could benefit you?"

"Perhaps I should explain the benefits tae *you* since you've brought up a verra valid point. Why should you choose me? Shall I explain that so there is no confusion?"

She took the bait, straightening and leaning forward. Clearly he had her interest now. "Very well. Perhaps you should endeavor to explain that to me."

His thumb roved over the inside of her wrist. "I'm offering you a chance at a new life. Away from boring, oppressive London." He paused, letting that sink in. "As my wife, you will have freedom. You can do more . . . experience more. Travel, if you wish. I will no' inhibit you. I ken that will make you happy. I can see it in your face. You've an adventurer's soul. Also, married tae me, you will never have tae worry about your tainted reputation returning tae haunt you."

She looked at him with a faintly mesmerized expression. He took that as encouragement and continued, "Do you want tae be a burden tae your family? Your brother and sister-in-law? The rest of your kin?"

"Of course not," she snapped with a touch of indignation.

"Then marry me and they shall never have tae bear that burden."

It was her Achilles'. He knew it because he knew she was a good person. Her family suffering because of her? She could not stomach that. Not if she could help it.

Her eyes flickered over his face for several moments until she finally shook her head, clearly reaching a decision.

"I can't." Inhaling, she squared her shoulders. "I respectfully decline your offer." Color flushed her face as she looked down at his hand on hers. That obstinate chin of hers inched higher. "Perhaps you should return to your lover and inform her of the news. I'm sure she will be quite relieved to know that you are unattached."

He adjusted his hand on hers until their fingers were laced. Stepping closer, he observed the way her breathing quickened with interest. She was not unaffected despite her rejection of him. That was something. Something he could cling to. "Are you jealous, Clara?"

She scoffed. "Of course not."

"You've no need tae be. I visited Catriona tae let her know that our association had come tae an end."

Association. He made it sound so very *un-*

loverlike. As though his relationship with this other woman had been a business arrangement. Would that be what their marriage was like if she accepted his proposal? She gave herself a mental kick. No matter. She was *not* marrying him. Ever.

"You told her your association had come to an end? Because of me?" Her nostrils flared and she shook her head. "Oh, that was very rash of you indeed. I do hope she will take you back, my lord."

He winced at her acerbic tone. "Clara—"

"No." She slid her hand free and sidestepped him, moving for the door. "You shouldn't have done that. I cannot marry you. I've thought about it and I cannot."

Frustration welled up inside him . . . and a bit of helplessness that he could not fathom. He hardly knew her, but marrying her, *having* her, had become like breathing to him. Urgent and every bit necessary. "But what about the child?"

She whipped around, staring at him in reproach as though angered he would remind her of her condition. "You needn't think on it." Her voice was as sharp as a blade. "It's no concern to you. I'm not your responsibility. I appreciate your kind offer, but I cannot accept."

She was all rigid formality.

"Clara," he began, "give it some more thought."

She shook her head. "No." Her hand clenched

around the edge of the door. "It's getting late. I should go."

"You should stay," he countered. "We can talk more—"

"No. We shouldn't be alone in here. 'Tisn't seemly."

He snorted. "I don't think you have tae worry about that."

Fire lit her eyes, and he knew he had angered her with this reminder of her status. Or perhaps it was simply telling her how she *should* feel. "You shouldn't remain here. It's unnecessary. You doubtless have things awaiting your attention at home. Please attend to your life and leave me to mine." A weighty pause followed, and then, her voice a whisper, she added, "Forget about me."

She departed swiftly with a swish of skirts, leaving him standing alone in the room.

Forget about her?

It was too late for that.

AS CLARA READIED herself for bed, she tried to will feelings of regret away. Rejecting his offer was the sensible decision. It was the only reasonable course of action to take.

When she'd heard that MacLarin had gone to visit his mistress, she had been unaccountably hurt . . . and worried. Had she misjudged the man? A man she had agreed to *possibly* marry?

She couldn't go through with it. She couldn't marry the man. It was mad. She'd only just met him. She couldn't trust someone that completely or that quickly. She wouldn't.

Marian helped her pull back the coverlet on her bed. "Well, I think you're merely looking for an excuse because you're frightened."

"Of course I'm frightened." She bit her lip to the point of pain, welcoming the punishment. "As I should be. Look where my recent choices have led me."

Marian stared at her with the bed between them. "You mean *here*? Potentially married to a very handsome man who is *much* more interesting than the fops in Town. Not a terrible place to be, in my estimation. I would not mind that . . . marrying a handsome and interesting man."

Clara looked with astonishment at her former governess. She had never heard anything resembling regret or longing for something more, something other than her current life, from her friend. Marian was always so practical. As the oldest of her siblings, Marian was accustomed to responsibility, to sacrifice. As soon as she was old enough, she had sought employment to alleviate the burden on her family. Clara also happened to know Marian sent home part of her wages.

"I thought you never wanted to marry?" she asked.

Marian shrugged. "Well, I can't be your companion for the rest of my life, now can I? I was your governess. Your mother should have released me from service when you turned eighteen. You don't really need me. Not anymore. I should be a governess to someone else and actually earn the money you pay me."

Clara shook her head. "You earn every bit of your wages. I do need you. You cannot leave. You are family."

Marian smiled. "You are too kind, but this cannot last forever. I serve no purpose here."

"You keep me balanced. Why should you ever have to go? If you insist on being a governess, you can be a governess to Marcus's children."

"Hmm. Or yours?" Marian queried with a suggestive waggle of her eyebrows.

"No. I will not marry. Not to MacLarin or any man." Clara strode to her vanity table and sank down on the bench and tried not to feel a stab of disappointment at the words. "Given my situation, there will be no more offers forthcoming."

"But you have an offer right now. Men have mistresses, Clara. I think it was rather courteous of Laird MacLarin to call on this woman personally to end their affair. It does speak to a sense of honor."

Clara set her brush down with a clack on the vanity table, wishing to stop talking about Mac-Larin and his viability as a husband. She grew weary of it all. "It's late and I'm tired, Marian. Can we continue this discussion tomorrow?"

"Very well." Marian opened her bedchamber but paused before stepping out in the hall. "It's not too late."

"It is. I've declined the offer."

"People change their minds all the time."

"Good night, Marian." Clara pulled back the bedding.

"Good night," Marian said, her voice reluctant. Clearly, she wanted to continue with this conversation.

Sleep evaded Clara. The fire in the hearth cast enough light to save the room from complete blackness. Perhaps she could have slept if not for the soft light tossing over the walls and casting flickering shadows.

She had overreacted in her encounter with MacLarin, letting her emotions get the best of her. He'd asked if she was jealous because she had been behaving, regrettably, as though she was.

She didn't regret declining his proposal. She only wished she had not done it in quite so ardent a fashion.

She should have been all coolness. As haughty

as Enid. A polite rebuff from her and no more. No more words had been needed.

All day she had been stewing and she let him feel her ire when she finally came face-to-face with him.

Soon after waking she had learned that Mac-Larin rode out at first light. The maid who arranged her hair for the day informed her the laird had a lady love in the area. Unaware that Clara had an understanding with him, the maid had spoken freely. *He must be calling on her. Och! But the men flock tae those redheaded lassies. They do, indeed. I wish I was blessed wi' such siren's locks. One of the stable lads spotted the Laird heading in the direction of her cottage in the early morning light.*

Clara tried not to show any reaction as her hair was tugged into a dark coronet, but she was fuming inside. The gall of that man! To propose to her and not one day later take to the bed of his lover.

She'd shared what she learned with Marian . . . who then carried forth her own investigation. By noon, Clara had the full story. The laird's lover was widely known throughout the Fife to be barren. Naturally, she would appeal to a man afraid of fathering a child.

"He should marry *her*," Clara muttered, flinging back her covers and climbing out of bed, quite done with trying to sleep. There was no chance of sleep any time soon. Her mind was overwrought with feverish thoughts.

She donned her dressing robe and departed her room. She had not eaten much at dinner, too preoccupied with the empty chair at the table. Her brother and Alyse had worked hard to fill the meal with lively conversation . . . never mentioning their absent dinner guest, which only made his absence ever more glaring.

Now her stomach made its unhappiness obvious.

With her robe belted snugly about her waist, she slipped on her boots. The kitchen was out of doors as was the case with many older buildings. Despite how much Marcus and Alyse had modernized the property, the kitchen still remained in its original location.

She made her way through the great hall, passing silently into the gallery and out the side door. She sucked in a sharp breath at the sudden cold. It was a short walk thankfully. The path was freshly paved with stone and covered with a roof so that the worst of the elements were obstructed. She was only briefly subjected to the frigid night before plunging into the warm kitchen.

The delicious scents of the day's meals still lingered in the air, as did the smoldering logs in the great hearth. She moved quietly so as not to wake the serving girls sleeping on cots along the wall.

She located a fresh loaf of bread and tore off a hunk of it. She inhaled the wonderful yeasty aroma before taking a moaning bite. She moved on, finding an assortment of lovely golden brown meat pasties. Placing the plumpest one on a linen, she continued, investigating what was on hand to drink. She knew she shouldn't, but she poured herself a glass of wine. A full belly of food and drink should do the trick and put her straight to sleep.

Clara rotated in a small circle, surveying the shadowed space, looking for a place to settle down to eat. A hammock hung in the corner, unoccupied. It was likely there for one of the kitchen staff, but she took advantage of the vacancy.

Sipping deeply of her wine so that it wouldn't slosh over the rim, she hesitated, poised above the hammock. Satisfied that the cup was now half-full, she sank down into the cloth, releasing a soft yelp when her sudden weight immediately set it into motion.

Her yelp faded as she wiggled about until she was comfortable, her body molded into the hammock's cocoon. Once settled, she ate her meat pie bite by savory bite, staring into the low-burning logs until her eyelids grew heavy. She finished the rest of her glass and let the empty vessel rest against her side. The hammock was so comfortable, she could imagine how people used them for beds. It seemed a great deal of effort to work herself free of its snug embrace. So much work that she decided to stay put just a little longer.

A little longer and she would return to her bed.

SHE WOULDN'T HAVE him.

Damnable gossip. Someone had carried tales of Catriona, and Clara completely misread the situation. She thought the worst. She thought he had left Kilmarkie for the day, left *her*, all because he wanted to dally with another woman. She thought that lowly of him—that he would propose to her in one breath and rush off to hop into bed with someone else in another.

It was laughable to consider. He was hardly driven by his baser needs.

He'd practiced abstinence for most of his life. Other than those few indiscretions during his adolescence—punishments, he now knew, that were intended for his mother, who would not cease her drunken rants of Hunt's imminent doom—he had adopted a policy of no physical relations with women.

Until Catriona approached him with her very tempting and reasonable proposition.

Following that, he'd lived with a steady diet

of sexual congress, but lately . . . He'd been seeing Catriona less and less. He'd assumed it was typical. The way it was with everyone after a time.

When he and Catriona began their affair, it was new and fairly exciting. That had not lasted long, however. Soon, it had become ordinary. A pleasant way to pass the time, but not something he required with any overwhelming urgency. In fact, he had never felt as though he *needed* to be with Catriona. *Need* had never entered into it. Their relationship had been about convenience. Indeed, his last few visits with her had felt more like a chore. An obligation to be fulfilled . . . and, truthfully, not so convenient anymore.

He'd just as soon chase down his missing bull than go out of his way to spend the night with Catriona. Clara, though, woke something in him.

Already he yearned for her. The moment he had come face-to-face with her at the inn, he felt as though he were emerging from a fog, or a great long sleep. He felt a hum in his skin. A coiling in his muscles. He didn't know why. He didn't care to examine it.

He only knew he wasn't ready to walk away from her. Not yet.

She knew so little of him. Only what gossip had supplied.

She'd been hurt recently. She had been *failed*.

Naturally, she would be on her guard. Skittish. It was only wise of her to reject him.

He needed to do the one thing he had never done before to any woman—woo her.

For no other reason did he find himself before her door in much the same manner as when she had invaded his room the night before. He rapped twice.

No answer.

With a furtive glance up and down the corridor, he knocked again, as loudly as he dared. The door suddenly parted with a creak. It had not been fully shut. The force of his knock pushed it inward.

He hesitated and then poked his head inside the chamber. There was enough light to see that she wasn't in her bed. The covers were flipped back, revealing a wide expanse of bed but no Clara. A deeper survey of the room revealed it to be empty.

Where was she so late at night?

He knew it wasn't his business. *She* wasn't his business. He had no claim on her. She had made that abundantly clear today when she told him to go home.

The question of her whereabouts niggled, however, gnawing at him until he had to act.

He made his way downstairs. He checked the library. The room was dark. He inhaled the scent of leather that swirled about the space and peered through the gloom, making certain he was not overlooking her tucked away in some corner.

Failing to find her there, he stepped out into the hall, feeling strangely unsettled. Perhaps she was in her companion's room. He wasn't about to go knock on *her* door. Knocking on her door late at night could only be misinterpreted.

Accepting that he could do no more, he turned back for the stairs but stopped with one foot on the bottom step.

Everything in him tensed. His nostrils flared, taking in a new scent. Bitter and acrid, faintly stinging in his nose.

Smoke.

Chapter 10

*C*lara woke disorientated, certain it was a dream. The air was thick, opaque. And it was noisy. Her ears throbbed with a rumbling roar layered with intermittent pops.

She coughed, which only seemed to incite more violent hacking.

Smoke. Her heart jumped to her constricting throat.

Fire.

She tried to stand and discovered she was stuck. She flailed, bewildered, panicked, coughing up her starving lungs. Then she recalled she was in a hammock. She'd gone to the kitchen and she'd fallen asleep in a hammock.

She twisted her neck about wildly, identifying a red-gold light. There was a rippling wall of heat where the fireplace had been, obstructing the door that led to the outside pathway. It ate up the walls around her like a red-orange river. That half of the room was engulfed, barring her escape. *Oh. God.*

She continued to cough, gasping and choking through the haze. Her eyes teared so badly it was hard to see.

She was trapped.

Was this it? How she would end? Perish in flame?

Screaming penetrated over the roar of fire. She searched and spotted the once sleeping serving girls up from their beds, pounding with their fists at the large mullioned window. They rattled at the latch, which only pulled the glass down partially, a fraction, a mere crack through which nobody could pass. A child's body perhaps, but not either of the girls.

Not her.

They were trapped.

As they cried for help, Clara flung herself from the hammock, spinning to the floor and landing with a jar. The force brought her teeth clacking together. She bit her lip. The copper taste of blood rolled along her teeth and washed over her tongue.

She didn't care. Smoke billowed thickly toward

her. She had bigger problems. The heat reached
her, singeing her face. Wiping at the back of her
mouth, she scrambled to her feet and joined the
girls at the window.

With the windows parted, the fire only seemed
to worsen, spreading faster, a scalding beast
growing at their backs.

She groped at the latch, screaming hoarsely
for help.

She was going to die.

Not like this. Not like this.

She turned, searching for something to use to
break the glass.

She spotted a heavy wood rolling pin on the
work table and leapt forward to grab it. Returning to the window, she attacked the glass, cursing
the grid system of muntins that prevented the
glass from breaking as it would if it were one
great panel of glass. The serving girls followed
suit, grabbing weapons to break the glass. The
sturdy iron muntins, however, remained mostly
in place.

Coughing through the thick smoke, she broke
several small panes of glass, hoping the iron
dividers would soon weaken and give way. No
such luck. A sob of frustration welled up in her
chest.

This could not be happening. Please. *No.*

She had not come here to die. Scotland was

supposed to be her salvation, not her demise. She was not ready for death. She had so much life yet in her.

Her tearing gaze searched through the stinging smoke. It would take something large and heavy to break the entire grid free. They were essentially caged within a burning prison.

She went back to work, whacking at the iron grid, her entire body growing heavy and sluggish, unbearably tired as she struggled to work through the darkening smoke. Her head throbbed. Her watering eyes burned. Her skin stung. Her lungs withered, starved for a taste of air. Sweet life-giving air.

A groan rumbled over the roar of fire like the advance of an incoming train and a crash boomed behind her. A quick glance revealed a portion of the ceiling had collapsed. Dear heavens. It wouldn't be long before the rest of it caved in on them.

They were going to burn.

She whirled back around to the window, stabbing frantically at it with the rolling pin, determined to fight; determined to live. She screamed with everything she had left. Her hoarse voice ripped from her raw throat.

She stalled altogether when she noticed something moving on the other side of the window. A figure.

"Stand aside!" came the deep shout.

A man moved out there, holding something. Something large.

"Help!" Her voice escaped in a pathetic croak. "Here!"

"Stand aside!" he bellowed again.

Her arm flew out to the girl beside her. "Back away." She forced them back, into the clawing heat. It went against instinct. Against the fear choking her along with the smoke.

Wheezing, the three of them clung close, jumping as a large stone burst through the window, taking a good portion of the pane out, iron grid muntins with it and all. The hole it made was not quite big enough for a body to pass, but close.

Not that it appeared to matter to the person on the other side. He pushed through the irregular-shaped hole, regardless of the jagged bits of glass and steel stabbing at him.

The man dropped down lightly on the other side. Through the haze, his face took shape. *MacLarin*. Her heart lurched at the sight of him. He reached for her. "Clara! Come!"

Clara turned and pushed one of the other girls forward. MacLarin scowled at her but didn't protest. He seized the female and lifted her up through the window.

The second girl was ready for him when he turned back around. He soon had her out as well.

Clara had scarcely taken a step forward for her turn before his hands were on her waist and he had her up and out of the window.

She landed on her feet on the other side and whirled around, waiting for him to emerge, holding her breath until he did so. Until he was standing safely on solid ground before her.

He reached for her, but not soon enough. Her legs gave out, too weak to support herself.

He caught her up the moment before she struck the ground.

"Clara!" He spoke into her face, his arms wrapping around her.

She tried to answer. Her throat muscles worked, but only a pained whimper escaped.

With a stinging curse, he lifted her up and moved her far beyond the burning kitchen.

People were everywhere now. All around them. A loud and frantic press of bodies. Someone was crying nearby. She heard all this over the roar of the hungry fire. She sensed their movements as she stared straight ahead at the laird's soot-marked face.

He came. He saved my life. Mine and the other girls'.

"How did y-you—?" She stopped. The words hurt too much in her throat. They felt like a knife scraping the inside of her throat.

"Shh," he soothed, holding her tighter in his arms.

She swallowed, wincing at the effort as he carried her back toward the house. "MacLarin."

"Dinna speak. Rest your throat. You inhaled a great deal of smoke."

He was right, of course. She should rest and let her throat mend. She *should* wait until after she was tended and she didn't smell like a fire pit and wasn't covered head to toe in cinders. A blessed drink of water wouldn't be unwanted either.

But not yet. Not until she said what she had to say. Before she lost her nerve.

"MacLarin . . . Hunt."

"What is it, lass?" He glanced at her before looking ahead again, minding his steps.

"I will marry you."

He stopped hard, his arms tightening slightly around her. He didn't so much as blink as he looked down at her. "Are you . . . Did you knock your head?"

She smiled and imagined she looked quite the mess, smoke-blackened and reeking of charred rubble. She was hardly a prize, even before her present condition. "My head is fine."

Very fine indeed. She'd be a fool not to marry this man. He'd saved her life at his own peril. She had been on the brink of death, tottering at the precipice, and he had yanked her back.

He was nothing like the fops back in Town. Her

brush with death made that abundantly clear. He was a man in possession of honor and strength. He was willing to take on another man's child. That said a great deal about him . . . *and* there was the not-so-minor fact that she was attracted to him in a way she had never felt before. *Achingly* attracted to him.

The only mark against him was that he believed in silly curses, and was that really such an awful thing? She had lived around superstition before. Her own mother would go out of her way to avoid a black cat.

He couldn't help himself. She was sure of that. He'd been raised to believe in such rubbish. That would soon change. She'd show him curses didn't exist.

She'd show him that they could build a life together.

And maybe, possibly, they could be happy.

THE MOMENT HUNT lowered Clara down onto her bed, he was ushered out by her companion and several servants. He had no time to talk to her further . . . not that he wanted to press her to speak. Not in her condition. She needed to rest her throat.

Maybe he could bring her quill and parchment and he could confirm in writing that she had in fact said she would marry him. He stifled a laugh at the ridiculous notion.

All giddiness fled as he paced in front of her door, thinking of how very ill she had looked when he left her. Ashen even beneath all that soot and grime. Her cough and croaking voice were worrisome. Only a temporary consequence of the fire hopefully.

She said she would marry me.

Equal parts elation and fear swirled through him. He wanted to barge through the door and make certain she was well—make certain his future wife and child were both well.

Alyse appeared. "Off with you." She shooed him away, motioning with her hands. "We will tend to her. Nothing for you to do lurking outside her door here. She will be well." Without another word, she entered the chamber, closing the door solidly in his face.

He stared at the thick wood a few helpless moments before realizing she was correct. He could be of better use elsewhere. Standing outside her door was helping no one.

He hurried downstairs to help the rest of the household put out the fire.

Autenberry was there in his trousers and boots. Shirtless as he'd undoubtedly been when roused from bed. He was oblivious to the cold as he worked in the bucket line.

Hunt joined him. He worked alongside the others until they had the fire contained. The kitchen was lost, but the fire was stopped from spreading. The castle itself spared. No one dead.

They worked until the light of dawn streaked the sky and the kitchen was nothing more than a smoldering pile of rubble.

Autenberry approached him, covered in sweat and ash. He wiped a forearm across his brow. "No one was hurt. That's the important thing," he said as though Hunt had voiced a question.

Hunt tossed aside his bucket and started for the castle, needing to see for himself that Clara was in fact unhurt. He ran inside and took the stairs two steps at a time until he arrived at her chamber's door just as her companion was emerging.

"Laird MacLarin, you can't go in there—" the lass, Marian, started to say.

He did not let her finish. He pushed past her, determined to set his mind at ease.

"Hunt." Alyse rose from the chair beside the bed where she sat. She motioned to her lips for him to be silent.

He moved deeper into the chamber and stopped beside the bed, looking down at a sleeping Clara.

Someone had washed her. Not an inch of soot present anywhere, but she was still pale.

"How is she?" His gaze traveled over her, assuring himself there were no visible injuries he had missed.

"Exhausted, but fine. Her coughing abated. She took down some water and fell back to sleep."

He reached for her hand where it rested limply by her side. He could not stop himself from touching her, from feeling her alive.

He dragged his gaze from her face to look back at the duchess. "What about the babe . . . no cause for concern there?"

Alyse looked startled for a moment. He imagined speaking so directly of Clara's delicate condition was off-putting, scandalous as it was, but since it concerned her well-being, he did not care for propriety.

Clara had agreed to become his wife. Her health and the health of her child were his chief concerns.

"The babe is fine. They are both fine, Laird MacLarin," Marian volunteered with a cheerful smile. "Much thanks to you, I understand."

He offered a shaky smile in turn. It was difficult to smile with Clara so wan in the bed only a few feet from him.

"What happened?" Autenberry charged into the room and dropped down beside his sister on the bed, evidently only now learning of her status.

"She was in the kitchen when the fire started. Hunt got her and the other maids out."

Autenberry's gaze swept over them all. "Why was I not informed?"

"Everything has been madness, Marcus . . . you had your hands full with the fire. She was in good hands with us," Alyse explained. "The fire—"

"It's out. We lost the kitchen, but the fire is out," Autenberry responded, his gaze still trained on Clara.

"That's a relief." Alyse sighed. "However did it start?"

"We'll examine for the cause later, but I imagine the fire set off a spark." He shrugged. "It can be rebuilt. Better. Safer. With a proper fireplace this time." He lifted his tired gaze to Hunt. "Thank you. For being there. For saving her."

Hunt nodded stiffly. Autenberry did not understand. Hunt did not need his thanks. There had been no choice in the matter for him; saving Clara had been as necessary as air to him.

"Come, Marcus. Let her sleep." Alyse tugged him away from the bed. "We would give her a fright if she woke up to all these faces."

"I'll stay with her," Marian said. "She shouldn't be alone."

"I will," Hunt announced.

Everyone stared at him as though he'd just uttered the most ridiculous thing.

"Have you seen yourself?" A smile played about Marian's mouth. "I'm afraid if you sit down you're going to ruin the upholstery."

He glanced down at himself, noting he was covered in soot.

"Bathe first at least," Alyse said. "She's not going anywhere."

He nodded, still reluctant to leave her but knowing he should.

They all filed toward the door with the exception of Marian.

At the door, he stopped and glanced back at the bed. "You'll fetch me if—"

"Why, Laird MacLarin, you're acting like a besotted lad." Marian's eyes glinted knowingly at him.

"She's going tae marry me." He felt compelled to say it, to establish this fact. Perhaps he just wanted to hear it out loud again. She was asleep now and he couldn't ask her to repeat herself. He could say the words, though.

She arched an eyebrow. "Is she now?"

"Aye. She said so."

"Did she? And when was that?"

"When I pulled her from the burning kitchen."

She laughed then, looking down at her friend fondly. "It took a near-death experience to bring her to her senses, did it?"

"I beg your pardon?"

"Never you mind. Just know this . . . if you wrong her, you'll have to answer to me."

"A fearsome fate indeed."

"It is. Especially considering I encouraged her to accept your proposal." Her smile faded away then. "Don't prove me wrong, Laird MacLarin. Don't you dare."

Chapter 11

They married two days after the fire.

It happened with such haste Clara scarcely had time to think and that was probably for the best. Less time to think meant less time to lose her nerve and change her mind.

Her voice had returned to normal by then and only a mild sore throat from her exposure to the smoke lingered. She was very fortunate indeed. All thanks to Hunt—a fact never far from her mind. The Laird MacLarin was a heroic man.

Marcus sent for the local reverend two villages away; otherwise they would have married the very next day with the smoke from the incinerated kitchen still a thick haze about the property.

MacLarin was eager for them to take vows. Clara assumed it was because he was sensitive to the fact that she was with child and they should marry as quickly as possible given her condition.

She winced. That misconception had to be remedied posthaste.

She was anxious to put the ceremony behind them, too. She didn't want her nerve to fail her, true...but admittedly, there was a certain amount of breathlessness when she contemplated marrying the handsome Scot. He excited her. Thrilled her in a way she had never experienced. Just one look from him made her heart race. There had never been that before and she wasn't certain how to cope with it. Surely it would pass. Surely they would reach a state of normalcy. Surely she would come to a point where she did not feel as though she were jumping out of her skin in his presence.

Of course, Marcus agreed they should act quickly. He was in full support of sending for the reverend. Only Alyse harbored reservations over the marriage, disliking that they hadn't disclosed the full truth to MacLarin.

Clara didn't like it either, but she had talked herself into it—with a good deal of help from Marian and Marcus. They were quick to remind her that MacLarin would be happy once he realized the curse wasn't real. Once he had sired his own baby. The prospect seemed surreal. She would marry this stranger. Take him into her body. Give him a child, if so blessed.

She told herself she'd do her best to be a good wife. To make him happy so that he would not care of her initial deception.

"Don't underestimate him . . . or yourself," Alyse had advised the night before as Clara readied for bed. "I've seen the way he looks at you, Clara. He is attracted to you and attraction can lead to fondness. Even love. There's a flame there between you both. Nurture it."

She hoped Alyse was right. That a part of him was marrying her for herself and not what he perceived she brought to him.

"When will you tell him?" Alyse had asked.

"After we're wed," Clara promised and meant it. After they wed. No more excuses.

They married in the morning with Marcus, Alyse, Marian and Hunt's man in attendance. She wore one of her finer day dresses—a deep rose-colored muslin sprigged with tiny rosebuds of yellow.

The maid took longer than usual on her hair, proclaiming it a special day. Marian seconded that opinion. Clara's poor bum was numb by the time she stood. But her hair was proclaimed a masterpiece.

It helped, knowing she looked her best when

she joined MacLarin at the altar of the small chapel. Fortified her somehow.

His gaze skimmed over her. Morning light from the single stained-glass window gilded his hair a rainbow of colors. In his eyes she thought she read the gleam of approval and that flushed warmth through her.

She liked him looking at her with admiration. In Town, her looks had not been very popular. Dark hair. Brown eyes. Skin less than the hue of milk. She was no classic English rose and often made to feel that lack. All the other girls especially made her feel that lack. Except in his eyes.

In his eyes, she felt admiration.

Together, they faced the reverend, and in that moment, she felt as though they were *together*. In this endeavor, in what they were committing to—they were equal and of like mind.

The reverend's accent was so thick, Clara had difficulty understanding him. There were times when she suspected he was speaking in Gaelic. She spoke up at the appropriate intervals, sometimes at the prodding of Hunt.

He stood proudly at her side, rigid as a soldier at attention. His hand brushed hers in those moments the reverend stared at her expectantly.

Those tiny touches made her breathing hitch. Everything else blurred around her. He towered over her, his shoulders so deliciously broad. She studied him from beneath her lashes, trying to memorize him, to freeze and immortalize this moment so that she would always have it. Come good or bad, she'd have the sweetness of this moment . . . the tender uncertainty where she felt as exhilarated and raw as an infant entering a new world, full of hope for the future.

His rich brown hair was shot with brilliant highlights of gold. It fell low over his forehead. She studied his lips as he spoke, forming the words that bound her to him.

Dear. God.

She was marrying this alarmingly attractive man.

She'd come north thinking she was entering into a life sentence of solitude. Now, instead, she was marrying this virile man who sent her heart pounding every time he came within proximity. She was his now. A part of her rebelled at this while another part simultaneously reveled in the knowledge. There was a part of herself, buried deep, that wanted to be claimed by this man in the most primitive fashion. As though he were a Viking marauder from old.

The reverend finished and MacLarin was pressing his cool lips to hers. Perhaps only cool because the rest of her was so overheated.

The kiss was over as soon as it began and they were surrounded with well-wishers. Marian was weeping. Over her shoulder, Clara watched as her brother clapped her husband on the back.

Her husband.

Husband.

They were married. She was a wife.

Dear. God. What had she done?

Hopefully the right thing. Hopefully nothing she would come to regret.

MacLarin's gaze found hers, deep and probing as though he sensed the panicked flurry of her thoughts. Who knew? Maybe he felt some of the same sense of panic?

Alyse had arranged for an impressive breakfast, a full spread of every sausage and sweet roll imaginable. Marcus gave a lovely toast—words she could not be counted on to remember at threat of life. Were wedding days supposed to be memorable? She felt rather numb, as though she were watching everything from under water. She doubted she would ever be able to recall any of it.

She hardly remembered tasting anything although she ate, sampling the array as she sat beside her husband.

Husband. Husband. Husband.

She knew it was early yet, but she longed for some of Mama's Madeira to relax her overwrought nerves. Although that was probably impossible. No drink could relax her. She sat stiffly, her stomach churning.

MacLarin turned to her after they'd feasted for what felt like forever. "Are you ready?"

She blinked. *Ready?* For what?

The image of her bed upstairs immediately filled her mind—but then she understood. He was not talking about *that*.

He wasn't some ravenous wolf ready to pounce on her. He wasn't that manner of man. No, desire did not enter into this. It was not what motivated him. He married her because she was the safe choice. She was already with child and he needed, or rather wanted, a child. She could give him that, as well as a fortuitous alliance with his lofty neighbor.

No, he was asking if she was ready to depart. He wanted to return to his home. He doubtless had matters that required attending, including introducing her to his grandmother and the rest of his people before word of their marriage got ahead of them.

His people. That rolled around in her mind. It was a reminder that he was a man of importance in this area. She hoped his people accepted her. She hoped his grandmother liked her. Life could be difficult otherwise. She hoped that his home would soon feel like her own, that one day she would wake and not feel like a visitor in a strange land.

Her nerves returned tenfold with her useless hoping and longing. It accomplished nothing to ponder such things. She forced a nod. "Yes. I am ready."

She said her farewells, giving her sister-in-law a lingering hug. "You will send word at once when your time arrives? I will come."

"Of course," Alyse said. "And you must visit often. Not only then, you know. Other occasions, too. We didn't have nearly enough time with you."

"No, we didn't," Marcus said gruffly, tugging her in for an embrace. "We thought we were going to have you with us forever here." His voice ruffled her hair as he spoke. "We will see you soon . . . and often."

"Count yourself lucky that you are not stuck with me forever," she teased, hiding how very nervous she felt at the prospect of leaving them, at placing herself among strangers. At least she had Marian for company. She would not be totally alone.

She had entered into this marriage voluntarily, but in this moment, with her thoughts spinning, she could only taste the fine edge of panic threatening to engulf her.

She took a breath and stepped away, but the sight of her brother's somber countenance gave her a pang of sadness. Silly, of course. He would be living a stone's throw away—so much closer than before. Before when she lived in London. Before when she was unwed and lived in London.

That was the difference. That was everything. The crux of the matter. Everything was different now.

Now she was married to a Highland laird. Maid no more. No longer even an Autenberry. She was a MacLarin now. Bound forever to a man she had known barely a week. She'd likely never see London again.

Suddenly her mouth dried and she felt dizzy. Something must have been reflected in her face. MacLarin was at her side at once, pulling her close, a solid arm sliding around her waist and that was its own cause for dizziness. Heavens, he smelled good. Like soap and clean air, wind and rain.

In London, the ballrooms had always been jam-packed, the men smelling of sweat that reeked slightly of onion, their breaths sour when they spoke close.

This was heady. *He* was heady. His deep brogue rumbled in her ear. "Are you unwell?"

"No," she breathed, but the air was tight in her chest, elusive. "I mean y-yes." She gave her head a small shake, attempting to clear it of his thrall. "Yes. I'm fine."

She forced a bright smile for everyone who watched her with such concern, feeling pinned beneath MacLarin's sharp gaze. She didn't want anyone to worry on her account. Especially him. Those eyes of his saw too much, too deeply. He needed to shift his attention elsewhere so that she might breathe again.

She settled into the carriage across from Marian, sighing with relief as soon as the door snicked shut after her. Hunt would ride alongside the carriage with his man, Graham.

"Try *not* to look so obviously thrilled to be getting away from your new husband," Marian chided as the carriage began moving. "You've only consigned yourself to spend the rest of your life with him. You should not look ill hours after your vows."

"I'm sure I don't know what you mean," Clara lied. She knew exactly what Marian meant.

Marian snorted. "I'm sure you do. And need I remind you that you're about to spend the night with him? Oh, and he thinks you're an experienced woman. You really should not look so green about the gills."

The blood rushed to Clara's face. "Dear heavens. You're not helping. Why would you say that to me?" She would be alone with him in a bedroom tonight—in a bed. Why had she not thought about that before? It seemed like the one thing most newlyweds would be thinking about on their wedding day and yet she had not. Not until now.

"Oh, dear. Don't faint." Marian scooted across the carriage to sit beside her and patted her hand.

"I'm not going to faint," Clara grumbled. "Have I ever been the swooning sort?"

"You look pale."

"I'm not some meek mouse of a girl."

"Of course not." Marian nodded agreeably.

"Look at the bold action I took to avoid marrying Rolland."

Marian continued to nod. "You were very bold in that regard, to be certain."

Clara still was bold. Look what she had done. She had married a man to save her reputation and spare her family. And because she believed him honorable . . . and he made her pulse race. She was no shrinking violet.

She inhaled. "I will simply tell him. Tonight." It was her turn to nod. Once. Twice. Decisively.

"So soon?"

"We're wed. 'Tis done. I always planned on letting him know the truth." Once he knew, there would be nothing more between them. They could begin their marriage honestly.

"I thought you wanted to convince him the curse doesn't exist."

"I shall do that, of course. Time will assist in that endeavor. He has married me. He will not die from it. 'Tis done. It cannot be undone at this point."

"My, my. How romantic," Marian murmured wryly.

Clara shrugged. "Our union can never claim to be founded on romance."

"Hmm." Marian reclaimed her seat across from Clara. "But perhaps it will end there. After tonight, eh? One never knows."

"You are the romantic one," Clara accused, resisting the niggle of hope those words elicited.

"Me? Not even close. I'm a realist. The fact holds true, though . . . before the night is over, the two of you will be sharing a bed."

The air fled from her lungs. "You needn't be so blunt."

"In the absence of your mother, as your former governess, I feel this is the moment I offer sage wisdom and advice, but I know little more than you do." Marian shrugged apologetically.

"Please. No advice." She held up a hand. "Mama already put me through that awkward conversation when she thought I was to marry Rolland." Her mother had equated Clara's body to a flower and Rolland the pollinating bee. She shuddered. "It was difficult to stomach."

Mostly because Rolland had been the man called into reference, and a part of her already knew then that she'd made a mistake accepting his proposal. The idea of living with him, sharing *his* bed, had started to make her skin crawl. A grim portent. Reflecting on that now only confirmed that she had done the right thing to escape her fate. No matter what it took. No matter where it led her.

Here. It has led you here, to tonight . . . to the bed of MacLarin.

Chapter 12

*T*hey stopped for the night at an inn halfway between Kilmarkie and Hunt's home.

They'd departed too late to make the trip in a day and the journey from Kilmarkie to his home was a definite push in that short time anyway. It required a hard, full day's ride by horseback. It was well enough when it was just himself or his men astride their mounts. They could press and make the trip in no time. It was another thing entirely for a gently bred lady ensconced in a carriage—and one who was increasing no less. He wouldn't demand such rigor of her. She'd already been through a great deal, nearly perishing in the kitchen fire. A half day's journey was best. He didn't want to overtire her.

Hunt knew the inn well. He saw to securing the appropriate chambers. Fortunately, the establishment was not crowded for the night, and there was plenty of room for all of them.

He and Clara would be the only two sharing a room.

The innkeeper escorted them to their chamber. "Finest one for ye and your lady, Laird," he proclaimed, moving to the window that overlooked the yard and pulling back the drapes to let in the waning evening light.

"My thanks," Hunt responded, his gaze fixing on Clara. His wife.

Wife. It seemed impossible. As though the word somehow did not fit into his vocabulary. Because it had been expunged. Wives were for other men. He'd been primed for loneliness, for eternal bachelorhood. It had been fed into his porridge.

The innkeeper left them with a promise to send up a couple trays of food.

Hunt did not spare the proprietor a glance as the door snicked shut behind him. "You look tired."

"Me? I'm fine. It's merely been a long day."

"That it has." They stared at one another, alone in a bedchamber, husband and wife. She did not look away from him. He would give her credit for that. She held her ground and stared back at him. The bed loomed close, a glaring reminder that they had every right under God's eyes to use it. To take to it together. In fact, they were expected to do that very thing.

He cleared his throat and rubbed a suddenly perspiring palm against the side of his trousers, marveling that he should feel so awkward. Like a green lad. "I'll just go check on the horses. Make certain they're tended for the night."

"Yes, of course." She nodded circumspectly, politely. As a stranger would. They still had a great deal to learn about each other. The prospect gave him a small thrill. He never had that before. Never had a future with a woman to look forward to, but he had that now.

"I'll be back soon."

He left her, wondering if he should have said something more to set her at ease, wondering if there was anything he could say.

Was she having second thoughts? Did she regret this day's deeds? Was she thinking of her lover, her child's true father, and regretting that Hunt was the man she had married?

Well, it was done and could not be undone now. If she thought he would fall on her tonight like some greedy beast, hungry to claim his husbandly rights, she was mistaken. He would do no such thing.

He was a man accustomed to restraint. He would wait until she was ready.

He would wait until she wanted him, and if that day never arrived, so be it.

THEIR TRAYS ARRIVED, but he did not.

Clara waited for him until pangs of hunger demanded she eat without him.

As the minutes waned, she tucked herself behind the dressing screen and changed into her nightgown for the night.

Perhaps he had decided to eat dinner downstairs. Perhaps he was in his cups with his man and had forgotten all about her.

Or perhaps she simply was not that important to him.

She decided against slipping into the bed. That felt too much like an invitation. She did not want to be waiting there like some manner of spruced goose ready to be plucked. Vulnerability was to be avoided.

She settled into an armchair before the fire after pouring herself a bit of mulled wine the innkeeper had been good enough to include with their dinner.

Soon her eyelids were growing heavy and she gave in, resting her head against the back of the chair. Whenever he returned, she would wake.

She would tell him everything. Confess all

and they would begin their marriage on a fresh page with no falsehoods between them.

"I CANNA BELIEVE ye did it," Graham proclaimed. "Yer grandmother will have much tae say on the matter. She might force ye tae take the lass back."

Hunt choked on a laugh. "I'm no' taking Clara back and returning her as though she's some bit of goods that did no' measure up. She's my wife." *Mine.* "I'm a grown man. Nana can't force me tae do anything I dinna wish tae." He downed his glass of whisky. Clara was his now. She and her child. Nothing could change that. Not even his grandmother.

She would still worry about the curse even once he explained his reasoning to her. Even though she had not behaved as his mother had, she was just as much a slave to it. Nana had lost her son and husband both to it. She had a healthy respect for its power. She would not trust that Hunt had found a way around it.

He set his glass down with a clack. "Well, enough. I'm tae bed."

Graham made a snickering sound and Hunt shot him a sharp warning glance. His friend looked contrite and pressed his lips in a firm line, uttering forth no further sound.

Hunt took the steps two at a time. He paused

briefly outside the door before knocking gently once. After a moment's silence, he turned the latch.

Clara was asleep in the chair before the fire. He could see the remnants of her meal on the table and he winced. He should have eaten with her. Nerves had kept him away . . . and in truth her earlier manner did not smack of eagerness for his company. She had been so stoic, reminding him of a man facing a noose. In this case, he was the noose. It was far from heartening. He had thought to give her time to herself.

He stopped before her chair and admired her for a moment. His gut tightened. She really was lovely. Wisps of dark hair haloed her face. Bending, he scooped her up and moved her toward the bed. She roused and stirred in his arms as he lowered her on the mattress and settled her beneath the covers.

Her lashes fluttered. She came to slowly, blinking inky lashes over warm brown eyes groggily. "Hunt?"

His skin tightened at the sound of his name. "Time tae bed." His voice escaped a bit gruffly, perhaps even sternly. He swallowed past the tightness in his throat and reluctantly slid his arms free of her body. "Shh. Rest now."

She sat up on the bed and looked around slowly as though reacquainting herself with her surroundings. "How long was I asleep?" She rubbed at one eye with the base of her palm. She looked very young and vulnerable with the loose plait of dark hair hanging like a rope over her shoulder.

"No' long, I think."

She covered her yawn with a hand. "We need to talk."

"It can wait until morning. You look ready tae fall over asleep." He felt his own yawn upon him. "I confess I'm tired as well."

She hesitated and then relented with a nod. "In the morning then. We will talk."

She lowered back down on the bed and snuggled deeper into the mattress with a sigh. Her eyelids fell shut again.

He stood back from the bed and stripped off his clothes, watching her sleep, her profile gentle and sweet in repose.

Dousing the light, he slid in beside her, careful their bodies not touch.

The sound of her soft breathing grew slower. She must be sliding into sleep. He held himself motionless, certain it would not be so easy for him to fall asleep. His mind worked feverishly, backtracking until he was standing in the chapel back at Kilmarkie with Clara beside him.

Her brown eyes had been twin moons in her

face as the reverend spoke over them—as though she did not quite comprehend. He could relate. He had felt some of the same shock standing before God and witnesses exchanging marriage vows. It was similar to the bewilderment he experienced now lying beside a woman who was his wife. It felt as though he were living someone else's life . . . a life in which he could have Lady Clara, the Duke of Autenberry's sister, as his wife. This girl with her liquid dark eyes belonged to him.

He realized with some start that she might not appreciate the fact that once she delivered her child they would have a name-only marriage . . . assuming they ever engaged in intimacy and she was not still in love with the father of her child. He would have to consider carefully when and how to introduce that news to her.

He didn't know the circumstances that led her to being unwed in Scotland. He only knew that it meant she was free to marry him. At least in name. He had no notion of the availability of her heart. That could very well be engaged elsewhere. Perhaps that was what she wanted to talk to him about in the morning.

Her past did not matter to him. He did not judge her for it. How could he? It was the very reason she was so appealing to him. He could not have asked her to marry him otherwise. And yet it stung to think she married him while in love with another.

He reminded himself of the purpose of this marriage. Her child would have a father and not face the stigma of illegitimacy. Clara would be respectably married. Hunt would have a child to claim as his own.

It was enough. It had to be.

He sighed and closed his eyes, willing himself to sleep.

HUNT WOKE SLOWLY to chirping birds. As he opened his eyes, faint sunlight greeted him and the scent of flowers filled his nose. She rustled beside him. A tangle of hair streamed across his chest. Dark as a moonless night. He threaded his fingers through it. Like silk. He brushed it aside and found himself staring at Clara. Her hair had come unraveled from its plait. She slept on, unaware of the strands of loosened hair everywhere, connecting them.

She wasn't aware of him at all. She slept blissfully ignorant that she had drifted toward the center of the bed, invading his space . . . invading *him*. One of her arms draped across his bare chest.

He was aware. Blissfully, wretchedly aware.

Her nightgown had bunched up so that the silken length of her leg wrapped around his hip.

He hissed out a slow breath, his body achingly alert to the proximity of sweet feminine flesh against him.

He fought to swallow. Her closeness was too much for any man to bear. He lowered a hand to the limb to push it off him, but then his hand lingered, luxuriating in the soft skin of her knee, the delicate bend.

She sighed and snuggled her face closer up his chest, right beside his face.

He reminded himself that she was sleeping. He told himself to let go of her knee. To remove her from him, peel her off and away.

Easier said than done.

He brought his face down to her neck and breathed her in. She smelled delicious. Like flowers and winter and soap all rolled into one welcoming package. He nuzzled her neck like he was some kind of purring cat desperate to get closer. And then he licked her. Tasted her warm skin with a small, satisfied growl. He followed the taste with a moist, openmouthed kiss on the side of her throat.

Her breath caught just above his ear, feathering his hair. He felt her swallow, her slender throat working against his lips.

Everything in him felt liquid-hot and melting . . . like his muscles had dissolved into heated butter.

He wanted to crawl inside her. Roll her onto her back and drive his body into hers until he experienced every part of her.

Every curve and dip and hollow. All her softness. His cock swelled, aching and eager to slide inside her snug heat. The core of her was so close, radiating heat, not far from his hip. So close. Her nightgown was already gathered high, her thigh flung around his hip. It wouldn't take much. A slight shifting and push and he could be inside her.

The sudden surge of need shook him to the core. It wasn't like anything he felt before. He'd always been strong and in control.

Right now he did not feel that way at all.

It dragged him back to reality, kept him from going further. It was enough. Enough to bring him back. He lifted his face from her throat and released her thigh . . . only to find a pair of unblinking brown eyes fastened to his face.

She was awake.

"Clara," he breathed her name like a benediction. That's how it felt on his lips. She was an answer to prayers. Prayers he had refused to think or utter. Somehow they had been answered anyway.

She didn't move. Not even a fraction of an inch.

Hunt waited for her to scramble away. Maybe even slap his face.

He watched her, waiting. "Good morning," he husked.

"Good morning," she whispered back.

He watched her lovely throat work as she swallowed. Then she shocked him by taking his hand and moving it back to where it had been on her knee.

He exhaled sharply as she settled his palm over the bend in her leg, pressing down so that he gripped her, so that his fingers splayed wide.

He read the hesitation in her face. She might be inviting him to resume touching her, but she was still frightened.

She moistened her lips with the tip of her tongue. "Why did you stop?"

Chapter 13

Clara could not have made the invitation any clearer.

She didn't know where such boldness came from within her. She had never forayed into intimacy like this. She didn't know she had it in her. She supposed it had something to do with the way he made her feel . . . something to do with the fire in her blood. Something to do with the fact that this handsome man was her husband. He was hers now as much as she was his, and she *could* do this. There was no reason not to.

He said her name again. "Clara." In that husky brogue of his. She felt herself melting, sliding deeper into a puddle of desire.

They hadn't even kissed. Not a true romantic

kiss. She did not count the chaste peck the morning of her wedding.

And heavens, she had wanted him to kiss her even then, in front of all those people.

She wanted his mouth on hers. She wanted to taste him with an ache that went bone-deep. Despite his gruffness, his mouth looked beautiful. There was a tenderness in the well-carved shape that she wanted to explore.

She inhaled a ragged breath, trying to calm her racing nerves. Desire rushed through her. Waking up to find him so close, touching her, licking her . . . She inhaled a shuddering breath. She should have been shocked or frightened, but he felt so good against her.

"Hunt," she whispered as she flattened a trembling hand against his chest. His heart beat hard against her palm, but hers beat harder.

She felt so awkward. She didn't know what to do next.

Instinct guided her and inched her forward. She pressed her mouth to his throat. He tensed as she feathered tiny kisses along the edge of his jaw until she reached the corner of his mouth. She paused there, suddenly seized with uncertainty.

His head dipped then, swiftly catching her mouth, claiming her for a kiss as though she might vanish from him.

Both his hands stole around her waist, pulling her flush against him, keeping her close so that their mouths remained fused.

She gasped and his tongue entered her mouth, slicked over hers expertly. She leaned in, moaning, tangling her tongue with his, faintly tasting the whisky on him.

She curled her fingers into his bare shoulders, clinging to him as though she couldn't get close enough, which was absurd. They were in a bed. Side to side and wrapped in each other's arms. How much closer could she get?

He made a deep sound in his throat and kissed her deeper, his fingers clenching her tighter. She touched his face, the scratchy growth of hair on his cheek a delicious scrape that vibrated through her.

They kissed and kissed and kissed. Mouths slanting in one direction and then another and another. She didn't know kissing could be this way. So intoxicating. So addictive. Endless and not enough.

She wanted more.

As though he read her mind, one of his hands moved up and palmed her breast through her nightgown. Sensation shot through her. Instantly she felt her nipple bead into a hard point. She moaned into his mouth, pushing her breast into his palm.

He released an epithet against her lips, pulling back.

She whimpered at the loss of him, but it was only temporary. He reached down between them and grabbed the hem of her nightgown. Seizing it, he tugged it up her body and over her head, leaving her naked as the day she was born.

His eyes traveled over her beside him in the bed, his blue eyes dark and intent on her. Her nipples tightened under his stare. Heat devoured her face. Her hands flew to her breasts, but his fingers circled her wrists, tugging them down.

"Don't," he commanded. "You're perfect."

Trembling, she didn't know if it was from his gaze or his words. The deep sound of his voice pushed her desire higher, the twisting throb becoming almost painful between her legs.

Still watching her, his fingers trailed down her belly to her thighs. He stroked and petted her until she was in a frenzy.

"Hunt," she sobbed.

In response, he shocked her by delving between her thighs and easing one finger inside her moist heat. "What . . . are . . ." She couldn't finish the question.

She flew out of her skin.

She had never felt anything like it. Sensations bombarded her as he stroked in and out of her, lightly circling a sensitive pleasure point above her folds. She writhed, small incoherent sounds bubbling up in her throat.

"Please," she begged, without modesty or any sense of dignity.

He finally took mercy on her and gave her body what it craved. His thumb pushed down on that spot and rolled it in a swift circle.

She arched against him, clawing his shoulders.

He added a second finger and thrust both of them inside her with deep, slow drags.

He caught her lips in another blistering kiss, drinking the sounds from her mouth as he worked her into a frenzy, his thumb pushing and circling.

"You feel so verra perfect, Clara." His guttural brogue only added to the delicious torment. She felt his voice as tangibly as his touch.

The deep, twisting pressure in her core built . . . and built.

"Come, lass," he growled against her mouth. "Let go."

Writhing, she shook her head, not certain what he was asking, what she needed to do.

Then his mouth was gone. He was gone.

Blinking, her head lifted, searching, bewildered.

"Hunt? What are you—"

All speech fled on a strangled shriek as his mouth landed . . . down there, where his hand had been.

She froze and tensed.

His lips closed around that nub and sucked, his tongue laving the little pearl buried in her femininity.

Pleasure exploded inside her, centered directly where his mouth fused so intimately on her. She fell back on the bed with a moan. Hot waves of sensation that seemed to go on forever rolled over her as he loved her so thoroughly.

She buried her hands in his hair and tugged hard on the ends, urging him on. His hands slid beneath her, gripping her bottom and hauling her closer to his mouth. He continued working his magic with his lips and tongue until she fell back on the bed, her chest heaving like she had just run a race.

He came up, crawling over her like a predator, looking very intent, his blue eyes gleaming darkly.

He looked tempting and masculine with his arms braced on either side of her, his biceps flexing taut to support his weight.

He traced a finger over her mouth. She snatched hold of it with her teeth. She didn't know where the impulse came from, but she bit down on the tip, enjoying the way his entire body tensed, muscles locking. She touched the tip of her tongue to his finger. If possible, his eyes grew darker. Unbelievably, the intense ache returned between her legs. She clamped her thighs together as if that could somehow assuage the throbbing there.

His hands moved to her face, cupping her cheeks, fingers burrowing into her hair as he kissed her again.

There was no such thing as too close. Her breasts mashed against his chest. She reveled in the hard strength of him surrounding her.

He dragged his open mouth down her throat, biting down where her shoulder and neck met. Not hard but enough for a moan to shudder out of her.

He closed both hands over her aching breasts and she arched into his palms. His head descended and his mouth closed over one nipple, drawing it deep into the warm cave of his mouth.

"Oh!" Clara cried, burying her hands in his hair and holding him to her. "Don't . . . stop."

He moved his mouth to her other breast, speaking around her turgid nipple. "No fear there, lass. I have no' even begun with you yet."

He settled between her thighs. She would have been scandalized, but his bigger body felt wonderful, hard and insistent against her warmth, and she ached. Her belly tightened with need and she wiggled desperately against him. She felt herself grow wet. It was mortifying and yet she didn't want to stop any of this.

Her fingers dug into his back.

She felt him then. The hard head of him at her entrance, sinking inside her, inch by inch. She gasped at the sudden invasion, at the sharp pain. It was too much. She felt stretched, full in a way she had never imagined possible.

Her arms wrapped more fully around him, desperate to hold on to him as she was impaled. He felt . . . huge.

Her gaze flitted everywhere, seeing nothing, *feeling* everything, both thrilled and scared at what was happening.

He groaned, dropping his head in the crook of her shoulder, his mouth moving against her humming flesh and sending delighted shivers throughout her as he added, "You feel . . . perfect. Like you are made for me, lass." His voice twisted into a gasp as she wiggled under him, acclimating to the size of him lodged inside her. It was a heady and alluring thought—that one person could be made for another. That *they* were made for each other. She liked that idea perhaps more than she should.

His hands slid to her thighs, anchoring her for his body, and then he resumed moving, thrusting with steady strokes inside her.

Her muscles stretched to accommodate him, burning and throbbing around his hard length. He looked down at her and smoothed the hair from her face. "Is this good?"

Instead of answering, she wiggled some more,

testing out the feel of him. Her inner muscles clenched around him and that shot sensation to every nerve in her body.

He groaned and bracketed his arms on either side of her, quickening his pace, his thrusts growing harder, each one driving a sharp cry from her.

She angled her hips, taking in more of him, following her instincts, searching for a way to bring him closer, deeper, to assuage that ache that only seemed to grow. "More," she pleaded.

She had to move. She lifted her hips to better meet his plunging manhood.

She whimpered at the drag of him against her aching flesh. The friction drove her wild. Pressure built at her center, coiling in her belly. Her body demanded more, needed it harder. Her hands moved to clench the firm flesh of his buttocks.

"Clara," he choked. "Please. I'm trying no' tae be rough wi' you, lass."

"I won't break," she snapped, her fingers digging harder into his backside.

With a strangled oath, his big hands slid under her bottom and lifted her higher. The angle changed everything.

Spots danced in her vision as he ground into her and hit some place deep inside that she never knew existed. She arched under him, her head dropping back on the bed as she cried out, tears leaking from her eyes.

She closed her eyes and felt him lean over her, his breath fanning her lips as he growled. "Open your eyes tae me now, Clara. Look at me. See it's me doing this tae you. No' him."

Her eyes flew open wide. His face was fierce, his eyes dark, devouring, demanding all from her.

Oh. God.

He thought she was maybe thinking of another lover. It was horrible. He thought she'd *had* another lover. He believed her to be experienced. Certainly *not* a virgin—and technically, she no longer was a virgin. Because of right now . . . because of Hunt.

She shook her head slightly, opening her mouth to say something, anything that could correct this wretched lie between them . . . but instead she sucked in a breath as his big, callus-roughened hand slid under her thigh, wrapping her leg around him, making more room for him between her thighs. He pumped harder, their bodies smacking together as they came together. Words were impossible. Confessions for another time, later—after this.

His face was so close. Eyes feral as they locked on hers. "You're mine now, lass."

She came apart in his arms.

He followed after her, shuddering with a bellow as his seed emptied inside her . . . and then he stilled, his chest lifting high with wild breaths.

She clutched him close, one hand buried in his hair, the other splayed wide on his back.

Their ragged breaths filled the air. She didn't want to break away and let go. She didn't want to face the questions that would come. The answers she would have to give that would change everything.

The fierceness faded from his gaze, replaced with something akin to tenderness. It was awkward . . . because she knew it wouldn't last. He rose up from the bed.

She tugged the bedding over her, modesty suddenly returning as she watched him dress. An ache twisted in her chest as she appreciated the hard lines and hollows of his body. Even looking at him now made her heart race.

She'd gone and done it.

Without first telling him the truth and beginning their marriage honestly.

Her throat thickened with dread. She'd intended to tell him last night, but they'd both been tired. She'd told herself it could wait until the morning . . . but then she woke up to his mouth on her throat, his hand on her knee, and she was lost.

She pasted a smile on her face and hoped it didn't look too thin. Clutching the bedding to her chest, she sat up and scooted to the edge of the bed, wincing at the vague soreness between her legs.

Once he was dressed, he stood in front of her.

"I'll go see tae breakfast and the horses and carriage . . . make certain they are ready so that we might soon be on our way." He smiled seductively as he looked down at her, scanning her, and she felt the pull of that slow grin affecting her, making her tingle all over yet again. "I could grow accustomed tae seeing ye this way," he whispered in an almost tender voice.

"What way?"

"Naked in bed, your face glowing from a thorough shag."

Her cheeks caught fire.

Tell him. Tell him now.

She opened her mouth but was silenced by his swift kiss. "As fetching as you are like this, dress yourself. I'll be back directly."

Then he was gone.

She got up to dress, marveling at the twinges between her legs as she moved . . . a lasting reminder that she had been claimed, thoroughly, by Laird Hunt MacLarin.

Everything was going to be different now.

Chapter 14

Clara was finishing packing her valise when Hunt returned, smelling of frigid wind and rain. No surprise, it was showering lightly outside the window, water pelting the glass in a steady patter. Surprisingly, she felt a little shy around him. Her cheeks heated and she knew she must be blushing. She avoided looking at him and rotated in place, surveying the room, giving it a final search.

"I think I have everything." She then spotted her hair ribbon in the mussed bedding. "Oh, my ribbon." She started to move toward it, but Hunt stood closer.

He moved, reaching the bed first.

"What's this?" he asked, flipping the covers back to reveal more of the bed. He stilled.

"Clara?" The tense sound of his voice made the tiny hairs on her nape prickle in warning.

She followed his gaze and her stomach plummeted. The bottom fell out of her world. There it was. As plain as the morning light streaming through the windows.

Blood. A small splash of crimson on the bed.

Oh, no no no no.

She knew what it was.

She knew what it signified, but she did not quite know how to tell him . . . how to explain. She had not imagined this would be the way in which she revealed the truth to him. No, it had not felt nearly as dramatic as this in her imaginings. Not as terrifying.

She started, "Hunt, I-I—"

He was all movement then, at her side in an instant. "Are you well?" He placed one hand on her back and his other hand flew to her stomach. Despite the intimacy established between them, she still hissed a breath at the familiar contact.

He appeared oblivious to her reaction. Concern was writ all over his handsome face. "The babe?" His hand shifted on her belly and a surge of memories assailed her. His hands on her, his mouth . . . everywhere. She gave her head a small shake and focused on his words. Now was not the time to feel arousal.

"Were we . . . was *I* tae rough with you?" His

expression twisted to regret. "I'm a right bastard. Forgive me, Clara. I was a selfish brute. Are you in pain? Should I send for someone—?"

"I'm fine."

His gaze flew back to the bed. "But the blood? I dinna think you are fine. We should call for a physician."

"No," she cut in. That was the last thing she wanted. "Please don't fret."

His voice lifted. "How can I no' fret? You're bleeding. Because of *me*!" His voice twisted at that last part and she wanted the earth to open up and swallow her. This was bad. Very bad. How had she reached this moment?

She closed her eyes in a long blink and blew out a breath. Opening her eyes again, she said, "It's not what you think."

He looked her up and down, alarm still all over his face. "What I think is that you're losing the babe and I'm tae blame."

"I'm not pregnant," she blurted.

He stared, his expression uncomprehending.

She moistened her lips and repeated, "I'm not pregnant."

He glanced to the bed again and she made a sound in her throat, wishing he would stop looking at it—the evidence of her perfidy.

"Do you mean tae tell me that you lost the babe already? Before we were together?"

It was time for directness. *Past* time. She took another breath. "No. Understand me now. I was *never* with child."

His head whipped back to face her. "What do ye mean *never*?"

"I was never pregnant."

His arms fell away and he took a step back as though she were suddenly something danger-ous. Something, or rather someone, he dared not stand close to.

"What do ye mean never?" His voice was rougher, thicker . . . his brogue more pronounced as he repeated the question. "Autenberry said . . ."

She moistened suddenly dry lips. "I wanted to tell you before, Hunt, I really did . . ." Her voice faded and she glanced to the bed again. "I wanted you to know before . . . before last night," she finished with an exhale of heavy breath.

She turned and moved toward the window, but his voice followed her, hard and demanding. "Clara."

Of course, he wanted answers. He deserved an explanation.

Answers she had meant to give sooner, but here she was.

She turned around and faced him with a brac-ing breath. "I was never pregnant. I invented the entire thing to escape a betrothal. It was the only way. My betrothed was very . . . determined." She winced, Rolland's reddened face flashing before her mind. She shoved the wretched memory aside. "He vowed never to let me go, so I made certain to make myself as undesirable as possible to him so that he would. I let him believe I cuckolded him." She shrugged as though it were the obvious solution.

Hunt blinked once. It was his only outward reaction. "And he believed you?"

She nodded. "Well. Yes. He was a proud man. He held himself in great esteem." To put it mildly. "I knew he would not be able to tolerate the slightest chance of disloyalty. He wanted nothing to do with me after that. I was ruined but free of him. It was worth it. I still believe that."

He swiped a hand angrily through the air. "You're telling me there is no pregnancy . . . no lover. That"—he pointed to the bed—"that right there . . . is your virgin blood?"

Her face heated at his directness, but she nodded.

"I took you like a well-seasoned woman, but you were, in fact, a maid?"

Mortified, she nodded again.

He dragged both hands through his hair and started pacing a swift line, muttering beneath his breath in Gaelic.

The more he paced, the harder her heart pounded. "Hunt." She attempted to catch him as he walked and force him to stop and look at her.

He ignored her, continuing with his self-inflicted rant.

"Hunt." She seized hold of his arm. "It's not the end of the world." She gave him a wobbly smile. "Is it?"

He stopped to face her and laughed roughly, brutally. "Oh, it verra well could be. The end of mine at least."

She shook her head. "No. The curse isn't real. It's just—just a fairy tale. Stories folk bandy about. You'll see." She smiled and nodded encouragingly.

He went utterly still again and she dropped her hand from his arm, backing up a step, suddenly nervous at the look of him.

"What do you ken of the curse?" he growled.

Too late, she realized her mistake.

Revealing she knew also revealed that she had set out to deceive him, that she had married him knowing they were at counter purposes.

But I meant no harm. I'm only trying to help him.

She clung to that reminder, wishing that Marcus were here so that he might support her through this confrontation with her husband. It was a cowardly thought, but she had never seen Hunt look at her as he was now—as though she

was the most treacherous creature on earth and
he wanted to be miles away from her.

Even when they had first met amid the brawl
at the inn, there had been humor and warmth in
his gaze when they sparred words, but now his
eyes were chips of ice, and she had no idea what
to say or do to thaw them.

"You knew," he whispered. "You knew and
you married me anyway."

She shook her head. "You cannot believe that
this curse is—"

"'Tis true." He closed his eyes in a long blink,
and she felt a stab of alarm at his obvious misery.
A niggle of doubt wormed its way inside her . . .
which was absurd.

He was mistaken. There was no such thing as
a curse. He was merely brought up to believe in
such things. She knew better. Soon he would, too.

It was a difficult thing to remember, however,
when he opened his eyes to look at her as though
she were something he didn't want near him . . .
as though she were a disease, a contagion that
had already infected him.

"You think me a fool who believes in nonsense?"

"We are talking about a *curse*," she snapped,
feeling her temper finally give way.

"Aye, a curse." He advanced with biting steps.
"One that has besieged my family for generations."

She tossed both hands up in the air. "I cannot argue with ignorance!"

A muscle ticked in his jawline. "Ignorant, am I? I'm surprised you would sink so low to marry such an ignorant man, much less take him between your thighs."

Her face burned. "I thought I could talk some sense into you."

"An ignorant oaf like me?" he sneered. "You should no' have had such high hopes."

She sucked in a deep breath, praying for patience. "I'm sorry, but put yourself in my shoes . . . does it not seem a small bit of madness to let superstition rule your life?"

He scoffed. "First I'm ignorant, now I'm mad."

Her temper flared higher. "I will not live my life at the whim of superstition and nonsense and neither should you."

He towered over her, his body seeming even bigger in his anger. "You make it sound so . . . meaningless." His gaze glittered with furious emotion. "The curse killed my father and destroyed my family. Superstition and nonsense it is no'."

She studied this man. He could not be swayed. They may have shared a bed last night, she might have given him her body, but she realized she still had much to learn about him. Except right now she felt the chasm widening between them.

He continued in a voice that had gone cold and

rigid, "You are right, though. The curse shall no' affect my life, because I will no' let it."

She shook her head. "I don't understand."

"I will never touch you again. This marriage is name only. As far as I'm concerned we are no' even married."

"Hunt," she breathed. "You cannot mean that."

He meant it. Staring at his still angry features, she read his resolve etched into the hard lines of his handsome face.

He nodded. "It will no' be so verra difficult. I am quite accustomed tae restraining myself." His gaze flickered over her and she had never felt so dismissed. As though what they shared did not amount to much of anything for him. The way he had made her feel, his desire for her, his possessive words. Vanished. All gone. As though it had never been.

He wanted nothing to do with her anymore.

"You are young," she appealed. "We've much life . . . many years left together. They can be good years."

Earlier, moments ago it seemed, the world had shone so brightly. The future an endless stretch.

She pressed on, "We could have a life together, Hunt. A good life." She believed that . . . especially after what had transpired between them, after the way she had felt in his arms. He couldn't mean he didn't want to have that again? Was it only within her? Did only she look at him and feel the desperate longing? The craving to repeat the closeness, the heady desire?

For a moment she thought he might relent, then his gaze hardened further. "No." He gave a swift shake of his head. "I can never have that kind of life. My mistake was thinking I could."

She waved to the bed. "And what about what happened between us? Are we to pretend it never happened?"

He flinched. It was a glimpse of emotion, but it lasted only a moment and then he was all coldness again. "A mistake, aye."

"Mistake," she echoed, the single word knifing through her. "If it's such a mistake, perhaps you should just take me back to my brother."

He shook his head once, but the motion was no less decisive. "Nay. You are my problem."

Problem. She was a problem.

That stung, and she didn't know whether to cry or scream.

"Take me back." Away from him. Away from this pain and humiliation.

"We said vows. 'Tis done. You should no' have lied tae me. We are stuck with each other now whether we like it or no'."

And he clearly did *not* like it. No. She was a *problem.* She would never forget that. Never not feel the pain of it.

But she didn't deserve this. She would own her mistakes, but she still deserved better than this. "And what of you? You lied to me," she accused, not about to let him behave as though she were the only one at fault for this unhappy situation.

"Me?" Astonishment cracked his stony facade.

"Yes, you." She stabbed a finger in his direction. "You omitted certain crucial facts. You made no mention of a curse before we married. When were you going to mention that, *husband*?"

"When it became relevant."

"And when would that be?"

He hesitated a beat before saying, "After you gave birth I was going to tell you."

After.

She felt her forehead furrow as that sank in. "Why then?"

He actually looked a little uncomfortable at this. "I would no' risk the curse once you . . ." His voice faded.

She stared, digesting what he was saying—and what he was *not* saying. Realization dawned. "You would only come to my bed while I was increasing? You mean to say that for the rest of our marriage you planned to keep yourself from me? That we would be a name-only marriage after I gave birth?"

"Aye." He nodded. "I would no' risk getting you with child again."

"Oh, that's rich! Did you think I would not mind? That I should be content to live out my life not as a real wife? To bear only one child? What if I wanted more than such a farcical marriage?"

More children. More of a husband.

More of a marriage than that.

"We would have had our time together," he countered, looking away as though he knew that was an unsatisfactory answer.

He intended to only give her a few months of himself . . . a few months of what a marriage could be.

Now they would not even have that. They would have a name-only union. It was certainly a grim picture of the future, but it was to be hers now. It was all he was offering. Oh, and without children since she wasn't actually pregnant.

She felt a clawing panic that wasn't dissimilar to the moment she learned Rolland was not who she thought he was. Familiar in the sense that the life she thought she had chosen . . . was not to be hers.

When that happened before, she had railed against it. She'd rallied and found a way to escape.

The question remained . . . what would she do about it now?

If she did not like her fate, it was up to her to change it. Somehow. Someway. She must.

"What if I want a husband in the truest sense?" she asked, lifting her chin defiantly, knowing a woman asking anything for herself was considered an act of defiance by many.

No matter her station in life, a woman's lot was straightforward. She went from belonging to her father to being the property of her husband, but she wanted to be more than one man's property. She would have more.

"Well," he announced, "we dinna always get what we want in life. I learned that at a verra young age. You might as well ken that lesson now, lass."

His condescension only angered her. "You're a coward for letting fear rule you."

The fury flashed hot in his eyes. "And what sent you running to Scotland? Was it no' fear driving you with your tail tucked between your skirts, lass?"

Oh! Her palm itched to slap him, but she refrained. She would not give him the satisfaction of knowing he affected her that much.

"At least I tried. At least I attempted to make a life for myself." *With you.* "I attempted to start a new life with *you.*" As he'd offered. Freedom. A choice. She blinked suddenly burning eyes. *Do not cry. Do not shed a tear.*

"Aye. I tried, tae." He looked her up and down again in a scathing survey, accusation thick in his brogue. "I thought you were someone else. I was mistaken."

"We both were mistaken."

Hugging herself, she looked away, but her gaze caught on the rumpled bed. A bad idea because she was suddenly assailed with memories of how they had occupied it only a short time ago and the bliss she had found in his arms.

"Aye," he growled, and her gaze swung back at him to find he was staring at the bed, too. Only there was no expression of longing on his face. "I've risked much."

She sucked in a sharp breath, understanding this new direction of his thoughts.

He meant if she was with child as a result of their tryst, he considered his life at end. Over.

She laughed.

She could not help it. It would be the height of irony if they had created a baby through their single coupling. Unlikely, but it would serve the fool man right. Then, eventually, he would learn just how wrong he was. Then he could beg for her forgiveness.

"Ridiculous," she managed to get out amid her laughter.

Incredulity warred with anger in the blue depths of his gaze. "You laugh?"

She held up both hands, palms out as though guilty—of laughing at any rate. "Nothing to fear," she mocked. "It's not likely. I doubt I'm *that* fertile. Especially if I'm anything like my dear mother. She faced many challenges in this, er . . . area."

He snorted. "Do no' think tae tempt me with the possibility that you are barren, Clara."

She stopped laughing. Oh, the cruel arrogance of him! "Tempt you! Ha! I'll not beg for you back in my bed."

Indeed not. He had demolished her pride this morning. She would pick up what scraps of it remained and keep them safe from him lest he do such a thing again. She had learned her lesson with him. She would not be so vulnerable again.

He shook his head, mockery glinting in his eyes. "The way you sighed so sweetly and melted under my hands? I could have you begging for me between your thighs again."

Oh! This time she could not stop herself. She slapped him.

His head turned from the force of the blow.

She waited, breath suspended, her palm tingling.

Slowly, he turned to face her again. Her handprint stood out in stark relief, an angry red mark against his flesh. The sight of it pricked her conscience.

She was not given to violence. She was a stranger to herself. A stranger she did not like very much at the moment. She had never struck another living thing and here she was, newly married and striking her husband. What was wrong with her? She really should return to Kilmarkie House.

She stood frozen, braced for anything he might unleash upon her. Certainly it would be his right. She was his wife now. No one would fault him for managing her as he saw fit.

She squared her shoulders and pushed back the fear.

He strode forward and she held her ground, and his gaze, refusing to look away. She'd read that in a book somewhere—how in the event of an attack it was important to hold your ground. She couldn't remember what manner of animal she had been reading about, but for some reason that bit of advice echoed through her mind right now.

"Such a temper, Clara." He tsked, reaching up to lightly finger his abused cheek.

"What can I say? You bring out the worst in me, MacLarin."

One corner of his mouth curled. "'No' always."

As soon as he said those words, he closed the last inch of space between them. His hand flew forward to slide around the back of her neck. He tugged her forward and she toppled against him, his hardness all at once familiar and unfamiliar.

They had never been like this. Never this close while standing upright. He felt so much bigger like this. Taller. Stronger. More intimidating.

He spoke against her mouth, his warm breath fanning her suddenly trembling lips. "I thought I told you tae call me Hunt."

She opened her mouth to protest, but suddenly his lips were there. His teeth clanged with hers as his tongue slid inside her parted lips, tasting, seeking.

This was plunder.

She froze, her thoughts sluggishly attempting to form under this assault.

He doesn't want me. I'm merely a problem.

But his mouth was so hot. So thorough. So persuasive. Her limbs melted. His hands slid around her waist and down to her bottom. He grabbed her backside and squeezed. Just like that, liquid heat shot to her core.

She moaned against his mouth.

And then he was gone.

He stepped back abruptly. She staggered forward a step, off balance and seeking, hungry for the loss of him, her hands grasping air.

"There," he pronounced, looking quite satisfied. "I think I made my point."

"Er . . ." She stared at him blankly, her senses still muddled from arousal.

"We can both agree you would beg for it. Again."

Suddenly she was glad she had slapped him.

Smiling almost cruelly, he pulled open the

door and stormed out. The door shut just shy of a slam behind him.

Her legs were unable to support her weight. She sank down to the edge of the bed and brought trembling fingers to her lips, suddenly wondering if she had not misjudged him entirely.

She had underestimated his commitment to the validity of the curse. She knew that now. Because the man who had just left her showed no signs of yielding.

He had no tenderness in him at all.

SHE'D LIED TO him. Hunt stormed down the stairs of the inn and out into the yard. He walked through the village, ignoring people that called to him, including Graham. The last thing he wanted was to talk to him. His friend knew well of his family curse. Everyone did. Graham had looked at him like he was a madman to take Clara to wife. He did not want to face him now knowing he'd made such a colossal mistake.

He couldn't bear it just yet.

It was cold out and he realized he had left his thicker jacket back at the inn, but he wasn't ready to return for it just yet.

He left the village behind and strode into the trees. His breath puffed out before him in a cloud of white. With a growl, he stopped and flattened both hands against a tree, bowing his head, letting the rough bark scratch his palms and remind him that he was alive.

Alive was good.

His wife, unfortunately, could put an end to that if he let her—if he let her *in*. No woman was worth dying for. He had a sudden memory of her crying out his name as she dragged nails down his back. He gave his head a hard shake. It had been incredible with her. Unlike anything he ever experienced.

But not worth dying for.

He had to remember that. His mother had told him that plenty of times over the years.

He'd never been tempted before to do anything that put himself at risk. Until now. Until that lass back at the inn with her soulful eyes.

He lifted his head and looked to the sky, to the canopy of trees overhead.

Now that he'd had a taste of her, it would be doubly difficult to avoid her—to keep his hands off her.

Unless she hated him. Unless he made himself the most disagreeable man in Christendom and then she would never let him near her.

He stood back from the tree, newly resolved. Dragging his hands through his hair, he turned back for the village, a plan in place.

It was time to go home.

Chapter 15

They arrived at MacLarin Keep later that day.
It was a castle, but this one looked older than
her brother's home, as though it had been here
long before the Romans ever set foot on this
island. The stone was dark where ivy didn't
cover it. The ramparts loomed tall but not as tall
as the anchoring towers stretching into the sky.
She lost sight of the towers as they rolled over the
bridge and beneath the portcullis, passing into
the courtyard.

Their carriage pulled to a gradual stop, the
wheels clattering loudly and announcing their
arrival. As she and Marian descended, she
searched for a glimpse of her husband, but he
was nowhere in sight. Husband? No. That felt

wrong—it felt untrue. He'd ridden ahead of them. She'd last seen him outside their window an hour ago.

There was only an old woman, waiting in the great threshold of the double front doors. Clearly, Clara was expected. A result, she could only assume, of Hunt's earlier arrival. He'd alerted the staff. Perhaps this was the housekeeper.

The woman studied Clara with a narrowed rheumy gaze.

"So ye be the one," she declared in a cracking voice, her brogue perhaps the thickest Clara had heard yet since arriving in Scotland.

Lifting her skirts, Clara ascended the steps and exchanged an uncertain look with Marian before facing the old woman again. "I beg your pardon?"

"Ye be the one."

Clara shook her head in bewilderment. "The one . . . who, ma'am?"

"The one tae murder my grandson."

CLARA WAS SHOWN to her bedchamber by Hunt's grandmother. The woman did not even attempt to hide her dislike. She pressed her lips together until they resembled the dried-up skin of a date.

"This be yer room. Mind ye, 'tis no' the master

chamber. Ye will no' be sharing a bed wi' my grandson." Those rheumy eyes snapped in challenge. As though Clara was intent on molesting her grandson. She had to bite back a hysterical giggle at the image of herself creeping into Hunt's bed and attacking him unawares.

"Ye understand, lass?" the woman persisted.

Clara's face heated, but she nodded. She had no idea how to respond. No idea what Hunt had told his grandmother about her.

The old woman had been mercenary in her speech and manner since that first greeting in the doorway. The entire trip to Marian's room, she had muttered in a mixture of English and Gaelic about the damnable English.

Now, as they stood in the center of what was to be Clara's room, the woman dealt her a cold survey. She missed nothing, inspecting Clara from head to toe. "Ye are no' much tae look at. I canna see wot prompted Hunt tae forget himself and wed ye."

Clara lifted her chin defiantly. "You refer to the curse."

"Aye," the woman said slowly, nodding. "The curse."

"Perhaps he married me because deep down he knows it's rubbish."

The old woman's eyes flared wide. Shaking, she stepped closer slowly, as though her old bones could not move any faster. She lifted a hand, pointing a trembling, gnarled finger at Clara. "Is that wot ye told him?"

Clara felt a stab of fear that Hunt's nana might drop dead in front of her. That would not go over well. Clara nodded once, feeling suddenly uncertain beneath the woman's wrathful gaze.

"Well, stop it," Nana bit out. "Dinna speak such things tae him, do ye understand me, lass? Dinna fill his head wi' such lies and rot."

The woman was shaking even more now. Clara reached for her arm in concern. "Would you care to sit down?"

She yanked her bony arm free and started clomping toward the bedchamber door. "Nay! I'm no' feeble in body or mind, thank ye verra much, but ye may be if ye treat me as an invalid."

Clara pulled back, wondering if that was a threat or just the ramblings of a distraught old woman.

The elderly woman stopped at the door and turned to focus her cloudy gaze on Clara once again. "I buried my husband and son. I'll no' live tae put my grandson in the earth as well. Ye hear me? I'd just as soon it be ye in the ground."

Well, then. Definitely a threat.

"I understand you perfectly," Clara answered. It would be difficult not to. "And you have nothing to worry about. Hunt and I will not be living as a true husband and wife." He had made that abundantly clear.

"Humph." She didn't look convinced.

Clara spread her arms wide. "Do you see your grandson here? He's nowhere near me because he regrets marrying me."

"But he married ye," she announced as if that was threat enough.

This was madness and this was Clara's life right now. For the time being at least. Until she found a way out of this mess.

"Did he lie wi' ye?"

Clara gasped. Her face caught fire and she sputtered, "That's none of your—"

Nana shook her head. "Aye, of course he did, foolish lad." She swept another withering examination over Clara. "Time will soon reveal if he's gone and killed himself."

"He did not kill himself," Clara snapped. "You will see, madam."

"Aye." She nodded. "That we will."

Apparently satisfied their conversation had come to an end, Nana turned for the door.

Before she departed the chamber, Clara could not resist calling out, "Where is he? Where is Hunt?"

His grandmother stepped out into the corridor and peered back inside the room. "Far from ye. He's gone far from ye, lass." She stabbed a damning finger at Clara. "If he's wise, when he comes back he'll send ye away where ye will do him no harm." That said, she shut the door, leaving Clara alone.

Blessedly alone. Wretchedly alone.

Alone in her chamber, Clara wondered if Nana's cruel words weren't perhaps the best solution. Perhaps she should leave.

Of course she knew staying here would do Hunt no harm. No more harm than a monster under the bed would do.

No, she feared the harm it would do to her if she remained here.

There was dying without actually dying. Being a wife to him and treated like a pariah . . . that would be one manner of death, and Clara had no intention of dying any time soon.

HUNT STAYED AWAY a fortnight before he accepted that he had to return. He had taken up residence at a hunting lodge that once served as a retreat for previous generations of MacLarin men. All of whom had died prematurely, of course, after siring their one son. He wondered how closely, if at all, he was following in their footsteps in seeking refuge there.

Had they, too, sought solace at the lodge? Whatever the case, Hunt knew it had not saved them. They'd married. They had begot sons. They had died. And all before their sons took their first breaths.

It was a dismal thought to think he was repeating their mistakes. He had thought himself smarter, more informed from the past and above lustful urges.

But he could not hide away forever. He had property to attend, as well as the needs of his clan. A late freeze had arrived whilst he was gone. He could no longer ignore his duties.

He could not simply disappear indefinitely. Although his grandmother might disagree. She had been furious with him. Growing up, she had not harped on him as his mother had. She'd been much too practical for that. Only his mother had wallowed and bemoaned her fate to all and sundry, prostrating herself, unable to move more than a few feet a day due to her overwhelming grief. In his earliest memory as a young boy, he remembered burrowing under the covers as he heard her wails echo through the castle, convinced it was a ghost haunting the place and come to get him.

Nana had gone about living. She'd been more mother to Hunt. When he arrived ahead of Clara and informed her of his nuptials, she had been direct with him.

Ye damn fool. What have ye done?

She never had been one to mince words. When

he suggested he leave for a respite, she had whole-heartedly agreed. *Mayhap time away from this lass who has bewitched ye will do ye some good.*

He'd experienced a touch of desperation knowing that Clara was close behind. He wasn't proud of the emotion. He felt like prey in a trap, the urgent need to run pressing on him like a great weight. However much he mocked her, insisting that she couldn't resist him, it was the other way around. He feared he could not resist her.

Anger welled up in him. How could it be that only the night before he'd felt such pleasure, such—dare he say it—joy?

Now there was only disappointment keener than any he'd felt before, and since disappointment was a way of life for him, he knew a great deal about the feeling. Enough to know that he despised it.

She'd done this. She'd brought him to this state. Another reason to resent her. To get away from her . . .

Aye, keep away from the lass. Or better yet send her away. Ye may still have a chance then.

He stopped his mount in thick woods, on a rise that looked down at his keep. Branches creaked all around him, burdened with newly formed ice.

His heart swelled, lightened to be back even if it meant facing his wife.

He loved this place. It was his heart. Other men built families. He built this place, this community. It was his purpose. He kept it going, thriving.

The castle was bordered on one side by a small village and white-frosted fields on the other. It was prosperous. Despite the personal hardships to befall the MacLarin men, the lands and people always managed to flourish. Even during the worst of times, during the battle against British tyranny at Culloden. His great-grandfather had died shortly before the battle, as a result of the curse, keeping them from getting embroiled in tensions with the English, and thereby saving their lands from being confiscated. It was probably the only time in the history of the MacLarins that the curse served to do anything good.

He thought of his grandmother's suggestion to send Clara away and shifted uncomfortably in his saddle. He did not care for the notion. They had taken vows . . . and he had promised her brother he would see to her care. Sending her away ran counter to that. Honor demanded he keep her here as his wife and not run her off like some wretched shame that must be expunged from his life.

And yet he had also decided to avoid her.

When that was impossible, he would keep his manner cool and give her no reason to like him. Shouldn't be too difficult. He was unaccustomed to charming women. Repelling this one shouldn't prove a challenge.

He spurred his horse ahead for home, an anxious buzz traveling along his nerves. He told himself it was because he must face the wrath of his grandmother again and not because he would soon see Clara.

Nana was equally respected and feared in these parts, considered a witch by many, but he had never feared her. She was kin. She could make a nuisance of herself to be certain, but fear did not enter into it for him.

Nay, he could not lie to himself. It was the prospect of facing Clara again. Despite their ugly words that day at the inn, his most resounding memory of her was how she had felt in his arms. How very different . . . how very right. He never knew it could be like that. The tups in his adolescence had been just that. Meaningless tups. Catriona had been nice. Comfortable.

Being with Clara had been like diving off a cliff. Exhilarating. Decidedly *not* comfortable. *Not* meaningless, if his inability to stop thinking about her was any indication.

Clara was the first woman he chose, he realized with some start. That made all the difference.

He'd been attracted to her. He desired her. He pursued her and won her.

Now he knew what it could be like. How good it could be. Being with someone *he* chose eclipsed every other encounter in his life.

Nana was right. The lass was dangerous indeed.

A stable lad rushed to greet him in the court-yard. Hunt tossed his horse's reins to him.

He approached the main doors, but paused before entering, hovering at the edge of the arched porch. Inside was his wife. It was still the strangest thought.

The door opened. As though Nana had sensed his arrival and been summoned, she stood there, assessing him critically.

She crossed her arms over her thin chest. "Wot are ye doing here?"

"And good day tae you, madam. I live here. Remember?"

"Humph." She rocked back on her heels. "I thought ye were going tae stay away."

"I could no' do that now, could I? I'm the laird."

Her head bobbed like a pecking bird. "Aye, ye be the laird, which is why I thought ye would have more sense tae go and marry that lass. Well, I've given it some thought and there is one obvi-ous solution tae this."

"There is?"

"Aye." She nodded, the motion not ruffling a

single silver hair within the tightly coiled plaits atop her head.

He stared at her, hope drumming through him at the possibility of a solution. He knew Nana well enough to know she would not say such a thing lightly. She'd always been the one to make things right in his life. When his mother would vent her spleen in a drunken rage, tossing and breaking items, Nana would take him off somewhere so that he would not have to witness it. She'd take him for a ride or a walk or fishing in the loch.

"Well?" he pressed. "What is it?"

"Get her wi' child."

The hope deflated in his chest. He snorted, certain old age had finally addled his grandmother's head. "Ye ken that is the heart of the matter. I canno'—"

"Nay. I'm no' speaking of ye. Some other man. Graham, mayhap? Or another of our clansmen. Any of yer men would do it fer ye if they thought it would spare yer life."

He stared aghast at his grandmother.

The notion of handing Clara, his *wife*, over to another man, enraged him. For a long moment he could not even find his voice.

At last, he responded. "Of course any one of my men would *do* it if I asked them," he growled.

"What man would turn down the offer tae bed a beautiful woman? It would be no hardship." He scoffed, his hands clenching at his sides. His grandmother was daft if she thought he would allow another man to touch Clara.

She was his.

"Och. Wot be the difference? Ye married her thinking another man had already done the deed by her so why—"

"That was *before* I met her. It was in the past." It was different now. Colossally different.

Nana lifted her bony shoulders in an indifferent shrug. "It should no' matter."

"It matters," he insisted, a shudder racking him at the image of Clara in another man's bed. He couldn't stop his imagination from running wild, envisioning Graham kissing her, his friend's hands caressing Clara, touching her where Hunt had touched her.

The notion made him sick.

Nana shook her head stubbornly. "Unless ye love her, why should ye care whose bed she shares?"

Heavy silence descended.

Nana stared at him in challenge. Her words hung thickly between them, the accusation a throbbing pulse in the air.

At last she tsked and shook her head in disgust. "Och. Ye do. Ye love her."

He came awake. "Dinna be daft."

"I hear no denial."

"You shocked me. Of course, I deny it. Obviously. But the topic is pointless. I cannot just give her tae someone. She's a person. I do no' own her."

"Don't ye? She is yer wife now."

"I won't give my wife tae another man and that is the end of the subject," he said tightly, barely checked fury radiating through him.

Nana huffed and shrugged. "Just like yer da, ye are. Lost yer head over a woman. She will be the death of ye, lad." Her eyes misted and she looked away, blinking fiercely.

"All will be well. You will see." He shrugged. "Mayhap this time will be different." He didn't know where the words came from . . . he had not allowed himself to think such a thing, but apparently he had been.

"Nay!" She wagged a finger at him. "Dinna ye say that! They *all* said that. Every one of them."

He sighed and shook his head the precise moment tearing pain lanced the side of his head.

"Ow!" he cried, staggering to the side, one hand flying up to clasp his head where the pain originated.

"Hunt!"

A sharp sting throbbed in his skull. He pulled back his fingers to see a smear of blood. *His* blood.

"What the devil . . ." Sudden dizziness swamped him and he took a shaky step.

Nana arrived at his side with far more speed than he would have expected for her advanced years.

She wrapped a bony arm around his waist to support him. He tried to shrug free of her, pride demanding he take no assistance from his frail grandmother, but the damnable dizziness forced him to lean into her. She took his weight with surprising ease.

"There!" She pointed a gnarled finger down to a chunk of ice on the ground. Half of it, the sharp tip, was stained with blood. "An icicle."

Ignoring the throbbing pain in his head, he looked up to where several icicles hung from the stone archway in the shape of daggers.

"Ye could have been killed!" she exclaimed.

"It was an accident. I'll have someone come clear the rest of those away so no one else gets hurt."

"'Twas no accident." Her pale eyes glittered and her voice fell to a solemn hush. "'Tis the curse."

"Ah, Nana. You are reaching for what is no' there. This was a simple accident . . . it could have befell anyone."

The worst of his dizziness had passed. He set Nana aside and entered the house, wincing and pressing his hand to his head in an attempt to stanch the flow of blood.

He did not make it far into the hall before Nana interceded him. "Come. Ye require stitching."

"Verra well, but I'm famished. Do your work on me in the kitchen, if you must." He pressed a kiss to her papery-thin cheek and moved ahead toward the kitchens, looking forward to eating something he himself had not cooked.

She followed on his heels doggedly, grumbling, "Ye should no' be here. Should never 'ave returned. No' whilst she is here."

He didn't bother commenting. The argument was becoming old. He wanted to lose himself in good food and better whisky and not have to talk or think about anything.

Upon arriving in the kitchen, he greeted Cook, who quickly began arranging a platter of food for him. He was a fine chef, well acquainted with all of Hunt's preferences. Cook set a selection of several meat pasties, dried fruit and some delicious-looking iced biscuits before him.

"Och! Wot happened tae yer head?" Cook inquired, adding a tankard of ale to the fine fare laid out before him. Several kitchen maids halted amid their duties to eye him curiously as Nana dabbed clean the blood from his temple with a less than gentle touch.

He grimaced at her ministrations but knew better than objecting. She would have her way.

"'Tis nothing." Hunt waved off the concern and bit into a piece of dried apple.

"Nothing, he says." Nana huffed, sifting through the hair of his scalp to better peer at his wound.

Footsteps clattered against the stone steps leading into the kitchen from the side door. The tread was accompanied by cheerful feminine voices.

He tensed and stilled, a biscuit en route to his mouth. They weren't ordinary female voices. They were English. There could not be many Sassenachs wandering about—of that he was certain.

My Sassenach.

Clara cleared the doorway with her friend close behind her. Her cheeks were pink from the cold or exertion, her dark eyes shining. His stomach clenched. Aye. Nana was right. He should not have come back here. How could he keep himself from her?

"Speak of the devil," Nana grouched.

Clara pulled up hard upon seeing him. "Oh." It was the only sound to escape her—a breathless little mewl that tightened his skin and increased his awareness of her. She might be covered from neck to hem, but he remembered the hue of her skin, the taste of her breasts, their shape and texture in his hands. Hell. He was getting hard just looking at her. Even with pain knifing his skull, the sight of her filled him with hunger.

Her knuckles whitened where they clutched the handle of a basket. Clearly she was about some task and he didn't know what to think about that. He'd imagined her prostrate, locked away in her room from the world, but here she was, flushed prettily from her jaunt.

"Oh, 'tis ye," Nana grumbled, glaring across the room at the two females.

Clara's gaze roamed over him, arresting on his head. "What's happened to you?" She hurried forward as though all rancor was forgotten between them—as though they had not parted in a maelstrom of harsh words.

She lifted a hand to his head, wincing as though the injury had been done to her.

He pulled his head from her reach. "Just an accident."

Nana snorted.

Clara sent her a glance before looking back to him questioningly. "What kind of accident?"

"'Tis no accident—"

"Nana," he rebuked.

Clara studied him for a moment, her eyes widening. "You think this is my doing?"

The entire kitchen fell silent, watching the exchange avidly.

"It was an accident," he repeated loud enough for everyone to hear. "Nothing more."

Clara continued to stare at him. After a moment, she reached for his head again as though to examine him herself . . . as though she might find the truth there.

He jerked away, reminding himself he must not invite her attention. For her or himself. It was best they didn't touch in any fashion.

She lowered her hand back down to his side. "I only want to—"

"That's no' necessary. I do no' require your assistance."

Hurt flickered across her face and he felt like a wretch—until he reminded himself that he did not want her to like him. In fact, it would not be remiss if she hated him. That would be for the best.

She lifted her chin. "Of course, it was an accident. What else could it be?" Her eyes sparked with challenge. She looked back and forth between him and his grandmother.

True to form, Nana took the bait. "Ye ken exactly wot it could be!"

Clara shook her head. "Stuff and nonsense."

"Impertinent lass," Nana sputtered.

"Enough," he thundered, leveling a look at both of them. "This is no' the workings of the curse. Nana, you forget she would have tae be wi' child for the curse to be at play here and that is no' the case."

His grandmother jutted forth her chin defiantly.

"Is that no' correct?" he pressed.

Nana gave a reluctant nod and a grunt of affirmation.

"Verra good," he finished, glad that was settled.

His grandmother, however, was not finished. She continued, "But do we ken fer certain that she is no' carrying yer child? Because unless she can attest tae that, 'tis verra possible the curse *is* at work here."

With a sigh, he turned his attention back to Clara, waiting to hear her reassurance. Instead he only found her studying her shoes.

"Clara?" he prodded. Her gaze snapped back to him, the color high in her cheeks again. "Can you please assure my grandmother that she has no fear on that score and she can put her mind tae rest?"

She exchanged a quick glance with her friend, scanned the room uneasily and then cleared her throat. "Well, I don't rightly have the answer to that matter. Yet." The color in her cheeks deepened to scarlet. "It's only been a fortnight, you see." Her slim throat worked as she swallowed. "I cannot know yet."

His gut clenched. "I do see."

She was saying it was not likely, but not impossible either. Odds he did not like.

"See!" Nana proclaimed.

He glanced around, suddenly aware they had quite the audience. With an epithet, he reached for Clara's arm. "Come. Let us have a word."

He was not certain what he hoped to gain by further conversation with her on the matter. Assurances, he supposed. He led her from the kitchen, feeling the eyes of everyone on their backs as they went.

"What about yer head?" Nana called.

"I'm fine." It still stung, but the bleeding had stopped at any rate.

"You should have that stitched," Clara contributed.

"When are your courses due?"

"I beg your pardon?" She tried to pull her arm free as he led her across the gallery to the staircase leading to the second floor.

He tightened his grip. "You heard me."

"That is none of your business, sir."

He released a single bark of laughter. "*Sir*, is it? And no' my business, is it?"

They started up the stairs, moving in unison. "You forget yourself. You excused yourself from the privilege of being my husband."

"Privilege?" He chuckled and slid her a glance,

admiring the lift of her chin and her mettle. She was no cowering female. "Och, are you no' a lofty one?" He climbed the stairs quicker, his longer legs moving faster than hers, forcing him to practically pull her after him. He knew he should shorten his pace, but he was feeling impatient. "The fact remains that we are wed. We consummated our marriage and I would like tae ken if there are consequences to that night, Clara."

She huffed out an indignant breath. "I don't keep proper track of such things. Never had cause to before . . ."

Before him.

And that warmed him with unjustifiable pleasure. It shouldn't matter and yet it pleased him to think he had been her first. "When was the last time?" He glanced at her profile. "Your menses? When did they last occur?"

She flinched. "It was before I arrived at my brother's."

"On the journey here then?" He glanced at her beside him.

"Uh." Her expression turned nervous. "At the beginning of the journey, I believe. Before we crossed into Scotland."

"The beginning?" he pressed, calculating the days. "That was some time ago then, was it no'?"

He stopped on the landing and turned so that they faced one another.

She expelled a breath. "I don't think I'm late." She winced. "Yet."

"Yet." The word escaped him with violent force for all that he uttered it quietly.

He dragged a hand through his hair and stepped back a pace to lean against the banister.

A splintering sound registered seconds before he felt the rail at his back give way. One moment the wooden banister was there, supporting his weight, and then it was falling away, breaking.

He saw a flash of Clara's horrified face.

Heard her scream.

His arms sawed through the air, seeking purchase, groping for anything to grab.

Except there was nothing.

Only air.

Chapter 16

Clara seized hold of his arm, a desperate cry on her lips. "Hunt!"

He was a great deal heavier than she, so she started to go with him, her slippers sliding over the runner. It all happened quickly, in the span of moments, but it felt like a prolonged fight—a battle for his life. She dug in her heels and yanked hard on his arm, pulling him until he changed direction and fell forward against her.

Her back struck the safety of the wall. Hunt followed, collapsing against her with ragged breath.

Her own breath fell fast and hard, as though she had just run a great distance. Her blood pumped swiftly, the panic of the past few moments not even close to subsiding, coating her tongue in a sour film.

"What . . . happened?" she panted.

He glanced over his shoulder. "The banister gave way." His gaze came back to rest on her face, widening ever so slightly at whatever thought tracked through his mind. "I would have fallen if you had no' grabbed me."

She shook her head and let out a shaky breath. "But you're fine."

"Twice in one day," he muttered. His gaze crawled over her face, searching, it seemed. As though the truth hid within her.

Her stomach knotted.

He looked back behind him. "The banister was strong oak. There wasn't the slightest wobble to it."

"What are you saying?"

She thought she knew what he was saying and it was impossible. She would not believe it. Accidents happened all the time without reason. That's why they were called accidents.

Footsteps rushed below.

He dropped his hands from her arms.

She released the air from her lungs and inched away from the wall to peer down at the remnants of the banister and balusters littering the floor.

"Och!" Hunt's grandmother jerked to a halt below. She eyed the debris and then looked up where they loomed. "Ye almost fell?"

He didn't answer, merely stared grimly down at the old woman. It was answer enough apparently.

"It happened again!" She shook a fist up at them. "Twice in one day ye nearly died!"

Hunt turned his grim gaze on Clara.

She shrugged inadequately. "A coincidence, surely." Even her voice lacked conviction.

"Perhaps," he replied, his voice flat and equally without conviction. He looked shaken; his features drawn.

Nana's voice rose from below. "She's wi' child! Just as I said. There be no other reason for this."

Murmurs broke out among the servants gathering below.

"It has begun!" she called up at them.

Clara shuddered at the ominous words. *It has begun.*

It could not be. Her hand went to her stomach as though she could verify this from one brush of her hand to her belly.

"Perhaps," he said again and there was such a dead look to his eyes that she wanted to flee to her room and shut the door on him. On this strange place where people believed in a curse and they actually had Clara herself wondering if there was some veracity to it.

She'd dreamed of motherhood, of course. She'd had a brilliant mother . . . and now watching her mother with the twins, even being on hand for so much of their upbringing . . . well, Clara had looked forward to her own turn one day.

When things ended so badly with Rolland she had accepted that motherhood would not be in her future. She'd accepted it and refused to allow herself to dwell on the unfortunate circumstance.

And yet here she was. Perhaps, quite possibly, increasing with a child.

And this man loathed the idea. As he loathed her. It was unbearable.

"But likely not." She nodded toward the space where the banister once stood. "It was simply loose. Clearly in need of repair. It's an old castle," she offered, letting that implication sink in and hopefully sway him against notions that the curse was in effect.

That she was with child.

He nodded once in seeming agreement. "It *is* an old castle. Some things are in disrepair, of course, and require tending."

"Of course," she echoed, except she knew that he did not believe what he was saying one little bit. *The banister was strong oak.*

"In any event, you will keep me informed . . . of your condition."

She nodded. "Of course. I am certain in a few days' time you shall rejoice at finding yourself still with no progeny in sight."

DAYS PASSED, AND she had no news to impart that would bring about rejoicing, which was an odd thing. Didn't people usually rejoice when they learned a child was on the way? Clara was secretly rejoicing, marveling at the life inside her. Was it a boy? A girl? What would he be like? Could he have blue eyes like his father? Would *she*?

"Will you tell him?" Marian asked.

She shook her head, her stomach churning. "I do not know for certain."

"Clara," Marian chided gently. "You know it is so. Why do you dally?"

She nodded. Yes. She knew. Even if time had not passed without nature's evidence presenting itself, there was the fact that her breasts were tender to the touch and it was near impossible for her to get comfortable at night. She tossed and turned in her big, empty bed. There was a general achiness and soreness about her hips. She had never experienced such symptoms before. It hinted that her body was undergoing some manner of change—such as readying and making room for the baby growing in her womb.

"Hello, there." Marian lightly tapped her beneath the chin, regaining her attention. "This is a blessing. You're to have a child."

"Yes. I know." Clara nodded, feeling the irrational burn of tears.

"And that husband of yours will soon see the error of his ways when you deliver him a healthy babe."

She nodded again. "Of course." She believed that to be true . . . so why did a thread of fear lurk within her? "I will tell him tonight."

"There's a good girl."

"Marian." She cleared her throat. "You don't think there could be something to this curse nonsense. Perhaps it's not such . . . nonsense?"

"Don't tell me you believe it, too. What is it with this place? Is there something in the air?"

"Well, there were those two accidents . . ."

"Accidents. Nothing more." Marian pulled her into a hug. "You will see. All will be well. Now. Why don't we select a lovely gown for you to wear? You should look your best when you meet with that handsome husband of yours, no?"

"Yes." She took a fortifying breath, hoping Marian was correct. "The yellow one, I think." She always felt strong when she wore it, bright and cheerful.

"Excellent choice."

SEVERAL DAYS HAD passed and he'd only spotted Clara from a distance. They never spoke. When their eyes met, she quickly looked away.

That did not, however, mean she was not constantly in his thoughts. Her bedchamber was located only doors down from his. A mighty temptation.

He had a wife. A wife for whom he happened to possess a great deal of ardor. One could not merely snuff that out as one does a candle. They ought to be together. Truly. In the biblical sense. As God intended a husband and wife to be.

This argument warred within his mind, oftentimes threatening to win out over a lifetime of careful restraint, of telling himself that he didn't need the things other men had—a wife, children. Telling himself he could live perfectly contented without those things because it meant he would live. He had his home. His people. He was laird. That had always been enough before.

Of course, his very near brush with death yet again served as an effective distraction.

He stalked into his bedchamber, thankful his grandmother had not witnessed the latest incident—although he had no doubt she would hear of it and soon be after him. Perhaps he should take himself off again.

Only as soon as the thought entered his mind he rejected it. He couldn't run. Couldn't hide from this. It was the life he had been given and he would make the best of it.

Shaking his head, he exhaled and stripped off his jacket and shirt, stopping before the washstand. With a wince, he twisted around and examined the gash along the side of his torso.

Blood seeped from the jagged tear in his flesh and he reached for a towel hanging along the side of the washstand to sop up the oozing blood. The area around the wound was already an angry red and bruising to purple. A few more inches to the left and it could have been bad. It could have been fatal.

Pressing the towel to the injury, he held it there, applying pressure to stanch the flow of blood.

After a few minutes, he peeled back the towel and looked down, satisfied to see that the bleeding had stopped.

Tossing the stained towel aside, he bent at the waist and splashed fresh water on his face, neck and chest. He rinsed beneath his arms, ridding himself of the day's sweat.

When he'd decided to work in the stables, pitching hay for the horses with the other lads, it had seemed the perfect way to get his mind off Clara. He hadn't anticipated one of the lads tripping and running his pitchfork into him, very nearly spearing him. Hunt wanted to believe the lad's clumsiness was just that—clumsiness. Not the curse.

Not death coming for him.

He knew what his grandmother would say. Hopefully, news of this recent mishap would not reach her. Hopefully, there would be no more mishaps.

"What happened to you?"

He twisted around at the sound of the voice and winced from the sudden movement, the action pulling on the gash in his side.

Clara stood in the threshold, blinking owlishly, her gaze skipping from him to the bloodied towel on the floor.

In his haste to examine his injury, he had left his bedroom door ajar.

"'Tis nothing," he replied, his gaze feasting on her, missing nothing.

She looked as fresh as a spring flower. Her dark hair was pulled atop her head in gleaming waves. A few strands dangled free, framing her face in the most fetching manner.

His fingers tingled, yearning to touch her, longing to run his hands through that dark mass and free it all of its pins.

She was garbed in a gown of sunny yellow, the brightest thing in this room of masculine browns. The only other color present was the MacLarin tartan draped over his bed.

He had a sudden flash of her there, spread out on his tartan, stripped of her clothes, her soft skin beckoning.

Clearly Clara in his room was not advisable. "You should go."

Her eyes traveled over him and he was sharply aware of everywhere her gaze touched. His face, shoulders, chest, stomach.

Instead of obeying and going away, she stepped deeper into the room. Apparently his lack of clothing didn't deter her.

"Did you injure yourself?" She closed the last of the distance between them.

Again. She didn't say the word, but it hung between them. Heard even if unspoken.

"I had an accident with a pitchfork."

"A pitchfork," she exclaimed, her hand reaching out to touch him. Her shaking fingertips brushed along his rib cage and he hissed in a breath that had nothing to do with pain.

His hand shot out to seize hers, stopping those slender fingers from exploring him further. Her touch was a torment—but then that left them holding hands. Still much too intimate. Still connected. Still a torment.

His thumb grazed her pulse point at her wrist. It was racing, but then so was his. She froze, her eyes flaring wide and locking on him.

She glanced down at the gash on his torso. "How did that—?"

"'Tis no' important." He shook his head. It was too unbelievable even though he'd been there, even though he had been the one struck by a pitchfork.

It could have been worse. He could have been impaled.

"Another accident," she murmured with a small shake of her head, the color draining from her face. "It could have killed you."

"It could have," he agreed.

She looked stricken. She turned and paced a short line, wringing her hands together.

His stomach knotted. "What is it?"

"Oh, no," she whispered brokenly.

"What?"

"Another accident. It can't be. This can't be happening." She hugged herself as if needing the comfort.

"Clara. You're worrying me."

"I'm . . ." Her voice faded.

"Clara?"

"I'm pregnant," she blurted as she stopped to face him. "That's what I came in here to tell you."

The words should not have served as any surprise. He knew there was a chance of this. His grandmother had been certain it was already a fact and never ceased to bemoan his impending doom.

He was ashamed at how he had thought himself so different from his forefathers, so much better, stronger. He'd done it. The same thing his father had done. And his grandfather. And his great-grandfather.

"Hunt?" She shifted on her feet. "Say something."

He said the first thing to pop in his mind, his voice a grim whisper.

"You've killed me."

Chapter 17

Clara waited a few hours before dawn to slip away.

She and Marian had packed their belongings before they went to sleep, so they would be ready the instant they woke. Their trunks would have to stay behind. They stuffed what they most needed inside their valises. They could send for the rest of their things later.

Even though she had reached the decision to leave with steady conviction, Clara slept poorly, tossing and turning, seeing Hunt in her mind getting stabbed by a pitchfork. A pitchfork for heaven's sake! It seemed much too incredible. On the heels of the previous two accidents, it was just too risky for her to remain here. She would not take the chance. She would not place him in further danger. She couldn't. With any luck, distance from her would soften the curse's power. It was a chance. A hope.

It would be midmorning before anyone realized they had gone. Clara assumed her husband would give pursuit. It was the honorable thing to do, and he was the honorable sort, after all. He couldn't simply pretend he did not have a wife.

However, she would be safely ensconced at Kilmarkie House before he caught up with her, and then his objections to her retreat would be merely obligatory.

Marcus would not force her to return with Hunt nor would she change her mind and return. This was for the best. For everyone.

Even Hunt would understand that. He, better than anyone, understood the danger, the threat she presented. He didn't want her around.

This was for the both of them. For the three of them.

Three. Her hand moved to her stomach. She'd hardly had time to think of it. Of *him*. Or *her*.

A life grew there, within her, someone who would be part of her world for all the rest of her days, if she should be so blessed. A piece of Hunt even when she didn't have him. She felt a pang in her chest. She rubbed her fingers there, but it didn't help.

"Are we going the right way?" Marian called from behind her as they plodded along the lane. Early morning light streaked the sky above the treetops in shades of orange and pink. "Are you certain?"

"Yes. We left early and are keeping good pace. We should be there in time for dinner, if we don't stop." She tossed a chiding look over her shoulder.

"Very well," Marian griped. "I won't pester for rests, but can you mind the pace? Some of us aren't horsewomen. Not as you are, at any rate."

"And you grew up in a country village, you say?" Clara tsked. "What kind of country girl are you?"

"We lived *in* the village. Riding was not an everyday occurrence. If we wanted to go somewhere we had a pair of proper legs to take us to and fro."

Clara was smiling when the woods on every side of them suddenly came alive. Her smile shattered as horsemen bound out into the lane with raucous shouts.

Her horse whinnied and danced in distress. She hastily worked to get the beast under control. Clara shot a quick glance over her shoulder, concerned for Marian. Fortunately, she hadn't been thrown and seemed to be managing her mount adequately.

She turned to find a man astride his horse

directly in front of her. He was surrounded by several other men—and he was familiar.

He wagged a finger at her. "Now we've met before, lass." Evidently he recognized her, too.

She remembered him. He was the man from the inn. The man who Hunt had brawled with over his lost bull. She shifted uneasily in her saddle. He was no friend to her husband, so it stood to reason he was no friend to her.

"I'm sure I don't know you." She lifted her chin.

"A Sassenach," he proclaimed to his comrades, chortling as though she were some kind of amusing exhibition.

"Be so kind as to let us pass." She swept a frosty glare over the party. Right now dignity was the only thing she could cling to in the face of these rough men.

"Such verra fine ladies should no' be out here without escort." He shook his head in reproof. "I'm afraid I canna in good conscience abandon ye both."

"What could happen to us?" she sneered. "We come into contact with a group of unsavory men up to no good?"

They all guffawed at that.

"Indeed," Marian said in her sharpest governess tone. "What are all you men doing about this early? I don't believe this is your land."

Their laughter faded and they all exchanged calculating looks.

"Ye ken that then, lass, do ye?" Bannessy inquired with a tilt to his head, appearing impressed. "And wot would ye fine ladies be doing out here on MacLarin land?" He stretched his neck, taking note of their bags.

"We're aware," Marian snapped. "I just pointed that very thing out to you."

Clara sent her a quelling look, wishing she had not revealed quite so much. Too late, though.

Bannessy considered them with a speculative gaze. He looked down the road behind them, his expression growing ever more calculating.

There was only one thing behind them. MacLarin—his castle and the neighboring village. She knew this Scotsman was reaching that same conclusion. He knew where they had come from. He knew they were connected to his enemy.

Her stomach knotted.

"Ye come from MacLarin Keep," he announced.

This time, Marian held her tongue, as though realizing she had revealed too much moments ago.

Bannessy pressed on, "Wot business do ye have wi' MacLarin?"

Clara pressed her lips firmly shut. She could think of no valid story, no viable excuse. Only the truth and she would not give him that.

"I must confess ye have my interest piqued," he continued.

"I don't know why." Clara fought for a casual air. "We're just two travelers passing through."

He smirked. "Ye dinna expect me tae believe that. Nay. Until I find out yer connection tae Mac-Larin, ye best come wi' me."

"With you?" Marian cried in outrage. "We are going nowhere with you, sir, now move aside."

Clara stared at Bannessy for some time before replying to her friend through unsmiling lips. "I don't believe they're giving us a choice, Marian."

He nodded cheerfully, approval bright in his eyes. "That is correct. Ye are a clever lass. Now come along." He moved his mount closer to Clara. "Make room for me tae ride beside ye so that I may come tae know ye."

The party of men flanked them and they continued on their way. She tossed Marian a reassuring look—even if she felt far from re-assured herself—and faced forward again, de-termined that he never come to know her. She would tell him nothing. He was her husband's enemy. She'd give him nothing—especially her identity.

After all, he'd absconded with Hunt's prize bull. There was no telling what he would do if he discovered who he had beside him.

HUNT STORMED THROUGH the doors of Kilmarkie House. "Where is she?" he bellowed until Autenberry and Alyse emerged from the drawing room, their expressions equally bewildered.

"MacLarin? What are you doing here?" Autenberry's gaze flickered around Hunt, searching. "Where is Clara? Why've you come?"

Something cold and frightening seized inside him, ten times worse than when he woke to learn she was gone from his home—*their* home.

"She's not here?" Hunt glanced back toward the doors through which he'd just entered. The air was dark. Cold gusted in behind him. It was well past the dinner hour. He hated to think of her out there in this . . . in the dark. Where could she be?

She and Marian had left ahead of him. She should have already been here.

It was not until midmorning that one of the maids reported them gone and he could only surmise that they had quite a few hours' head start on him. They should be here by now.

Clara should be here. It was his only thought, pumping alongside the fear coursing through him.

"Clara?" Autenberry's face hardened and he suddenly had his hands on Hunt, thrusting him against the wall with violent force. "Where is my sister?"

"She and Marian rode out this morning. I assumed they came here."

"Why would she have left and returned here on her own? What did you do to her?"

Hunt pushed Autenberry off him. He didn't need Autenberry in his face to feel guilt. Or panic. He had felt all that and more the moment he realized she had left him—he *still* felt it. It had not abated nor would it until he had her safely back with him.

All this time he had been worrying about his fate. It had never occurred to him to worry for her.

Fear for her, he now realized, was so much worse than any fear he'd ever felt for himself. Bitter bile rose up in his throat. He wanted her safe before him.

"I dinna ken why she left," he said. Not entirely true, but it seemed too complicated and personal to explain. And it damn well wasn't Hunt's place to inform Autenberry of his sister's condition. Hunt would leave that to her. It was her right to tell, her news to impart.

Autenberry pointed a finger at him. "You promised me you would take good care of her."

"Aye." Hunt nodded. "It's a promise I intend tae keep." He turned for the door.

"Where are you going?" Autenberry called after him.

"It's late . . . and dark out there," Alyse chimed in.

"If she's no' here, then she's somewhere else." He spread his arms wide. "I intend tae find her." He'd not stop until he did.

"Not by yourself, you aren't." Autenberry pressed a quick kiss to his wife's cheek and followed after Hunt. "Let's go."

BANNESSY LIVED IN a smaller castle, essentially two tower houses conjoined by a timber structure. Like her brother's and Hunt's homes, a high curtain wall surrounded the residence so that livestock could roam within the space. Unlike Hunt's and Marcus's homes, the place wasn't very tidy. No one seemed to mind when the loose livestock wandering about the courtyard made their way into the house.

A couple chickens even strolled into the dining room where she and Marian took their breakfast, pecking at the crumbs scattered on the floor. Clara froze midbite, her toast inches from her mouth as she stared at one sharp-eyed bird.

"Are those . . . chickens?" Marian murmured.

Clara and Marian had shared a bedchamber the night before. Neither one of them had any intention of being parted in light of the fact that they had been abducted and trusted no one here. The housekeeper had scarcely grunted a word to them as she led them to their room last night.

None of the servants spoke to them. They were definitely considered Bannessy's captives.

"Yes," Clara answered, using the toe of her shoe to push one particularly aggressive chicken away when it decided to peck on the tassels on her slippers.

A maid stood in the corner of the room. She stared vacantly into nowhere, presumably not paying attention to either one of them.

Still, Clara leaned forward to whisper, "We need to get away."

Marian shot a furtive glance to the maid and nodded. "I'll see if I can slip away and assess the stables."

"Be careful."

"They're not watching me nearly as closely as you. Bannessy sees only a maid when he looks at me. He knows you're the valuable one, you're . . ." Marian's voice faded and she sneaked another look the maid's way. She wasn't going to risk voicing Clara's connection to Hunt even in a whisper. Bannessy could not know she was Hunt's wife. Clara had made certain Marian understood that once they were alone in their bedchamber last night.

"Ah, there you are!" Bannessy entered the dining room. He kicked a chicken aside as he strode across the room and pulled up a seat next to her as the bird squawked in outrage, ruffling its feathers as it sped around the dining room with its neck extended. "I hope yer breakfast was tae yer liking."

"Yes, thank you." She'd only sampled the toast, finding her stomach a little unsettled this morning, but he didn't need to know those particulars.

"Since we arrived so late last night, I was wondering if ye might like a tour about the grounds?"

She opened her mouth at first to reject his invitation. She was no guest here, after all. But then she realized it would be the perfect way to assess her surroundings so that she might later escape.

"That would be lovely. Thank you."

He beamed, looking a little surprised at her acceptance. "Lovely indeed. Shall we go now?" He glanced at her plate. "Are ye finished?"

"Quite so, thank you." She lowered her napkin to the table and sent an encouraging glance to Marian from under her lashes. Her friend frowned after her, clearly not liking this development, but she held her tongue—and her seat.

Bannessy offered his arm and escorted her from the dining room.

It did not take long for him to begin interrogating her, proving his motivation wasn't purely an innocent stroll.

"I've given some thought. A fine Sassenach lady such as ye . . . and the first time I laid eyes on ye was in that taproom, not far from Kilmarkie

House, near the Duke of Autenberry's property. It must have been yer destination. He's English like ye are. Could it be ye were visiting him?"

She hesitated, uncertain if it was wise to confess she was sister to the Duke of Autenberry. Bannessy could attempt to ransom her.

"Yer silence is verra telling," he added.

Quickly. Answer him.

"I was visiting his wife, Lady Autenberry. We are girlhood friends."

"Hmm." He mulled that over. "Then why did I find ye where I did? A bit far from Kilmarkie House. You appeared tae be leaving MacLarin Castle?"

They'd circuited the house and had now arrived in the front courtyard again, stopping beside a large neglected fountain. The water was green and a film of scum floated over the surface. The condition of the water did not stop a hound the size of a small horse from trotting up and drinking sloppily from it. Water flew and she scooted over to avoid the spray.

A sudden wave of nausea beset her and she closed her eyes against it, swaying on her feet.

Bannessy brushed a hand against her arm, gently holding her. "Are you unwell?"

She shook her head but could not yet speak. A swell of bile rose up in her throat and she feared any attempt at speech would have dire results.

"Lass, ye dinna look well." His concerned gaze flitted over her face and his light hold on her arm tightened into an actual grip.

She attempted to move a step, but her legs wobbled, threatening to give out under her. He caught her against him.

She blinked her suddenly fuzzy gaze up at him. "I don't know what's wrong with me." Her knees buckled and he caught her, sweeping her up into his arms.

"Oh!" She pushed weakly at his chest. "I'm fine. Set me down."

"Lass," he chided, "yer face is white as snow."

A violent pounding suddenly filled the air. Horse hooves on the packed earth.

Bannessy turned in the direction of the sound, still holding her in his arms.

Two horsemen galloped into the yard.

"Bannessy!"

Clara blinked, struggling to clear her blurring vision to make certain her eyes were not deceiving her. "Hunt," she murmured with a touch of awe as her husband launched himself off his horse before the beast even came to a full stop.

Marcus was with him, too, following a few paces after her husband.

Hunt charged toward them, stabbing a finger in their direction. "Let go of her, you bastard. Put her down!"

"MacLarin! How good tae see ye! And sooner than I expected." He adjusted Clara in his arms, bouncing her higher against his chest.

Clara closed her eyes briefly, not appreciating being jostled about in her present dizziness. She opened her eyes again to see Hunt studying her face with a near panicked expression.

"What have you done tae her? She looks ill!" He reached her side, tapping her cheek lightly, scanning first her face and then looking her all over. "Clara, love. Are you well? What is it? What's wrong with you?"

"I've done nothing tae the lass. I saved her from hitting the ground just as she was about tae swoon."

"I'm fine now. Really. I can stand," Clara insisted, her voice betraying her with a quiver.

"You heard her," Hunt growled.

"Put her down," Marcus added from behind him. "Now."

"Och." Bannessy looked down at Clara with new consideration. "Two men fighting after this wee lass. She must be quite the prize."

"She's my bloody sister," Marcus spit out.

"And my wife!" Hunter added in a growl.

"Your wife!" Bannessy's eyes boggled. "Ye've married!"

"Aye. And she's pregnant. Now give her back tae me before I tear you apart, man."

"Ye've married, MacLarin? And yer tae be a father?" Bannessy hurriedly transferred her to Hunt's arms as though he could not be rid of her fast enough. "Are ye daft, man? What of the curse?"

She groaned. Even Bannessy knew of it . . . and believed in it.

"The curse," Marcus exclaimed, looking incredulously back and forth between the two men. "Don't tell me you all think . . . you *believe* that rot to be true!"

"Marcus," she chided from her new position in Hunt's arms.

Her brother's eyes shot to her, seeing something in her face and at once understanding. "Don't tell me you believe it, too, Clara?"

She didn't know what to believe. She only knew that Hunt had three very close calls lately . . . and she had no intention of risking his life a fourth time.

"Och, coz." Bannessy shook his head. "What 'ave ye done?"

"Coz?" she parroted. "Coz? As in *cousin*? He's your cousin, you mean?" She punched Hunt in the chest.

"Aye." He shrugged. "We are practically all kin in this area. We share the same great-grandfather."

"B-but you *steal* from each other," she sputtered, her voice gaining shrillness. "You're family and you steal from each other?"

"Aye," Hunt and Bannessy said in unison, as if the practice was the most common thing in the world.

"What is *wrong* with you people?"

They ignored her question. Bannessy looked at Hunt with something akin to an apology in his eyes. "I had no idea she was yer wife. I would no' 'ave taken her, Hunt." Apparently certain things were off limits then. Bannessy shook his head in a proper show of contrition. "Why'd ye do it, coz? 'Tis suicide."

"Put me down," she commanded, having had quite enough of such a grim exchange. Even if it was true. *Especially* if it was true. She didn't want to hear of it.

Hunt obliged and her feet slid to the ground.

She stepped back, too quickly it seemed, for the world moved swiftly around her. She staggered with a small cry.

"Clara!" She was swept up in Hunt's solid arms again. "What ails you?"

She didn't even answer. She was too busy combatting the dizziness assailing her. Blast it. The world would not stop its moving.

She peeked her eyes open to see that it wasn't only her dizziness. They were indeed moving now.

"Where are we going?"

"I'm taking you inside. Tae bed."

"What for? It's the middle of the day, I don't need a—"

"You're clearly unwell so bed is where you belong."

"I'm not ill!"

He strode past gawking servants, marching up the stairs, not the least winded from his exertions. At the top, he stopped and rotated in a small circle, obviously unsure where to go.

"To the right," she snapped, pointing in the direction of the room she shared with Marian. "That one. Right there."

He carried her inside the chamber and set her down on the bed.

She looked up at him crossly. "Nothing ails me."

"You couldn't even stand."

"I'm dizzy. It's not so uncommon. I likely need to loosen my corset."

"A corset?" He scowled. "Remove the damn thing. Toss it out."

Before she could argue, Marian suddenly breezed into the room. "What has happened? I just saw your brother and he—"

"She's unwell," Hunt quickly supplied.

"Only a little dizzy," Clara corrected.

Marian sank down on the bed beside her. "Not

to fret. My mother suffered similar symptoms when she carried my younger siblings. Only in the beginning. She improved as she increased."

Hunt looked slightly appeased. "Rest now. Recover yourself."

"When will we go? I'm eager—"

"You will rest," he admonished.

Clara huffed in affront. "I do not need to rest."

He shook his head obstinately. "You'll no' leave this bed until a midwife has seen tae you."

"Oh!" she cried in outrage. "The nerve of—"

"It isn't a *bad* idea, Clara," Marian volunteered.

Hunter clapped loudly once. "A voice of reason!"

Clara turned on Marian. *"Et tu, Brute?"*

"Oh, cease with the dramatics," Marian admonished, removing a tartan from a nearby chair and tucking it all around Clara. "We shall all be much relieved to have you pronounced fit. You'll be relieved, too, when it's all said and done. You will see."

"She's right," Hunt seconded.

Clara crossed her arms. She couldn't argue with that logic. "So we stay here? For how long?"

"Until the midwife declares you well for travel," he answered, his gaze fastened on her as though she were some fragile thing that might shatter into pieces. Ironic, considering he was the one that seemed so fragile of late and destined for a dire fate.

She forced a smile—for him, for herself. "I'm fine," she insisted. "Healthy as can be."

He nodded, still looking uncertain, and a warmth suffused her to have him here . . . to see him so obviously concerned and solicitous over her. A marked difference from their last encounter.

Of course the matter of the curse still remained, hanging like a dark pall. That had not gone away, so it meant she had to.

She still had to find a way to leave. That had not changed.

Chapter 18

*T*hey stayed a week. One endless and interminable week.

The local midwife had examined Clara and while she pronounced her hale, she suggested one week's rest was necessary. There was no arguing her recommendation. Hunt and Marian were in accord with the midwife and they made certain Clara followed her instructions and stayed put in bed.

Her brother had left the day he arrived with Hunt. He was understandably anxious to return to Alyse. Her time was approaching. Even though Clara had not changed her mind and fully intended to continue on and join him at Kilmarkie House, she let him go without protest. He needed to get back to his wife, and Clara did not need to worry him any more than she already had. She'd break free of Hunt and find her own way to her brother's home.

A week's rest in bed had very nearly finished her. It was tedious. She felt pushed to the brink of madness. Hunt and Marian had not allowed her up from bed, so she was quite eager to be free of her prison when her sentence came to an end.

Clara was up on the morning of the eighth day, not to be deterred. She was packed and ready to go when Hunt entered the room. He closed the door softly behind him and stopped before her.

Dressed and ready to depart, she wrapped a hand around the bedpost as though needing support in this confrontation with him—this man who was quite possibly cursed because of her.

She'd seen him throughout the week, of course, although Marian had continued to share the bed with her. Hunt had taken the room next door to them without seeming to mind that he was not sharing a bed with his wife. Perhaps because he didn't mind. He didn't care. As far as he was concerned she had killed him. He'd said as much. He blamed her. A pang punched her in the center of her chest at that reminder. That guilt was never far. She rested her cheek against the wood post, feeling wretched.

He frowned and stepped closer. "Are you well?"

"I'm fine." She exhaled. "What are we doing, Hunt?"

His gaze brushed over her face, searching. "We're going home, Clara."

"It's not my home. Your home is not my home." She spoke calmly, steadily. It was not her intent to start an argument or appear wrathful. She merely didn't intend to leave here with him and he needed to understand that.

His eyes sparked in challenge. "We took vows that essentially bind us. My home is yours. All that I have . . . is yours."

"I don't want it." *Not if it could cost you your life.*

His face did not react to that, but a sudden tension lined his shoulders that made her think she had wounded him somehow.

"A little late for that now." He waved toward her stomach.

"It's not too late. Mistakes happen. It's how we make the best of them that matters, that makes a difference."

His lips twisted. "Marriages happen all the time between people who like each other far less than what we feel for one another."

"Well, the marriage doesn't lead to the groom's death, does it?"

"Och, so you believe me now?" He chuckled.

She bristled. "It's not amusing."

"Aye." He laughed harder. "I ken."

She shrugged. "I don't want to rule out the possibility that it could be true. Given that, I think it best if I remove myself far from your sphere." She nodded resolutely.

"Ah. This is why you crept away like a thief in the night."

"You've suffered from three potential fatal accidents."

"Aye. The curse is at work." He nodded and looked woefully unperturbed by the announcement.

"Don't you care? If it's true . . . aren't you . . . afraid?" A lump rose in her throat.

"I've spent a lifetime trying to avoid and evade and trick it. It's actually a bit of a relief."

"A relief?"

"Aye. I dinna have tae worry about it anymore."

She released the post and lurched forward, grasping a hold of his jacket with both her fists. "Of course you should be afraid! You should be worried. You used to be. Where did that man go?" She shook him a little. It was as though he didn't want to live anymore and she couldn't have that.

He had to live.

He covered her hands with his own. "Come

home, Clara. It won't make a bit of difference where you reside as far as the curse is concerned. You're my wife. And you carry my child. Our child." His hand drifted down to cover her stomach.

She choked back a sob. It was the first time he had acknowledged their child directly.

"Dinna fash yourself, lass." He swiped his thumb over her cheek, and gave her an encouraging smile. "Don't run. I will only have tae chase you." He dropped his head until their foreheads were touching, lips so close, nearly brushing hers as he spoke. "Come home, Clara. It's your home now."

She released a shuddering breath, compelled and yet still so very uncertain, so very much afraid. "Very well."

THEY ARRIVED HOME just in time for dinner.

The midwife had recommended Clara abstain from riding, so Hunt secured his wife in a carriage with Marian.

Hunt rode alongside them, thinking on the future—whatever was left of it for him—and how he wished to spend it. It was a sobering internal dialogue, but perhaps one every person should have at some point. People died all the time, after all, young and old. Should not everyone live as though each day were their last? Was that not a proper philosophy?

Nana was there to greet them in the foyer. "Retrieved yer lass, did ye?" Her pale eyes gleamed in disapproval.

"That I did," he said.

He would not waste another day dwelling in miserable thoughts. His grandmother needed to be apprised of that fact because he was done talking about the curse. Done thinking about it.

Now he simply intended to live.

"We're famished," he announced, hoping to direct the conversation and detract his grandmother from contributing anything negative.

"Aye," she grumbled and turned to lead the way to the dining room.

They ate in relative peace. Hunt spoke of the coming planting and the festival they had every spring. Clara's eyes lit up as he described it, and he realized he enjoyed seeing the light shining in her eyes.

His grandmother sat in fuming silence, but he didn't care.

After they ate, he escorted Clara to her chamber. "Good night."

She smiled tremulously and he fought the urge to lean down and kiss those soft lips. He held back. She'd agreed to return home with him, to stay, but she had not agreed for more than that.

She had not agreed to alter their understanding of a name-only marriage.

"Good night," she returned.

They stood before her door hesitantly, each unmoving, and he felt like a boy before his first kiss. But there would be no kissing this night.

With a final smile for him, she slipped away inside her room, closing the door on him.

CLARA WAS READYING for bed when her chamber door opened and slammed shut. She spun around at the sound, the dressing robe she had just removed clutched to her chest.

"Oh." The breath rushed out of her. "You."

She knew she sounded surly, but she couldn't help herself. Hunt's grandmother did not like her. She had made that abundantly clear with each of their encounters. Nothing Clara said or did was going to alter that fact.

She went about slipping on her dressing robe, bracing herself for whatever was to come in this encounter.

It was rather freeing. Embracing her status as unwelcome, unwanted, reviled even. She was already at the bottom and she accepted there was no climbing up.

"Aye. *Me.* You came back." Nana crossed her arms in clear resentment.

"Yes, I did. Your grandson insisted."

"Of course he did. You've bewitched him."

Clara laughed. "That is hardly the case." Hunt was quite un-bewitchable. The majority of the time she could not tell what thoughts were playing behind those eyes of his.

Nana shook her head with grim disapproval. "Ye need tae leave."

"I tried that already."

"Try harder."

"Do you really think me leaving will make any difference?" Clara pressed a hand over her stomach unthinkingly. "It is done already."

Nana's gaze flew to her stomach. "Aye, but that can be undone, lass."

Clara sucked in a breath, perfectly aware of her meaning. Aware and horrified. Even so, she heard herself asking through lips that had gone numb, "What do you mean?"

The old woman advanced until she reached Clara. She stopped before her, her expression almost serene as she threatened in a softly sinister voice, "I will no' lose my grandson."

Clara nodded once, her body so tightly wound it could snap. "Understood."

And she did understand. Fully.

She understood that she was face-to-face with a desperate woman who would do anything to protect her grandson.

And that meant it fell to Clara to protect herself . . . and her unborn child.

HUNT COULDN'T SLEEP.

In his bed, he stared in the dark, his hand resting limply on his stomach, wondering crossly what the hell he and his wife were doing in separate bedchambers.

Wasting time we could be happily shagging.

He knew they had reached a truce of sorts. She had agreed to come back home with him, after all, but there was still much hovering between them. Much unresolved—bitter words they had spoken the morning after their wedding when he had confronted the evidence of her maidenhead on the bedsheets.

He had been the one to insist they would have an in-name-only marriage. That had been his decision.

He was a jackass.

He winced. He'd called her a problem. Damnation. He groaned and dragged a hand over his face, fervently wishing he could take those words back. He needed to woo her . . . to talk to her. Eat crow. Beg, if need be. That was if he wanted to resume conjugal relations. If he wanted to be close to his wife.

His hand slid down his stomach to fondle his

aching cock. God help him. He did. He ached for her. He wanted his wife again.

And why not? The damage was done. She was already with child. The curse had already been activated.

He tossed and turned, punching his pillow several times, trying to relieve some of his frustration. No good. He was still wide-awake and restless. It didn't help that his cock was perpetually at half-mast. He was like a randy green lad ever since she'd come into his life.

Somewhere in the distance, on the same floor, a door creaked. Someone was out of bed, and because he didn't have anything better to do, he hopped from bed to go investigate, pausing to hastily don his trousers.

He stealthily departed his room and peered up and down the hallway. The sconces glowed dimly, illuminating the empty corridor. No one was inside, nor could he determine which chamber door had opened. They all stood closed and silent in the dead of night.

He turned, prepared to return to his bed and give another try at sleep. That was when he heard the creaking step. Someone was on the stairs.

He whirled around and strode quickly in that direction.

Hunt stopped at the top of the stairs and

looked down, his gaze colliding on the backs of two women fleeing down the stairs.

"Clara!"

The women froze, but he only had eyes for one of them. Now at the bottom of the stairs, Clara turned slightly to look up at him. She lifted her chin proudly. "Hunt," she greeted as though they were coming face-to-face in a drawing room.

"What are you doing? Where are you going?" His gaze skipped to Marian, who had the sense to look a little shamefaced. She shrugged up at him.

"I changed my mind." Clara's voice rang out. "I decided it would be a good idea to leave, after all."

"And this is the way you do it?" He descended the stairs, his feet moving quickly down the familiar steps. When he reached the bottom, his attention turned briefly to Marian again. "You may go tae bed now. There will be no trips this night."

Marian turned to look at her mistress. "Clara?" she asked gently, clearly seeking word from her on the matter.

Clara nodded stiffly. "Do as he says, Marian. I will be fine."

With a brisk nod, Marian started up the steps, stopping for a moment and looking back down at him. "Mind yourself with her," she warned, indifferent to the fact that he was now essentially her employer. Her loyalty was to Clara, and he admired her for that. He wanted Clara to have supportive friends in her life.

"She will come tae no harm. Now tae bed with you, Marian."

With that reassurance from him, Marian ascended the stairs and left them alone.

He repeated his earlier question. "You thought this was the best way tae leave me?"

"Will there ever be a good way? An easy way?"

"Why?" he pressed, desperate to comprehend. "I thought we had reached an understanding. What has changed?"

"I just can't . . ." She shook her head, tension humming from her body.

"You *can't* tell me." That was the truth of it. Can't. *Won't.* He could see it in her evasion, in the way her voice wobbled and she shifted on her feet. He could look at her even in the gloom and know this. He was coming to know his wife and her habits. She wasn't being coy. She was . . . frightened.

The air left him in an angry rush. Why was she scared? Scared of him? He wouldn't have it. The idea that she could be frightened of him twisted his stomach. Clearly he had failed somewhere along the way if his wife was afraid of him.

"You have to let me go." Her dark eyes were like endless lochs.

Frustration welled up inside him . . . and a

sharp blade of panic. He could not lose her. However much time he had left, he wanted to spend it with her, getting lost in her, gorging himself on this woman that he had given up everything for. Feasting on her until he was satisfied and hungry no more.

"You ask the impossible."

Her head dipped as though she was gathering something from deep inside herself. "I know I said I would stay, but that was before . . . before . . ."

"Before what? What happened?" What could possibly have happened since dinner?

She shook her head. "I'm sure it's nothing, but your grandmother . . . She's obviously upset at this marriage, at me . . . at the prospect of this child."

"What are you saying, Clara? You're afraid of my grandmother?"

"There's more at stake here than your life now." In the dim light, he noticed her hand move down to hold her belly as if seeking to protect the life there.

He sucked in a short breath. "You're afraid of Nana? You think she might do something to make you lose the babe?"

"It would break the curse . . . and save you." She gave a hard nod.

"She threatened you? She threatened the babe?"

he pressed, seeking confirmation because it was so very unbelievable that his grandmother would betray him in such a way. His anger edged into fear. Fear for Clara and their child. *Our child.* He had not thought in those terms before but now he had and he could not stop.

"Not in so many words, but yes. She reminded me that something could happen to prevent me from having this child."

He stepped forward and took hold of her, his hands locking on her arms. "Nothing is going to happen to you. I won't let anything happen to you." His gaze flickered down and then came back up to her face. "I won't let anything happen to either one of you."

She sighed softly. "Me staying here . . . there's so much risk in it."

"The risk is worth it. You're worth it tae me, Clara. I will handle my grandmother. Aye, she is upset, but I will no' let her harm ye or this child. You have tae trust me." His hands flexed on her arms, trying to convey his sincerity. "Stay." It was a single word, but he put everything into it. Everything he was feeling. All his desperation. All of his need for her.

She took her time replying, and when she did her voice was small and dejected. "Hunt," she began, and he already knew he wasn't going to like what she had to say.

She wasn't going to stay. He had not convinced her.

Fueled by desperation, he hauled her against him and kissed her. Circled her neck with his hand and held her in place for his feasting mouth.

There was nothing soft or tender about it. He claimed her, his teeth tugging her bottom lip down. She opened for him with a moan and it was all the invitation he needed.

He picked her up, his hands guiding her legs around his waist as if she weighed nothing at all.

A few short strides and they were in the drawing room. On the sofa. He fell over her and yanked at her skirts, shoving them to her hips with rough movements. Her hands were there, trying to assist them.

Everything happened fast. His heart pounded, blood rushing to his cock.

His mouth fused hotly to hers, not even coming up for air as he worked to free himself from his trousers. Once his engorged member was free, he seized her hand to close around him. "Touch me," he pleaded in a hoarse voice.

Her fingers circled his hardness, her thumb dragging over the swollen tip of him, experimenting, rubbing his juice into the taut skin of his cock.

"Damn, lass," he muttered.

He broke away long enough to shove his trousers all the way down his hips.

He spread her thighs wide and reached down to tear the seam in her drawers wider for him so he could see all of her pretty quim. The rent of fabric on the air only inflamed his arousal.

It excited her, too. Her breathing quickened and her eyes dilated, glowing black in the firelight.

He touched her, running a finger over her folds. She was already wet for him. She cried out when he found the pleasure button at the top of her womanhood. He pressed down and massaged it in a firm, circular motion.

"Hunt," she gasped, arching up off the sofa. "Please."

Propping one elbow on the back of the sofa, he slid his other hand into her hair, his fingers locking in the silken mass.

And then he was driving into her, pushing deep.

She surged against the fullness of him, her head dropping back with an exultant moan as he sank himself to the hilt.

The sensation of her, so hot and tight, milking his cock, undid him. He didn't wait for her to catch her breath. He couldn't. He had to move. He pumped inside her, his desire for her savage as he worked to his own release. She clutched his biceps, as though needing something to hang on to as he pounded out his need.

Sharp little yips escaped her in conjunction with his every thrust and it only spurred him on.

Need drove him. Animal instinct. He flipped her over so that her back was to him, and he guided her to grip the back of the sofa.

He ripped her drawers in half, exposing her so that he could palm her lovely bum. Her cheeks were smooth and round and a curse of appreciation escaped him.

Adjusting her position on her knees to his liking, he slid into her quim from behind, the angle deeper, tighter, and they groaned in unison.

His hands gripped her ass, fingers digging into the sweet flesh as he dragged in a breath. He dropped his head to the back of her neck, his face burying in sweet-smelling hair. For a moment, his vision darkened. The pleasure twisted near to pain, it was so intense.

He pulled out almost fully and then drove back inside her. A rush of wetness met the thrust of his cock, and it was the final straw.

He took her fast and rough, spurred on by her pants and pleas and moans. Her sex clenched around his sliding cock. Her hands pushed against the back of the couch, and she pressed into him, meeting his thrusts in her own frenzied need.

She glanced over her shoulder at him and the sight of her heavy-lidded eyes, her expression that of a woman well-fucked, stripped away the last of his restraint. Turned him feral. He pounded into her. When her knees started to shake, he seized her hips, holding her upright. He leaned over her, his chest curving over her back. One of his hands slid around her hip and dove straight to the core of her, finding the sweet little nub, swollen at the top of her sex. He pressed down and rolled it deftly.

She came apart, jerking and convulsing, releasing a keening cry.

Still, he continued, hammering into her desperately, barreling toward his own release over the sounds of her gasps.

He found her ear and sank his teeth down into the lobe. And just like that she shuddered all over again, her body vibrating and humming as her sex squeezed around him.

He groaned. "That's it. Come again for me, Clara."

Then he reached his own climax, thrusting and releasing his seed deep inside her, shuddering into her own contracting body.

She turned her face to the side, still gasping under him. He held himself lodged inside her, bracing his hands on either side of her on the back of the sofa, keeping his weight from fully crushing her. His harsh breath fluttered the hairs at her neck. She brushed her fingers there as though it tickled.

He breathed into her ear, "Now you have tae stay . . . so we can keep doing this."

She chuckled lightly.

His chest expanded at the sound of it. In that laughter, he heard *yes*. He heard more than yes. She was his. And he was hers. She felt that, too, even if she didn't say it.

He flipped onto his back on the sofa, lifting his body off her. Even though they were still side by side, he felt the sudden loss. Was it mad that he wanted to be back inside her again?

She collapsed beside him. Both their chests lifted from exertion.

"Is it like that for everyone, you think?" she whispered over the sound of the crackling fireplace.

"No," he answered quickly. "It's not. This is . . . special." *Just for us.*

He held his breath, waiting for her to say something, to promise they could continue like this.

He rolled his face on the back of the sofa to look at her.

She had turned to study him. "You'll talk to your grandmother?" she at last asked.

"I'll send her away, if need be," he promised, meaning it. Nothing would pose a threat to Clara or the babe. No one.

Her expression turned solemn and she nodded slowly. "I'll stay."

Chapter 19

*N*aturally, Nana was asleep when Hunt entered her bedchamber, but he didn't care. He'd have an understanding with her this very night or she would be gone first thing in the morning. It was not the kind of thing that could wait.

He shook her awake, interrupting her snoring.

"Hunt?" she queried groggily, rubbing at her eyes. "Och." Her nose wrinkled. "You smell of her. I dinna need tae ask where you have been, now do I?"

"That's right," he said unapologetically. "That's because she's my wife and you best accept that and vow tae no' harm her."

Nana shook her head. "You damn fool."

"Indeed, I may be a fool. But it's my life." He

took a menacing step forward. "Hear me now, nothing will befall Clara. Not her or the babe, understand me? That child is mine . . . and your kin, too." He pounded his chest. "*My* heir. The future Laird MacLarin. Does that no' mean something tae you?"

Nana slapped her hand through the air. "Pah! Course it does. I will no' harm the girl or the babe. I was just trying tae scare her off. Mayhap I was a bit scared, too." She lifted a single bony shoulder in a shrug, as though hating revealing such vulnerability. "That child is a part of me. A part of this place. I would no' do anything tae hurt one of my own."

Hunt looked at her steadily, intently. "Clara *is* my own . . . and that also makes her your own now. Think on that."

Nana let out a gust of breath, her shoulders slumping. "Aye. I see that now. Verra well. Ye have made yer choice. I will no' interfere anymore. I will do my part, and I will be of assistance whenever I can."

Hunt leaned over and embraced the old woman, patting her on the back lightly. She was so frail he worried he might break a bone. "There, there, Nana. All will be well."

She sniffled against his chest. "I've heard that before."

"This time it will be true." Hunt wasn't sure if

he believed that or not, but Nana needed to hear it. He was at peace, content . . . anxious to get back to his wife.

Exchanging good nights, he left Nana to return to her sleep and made his way toward his bedchamber. He peeked inside, verifying that his wife was not there.

With a grunt of dissatisfaction, he ventured to her room. He strode inside without knocking, finding her in her bed.

He sank down onto the mattress. "Hello there, I think you're in the wrong bed."

She lifted her head drowsily. "Am I? I wasn't sure. I didn't know if you—"

He silenced her with a kiss, following her back down on the bed, coming over her. It was several moments before he broke away to say against her lips, "From now on you sleep in my room, wife. We share a bed." His hand moved to her breast. "We share everything."

She sighed and arched beneath his touch. "Hmm. That sounds lovely . . ."

"It will be lovely." His hand delved beneath her nightgown and cupped the heat of her sex. He gently eased a finger inside her. "Too soon, lass? Are ye verra sore?"

In response, she opened her thighs wide for his foraying hand with a purring moan. "Deliciously sore."

They kissed again . . . after a while though her lips slowed and stilled against his until she finally spoke. "Hunt? What of the future?"

"Shhh. We will not speak of the future. We will live only for the present." His finger increased its rhythm between her legs until she was gasping. "For this. For us. For now. Promise me. Say it."

Her head lolled on the pillow as her need grew, speech apparently too difficult for her.

"Clara?" His hand stilled its feverish work. "Focus for a moment. Promise me. Say it."

Her eyes sharpened on his face. She reached out to brush her palm against his jaw. "I promise we will live only for the present. No more talk of the future."

Chapter 20

$\mathcal{F}$or the next couple months, they did just that.

Clara kept her promise. They lived only for the present. They never spoke of the future. They never mentioned the curse.

A peace of sorts fell between them.

They fell into a routine. Hunt was gone through most of the day, tending to matters among his clan and caring for the livestock roaming his property, protecting them from the ever present threat of thieves . . . even if said thieves happened to be his rascally relations most of the time. Apparently this was just a way of life here and one of the many things she had to grow accustomed to.

Hunt's grandmother began teaching Clara the

day-to-day matters of running the keep. It was no small gesture when, over dinner one evening, Nana turned over the keep's keys to Clara. She dropped them heavily atop the old wooden table. The widening of Hunt's eyes only attested to the miracle of such an event.

"Thank you," Clara murmured, closing her fingers around the old iron keys, feeling the women, the many lives before her, that had possessed these keys. It was a fanciful notion, she realized, but the feeling was there nonetheless.

"Best get accustomed tae yer new role," the lady said. "How many more years can I have left? Twenty? Thirty?"

Hunt snickered and Clara smiled into her napkin, well aware the woman had to be nearing ninety years.

Nana's wrinkled lips twitched, clearly alert to her own joke.

It was strange indeed that it felt good jesting of one's own mortality. Clara slid a glance toward her husband. *Husband.* Another thing that felt strange even with their growing closeness.

She had accepted this man as her husband. She had accepted her life here. There would be no more running away. She would have her child and live out her days here.

"I am certain you have another thirty years, at least, Nana," Hunt agreed with a solemn nod.

The old woman cackled.

Clara felt the smile slip from her lips. Did Hunt have another thirty years? He should. He was a young man yet. There should be no reason he could not live to see his child grow to adulthood. No reason except . . .

Her stomach knotted as her mind traveled down that much-to-be-avoided path. He'd had no accidents lately. At least none that he had revealed to her. She knew he would not confide in her if he had, though.

She couldn't help wonder, however. Wonder and worry. Were things happening to him when he left for the day that he did not report to her? Was his life at continued risk? The very possibility made her sick.

Because they didn't speak of it, Clara liked to pretend the curse wasn't there. She told herself it wasn't real. She wanted to believe that the curse was forgotten for good, but she felt it hovering, like a monster waiting, watching in the dark, readying to strike.

As though Hunt could sense her thoughts, his gaze drifted to her where she sat across from him at the table. The slight curve of his lips faded as their gazes locked.

He knew. He knew her thoughts. He knew her worry—that she was contemplating his fate now that she believed the curse was something to be feared. He knew but said nothing. It went against the pact they'd made.

Live only for the present.

They finished dinner and retired to the drawing room. Nana worked on her knitting. She was determined that the baby have plenty of warm garments. Marian sat at the escritoire, penning a letter home to her father and sisters. Apparently one of her sisters was being courted by the local squire's son. There was much excitement over the courtship. Letters from various members of Marian's family showed up almost daily, all regaling her with the delighted particulars.

"How is your sister's courtship proceeding?" Clara inquired.

Hunt was reading near the fire, a glass of whisky held loosely between his fingers. He did not look up.

"Brilliantly," Marian replied, the letter crinkling in her hands as she lowered it to her lap. "Papa is anticipating he will offer for her soon. And he really is a fine young man. I remember him well. As a lad, he was always taking in injured animals and attending to those less fortunate in the village. He is a very kind soul and so is my sister. They are well matched. I can imagine no couple better suited." Her words dropped over the sound of the softly crackling fire.

Once the words were out, Marian's smile disappeared and her cheeks pinkened. Her gaze darted back and forth between Clara and the laird, well aware that in complimenting her sister and her suitor she had possibly offended them.

Clara shifted awkwardly in her seat and told herself not to look in Hunt's direction. Easier said than done. Impossible, actually. She was much too aware of him. Always. Even across the room she felt him. She felt his stare. She felt him like heat radiating from the sun, singeing her skin.

She looked up to find him studying her. She lifted her chin. Marian shouldn't be embarrassed. She said nothing wrong. She'd only been speaking of her sister.

It seemed glaringly obvious that she and Hunt weren't well suited. They were simply making the best of it.

"Of c-course, I don't venture out very much to make comparisons," Marian stammered, casting Clara a regretful look.

Clara gave a swift single nod, conveying that she should not worry about it. The state of her marriage with Hunt was not Marian's worry. Her friend need not try to make Clara feel better.

Clara rose from her seat. "I'm weary. I think I'm going to retire for the night."

"'Tis the babe," Nana volunteered. "Takes all yer energy. Ye need tae start taking naps in the day. Store your energy."

Hunt unfolded himself from his chair. "I'll escort you."

He always did that. Every night. As though she were some fragile creature that might fall to mishap. As though he was not the one susceptible to mishaps. After escorting her upstairs, he left her at her bedchamber door. He always did that, too.

Alone in the chamber, her maid soon arrived and helped her undress and unpin her hair. Nana must have spoken the truth because once Clara was snug in her bed, she was asleep in minutes, awakening only later in the night when Hunt joined her. This was becoming habit, too.

They were together like this at night. Every night they came together in bed. He might not be there when she went to bed, but he was always there, reaching for her sometime during the night. If she woke in the morning to a cold and lonely bed, it was just as well. He said they would not talk about the future. In fact they weren't talking about much of anything at all, but she had this. Every night she had this.

His arm slid around her now substantial waist and pulled her against him. She sighed and relaxed, her back nestled against his chest.

In moments she was asleep again, his hand cupping her belly and his breath warm on her neck.

When she woke he was gone and the maid was in her room pulling back the drapes. "Good morning! Or should I say good afternoon?"

Clara stretched and swung her legs over the side of the bed. The amount of sunlight pouring into the room told her it was well past morning. "You let me sleep so late."

"I am under strict instructions tae let ye sleep."

Of course. Hunt's grandmother wanted her to have more rest. "You don't need to listen to her when it comes to my sleeping—"

"Oh. It was the laird. He bade me tae let ye sleep."

Hunt? She mulled that over as the maid selected her garments from the bureau.

"I almost forgot! A letter came for you." The girl reached into the pocket of her pinafore and handed her a letter.

Clara eagerly tore into it. She scanned the contents and then looked up, one hand pressed over her suddenly racing heart. "It's from my brother. His wife has had the baby. We must go. We must leave for Kilmarkie House at once."

THEY LEFT THE following day.

They didn't travel with the same rigor as previously. They took their time, much to Clara's aggravation. She had never witnessed horses moving so slowly. She was quite certain she could outpace them with a brisk walk.

Hunt insisted on their dawdling pace. Despite her protests, he could not be swayed. He was not moved by her eagerness to reach her family and see the new baby. Due to her condition, he insisted that they take this ridiculous pace. Almost as though she were the one with a threat of death hanging over her head. It would be amusing if it were not so very real and so very sobering.

They stopped for frequent rests so they ended up needing two nights at an inn instead of the usual one. She and Marian shared a room. She was not sure where her husband spent his nights, and she told herself not to worry about it. He could take care of himself. At least she told herself that. She told herself that he would be fine. Perhaps their crawling progress benefitted him. There could hardly be any risk of accident when his horse ambled at a snail's speed.

Despite her eagerness to be on her way the final morning of their journey, no one woke her early and it was almost midday when they departed for Kilmarkie House.

Apparently she couldn't fight this chronic weariness. Perhaps she would have to start taking Nana's advice and nap during the day.

Riding through the gates to her brother's home, eagerness hummed along her skin. They were finally here. She glanced around thought-fully. Already the place felt different. Smaller somehow. The dark sea glinted in the distant ho-rizon beyond the house. She and Alyse had yet to take that walk along the shoreline and see the dolphins. She supposed that would have to wait. Given Alyse recently gave birth, she wouldn't be taking hikes any time soon.

Months ago Clara had thought she would return here without her husband. Now she was back here with her husband in tow and a defi-nite waddle to her walk. She couldn't see her toes anymore. Perhaps that was the true reason he had not shared a bed with her at the inn. Perhaps her appearance was no longer tempting to him.

They all stopped their mounts in the court-yard and she shoved the troubling thought from her mind. Hunt dismounted first and was at her carriage door, pulling it open and reaching for her hand to assist her down. She smiled down at him with a tentative curve of her lips. He smiled back, but there was something repressed about it. The smile did not quite reach his eyes.

The front door opened and her brother emerged, his expression eager and delighted. She didn't think she had ever seen him appear so happy.

"Welcome." He embraced her and kissed her warmly on the cheek, and she felt some of the tension easing from her shoulders. He looked down at her very swollen belly. "It appears that it will soon be your turn, dear sister."

She nodded cheerfully, resting a hand on her stomach.

"Come, come. Inside with you all. What would you like to do first? Rest and partake of refreshments or—?"

"Alyse and the baby," she exclaimed, lightly swatting him on the shoulder. "I want to see them, of course. Take me to them."

"Of course." He chuckled and led them inside. They quickly shed their coats and gloves and hats and then proceeded through the house until they reached the master bedchamber. Clara could scarcely contain her excitement as they entered the massive chamber.

Alyse was settled into the center of the large bed, looking dazzling with a baby nestled in her arms. Her face glowed, eyes shining brightly. A wave of emotion rushed over Clara. Happiness for her brother. Happiness for her sister-in-law. Longing for herself.

She wanted the same joy. She wanted the fear gone. Eradicated. She wanted to know she would have this day with *her* husband at her side. She was desperate for that assurance, but it couldn't be given no matter how desperately she wished.

Clara hastened to sit at the edge of the bed. For

a moment she could do nothing more than stare in awe, overwhelmed at the sight of her nephew. Finally, she regained her voice. "Oh, Alyse. He's beautiful." Her gaze shot to her sister-in-law. "You look beautiful, too. Radiant. You are well, yes?"

It was no exaggeration or empty compliment. Alyse was beaming. "We are both very well. Would you like to hold him?"

"Oh, yes. Yes." Clara nodded, resetting her weight and holding out her arms, thrilled to meet her nephew. She only wished Mama was here for this. She assumed she would be visiting soon with the rest of the family. At least her last letter had promised as much. Mama had her hands full with the twins. The rambunctious five-year-olds kept her occupied. Mama had never been the type to leave child-rearing to members of the staff, after all.

Alyse transferred the precious bundle to Clara's arms. He stirred lightly at the adjustment, his tiny fists jerking on the air, and then he settled back down, sweet little cooing sounds escaping him that melted her heart.

"He's just too beautiful. Even if he does have Marcus's nose."

"Hey," Marcus objected from the foot of the bed.

She giggled, hot tears pricking her eyes. She

teased, but emotion welled up inside her. "Simply beautiful." She brought her face close to his head and inhaled his pure baby scent. "He smells lovely."

Lifting her head up from the baby, her gaze caught on Hunt standing just inside the room. He stared at her with an elusive expression on his face, his eyes dark and unreadable across the distance of the room, lips unsmiling. What was he thinking and why would he not come closer?

The baby stirred and gurgled. She looked down at him again and stroked his tender cheek. "Now, now, everything is fine." The words rang a little hollow in her ears, and a deep ache throbbed in her chest. She wanted everything to be fine. She *needed* everything to be fine.

When she looked back up, Hunt was gone.

Chapter 21

*H*unt sequestered himself in Autenberry's study, deciding it best if he stayed out of the way. He had no wish to ruin everyone's joy with his less than cheerful face.

After helping himself to a drink, he settled himself in a wingback chair near the window that overlooked the gardens and, in the distance beyond the gardens, the sea.

He stared out into the deepening dusk, growing pensive as day disappeared into night.

Seeing Clara with the baby in her arms was a jolt. It was too much. A reminder of all he was going to miss. It hurt more than he ever could have anticipated. A dull ache pulsed at the center of his breastbone. He had convinced himself he was content.

Everyone had to die someday. At least he would leave behind a legacy. And there was Clara. She would live. She would go on. She would not be weak like his mother and break beneath the burden of her ordeal. She was stronger than that. She would be a good mother to his child, and he'd convinced himself that they could enjoy each other for however much time they had left together and he could be at peace with whatever happened.

Now it felt as though he had been lying to himself all along. He could find no contentment. Only longing. Only loss for what was to come. For what he would never have, for what he would never even witness.

Clara.

She was under this very roof right now, holding a baby and looking as natural and as beautiful with that babe in her arms as he had ever seen her—as he had ever seen any woman. But this woman, Clara, was his wife. She carried his child. In another life, in different circumstances, they could have been happy. They could have been in love. His throat thickened uncomfortably. It would be easy to love her.

He'd left her alone the last two nights as they traveled, permitting Marian to share the larger, more comfortable room at the inn with her each night. He had missed her those nights. Missed the warm and giving sensation of her body pressed against him. It seemed remarkable that he had gone so much of his life without her there in his bed. In a mere two nights he suffered the lack of her presence.

"MacLarin, what are you doing in here?" His brother-in-law entered the room, jerking him away from his troubling thoughts. The man looked happy. And why wouldn't he be? He had everything.

Autenberry clapped his hands merrily. "It's almost time for dinner. Shall we move into the dining room? Alyse is going to join us tonight. She insists she is ready to be up and about."

"We shall join them in a moment. First we must speak." He knew when he left for Kilmarkie House that he had to have this conversation with his brother-in-law.

Autenberry advanced into the room. "Very well. Sounds important."

"Aye. 'Tis."

Autenberry settled into the seat across from him. "Well then. Proceed. There's a fat pheasant begging for our attention."

"I need your assurance that you will help your sister."

"Help my sister?"

"Aye."

He shook his head. "What do you mean?"

"I want . . . nay, I *need* tae hear you say that you will take care of your sister and my child when I'm gone."

"Gone? Where are you going?" He chuckled. "You're not abandoning my sister, I hope. Because then I would have to track you down and kill you, MacLarin, and that would not do."

A beat of silence stretched between them and the mirth faded from Autenberry's face.

"I would never abandon your sister." *Never willingly.*

The duke looked no less uneasy at this declaration. "What are you saying?"

"I'm not abandoning her, but things happen. Things we have no control over." The sudden lump in his throat felt the size of a small boulder.

Autenberry stared at him with a furrowed forehead. "This is about the curse." The duke's expression was grim. "Have you not given up on that foolish notion? You're not going to die. Not for a great many years."

Hunt shook his head, unwilling to speak of it, unwilling to argue. He wasn't speaking of it with his wife. He most certainly wasn't going to speak of it with Autenberry.

The duke continued, "You know there is no such thing as a curse. Come, man. It's nonsense."

This was why he did not wish to speak of it. People, outsiders especially, could never understand. They never would. "I'm no' here tae convince you of anything. I am here tae have your word, your vow."

"To look after my sister?" Autenberry looked almost offended. He scoffed. "Of course I will. You need not even ask."

Hunt shook his head. "Let us be clear. She will be the mother of my child, the future Laird MacLarin. You must look after them. Protect them and the clan until my son comes of age. There are those who would try tae wrest all that belongs tae the rightful MacLarin heir while he is young and vulnerable."

Autenberry gazed at him for a long measuring moment before leaning forward in his seat and replying, "Rest assured, I will protect my sister and her child and your legacy. No one shall thieve from them and take what is rightfully theirs. Ever. Not," he added with heavy emphasis, "that I believe such an assurance necessary. You shall be around for a very long time, my friend."

Hunt offered an obligatory smile, feeling much appeased, if not outright better.

Whatever came to pass, Clara and the child would be well.

He could rest easy and go to his death knowing that.

Chapter 22

*H*unt didn't join them for dinner, convincing Clara that she had done something to displease him.

Or simply *she* displeased him now.

She kept a brave face pinned in place, smiling and chatting with her family. It wasn't until she was alone in her room that she dropped the ruse. A maid joined her, helping her undress and take down her hair, brushing it for her.

"Thank you. That will be all." Instead of climbing up into her bed, she settled into the chaise longue by the window that overlooked the night sea.

She listened to the waves lapping gently at the

shore and closed her eyes. For once sleep did not pull at her. She wondered where her husband was. Did he take himself to the village? Had he left? Returned for home without her? She knew she had wanted to be apart from him before when she thought it could save him, but now she couldn't bear the thought. She longed for him like her next breath. She really didn't know what to think.

She didn't rouse from the chaise as night descended. She snuggled beneath the soft blanket draped on the chaise, quite content to spend the night here.

Then the bedchamber door opened.

Hunt walked in the room.

Her chest ached at the sight of him, actually hurt as she absorbed his masculine beauty. "I thought you left."

He angled his head. "As in left here? Left Kilmarkie House? Left you? Why would you think that?"

She shrugged uneasily, feeling a little foolish. Even if she felt that he'd left, she should never have admitted that to him. Never revealed such insecurity.

He advanced. "I would never leave what's mine."

Meaning her? He hadn't been acting very possessive toward her lately.

He stopped a single pace from the chaise. His eyes appeared almost black in the shadows. "I'll never leave you."

Except in death. The thought popped into her mind, unbidden, and her eyes burned from the threat of tears.

He smiled then. "Stop thinking so much, Clara."

"Stop thinking?"

"Aye. You think too much."

She snorted. "How can I do that? It is not possible for one *not* to think."

"It is verra possible." Almost on cue, he smiled, and there was such wicked promise in his lips that she knew for certain that she did not displease him—that he would not be leaving her alone this night. His gaze dropped, skimming her body. "That's a lovely nightgown."

"T-thank you." He still had the power to unnerve her.

He closed the distance between them and his hand reached to toy with the tiny ribbon at the scooped neckline. It took her a moment to realize he wasn't merely toying with it. He knew exactly how it functioned, unraveling the bow with a flick of his strong fingers. Her nightgown gaped open, exposing her breasts. Breasts that had nearly doubled in size in the last few months. They were incredibly sensitive, the nipples larger, darker.

Before she knew what he was about, he dropped to his knees and took one breast into his mouth, sucking deeply at the tender nipple. She cried out, arching under him, her fingers flying into his thick hair, tangling there, pushing and pulling, guiding him in his expert ministrations.

He turned his attention to her other breast and she released a keening moan.

He growled in approval against her damp skin. "That's it," he crooned, biting down gently on the engorged tip.

Moisture rushed between her legs and she shuddered, climaxing in a hot rush.

His fingers moved to the hem of her nightgown. "As lovely as this is on you, it would look much better on the floor."

She giggled.

He bent slightly, watching her face intently as he clutched the hem. She lifted up, helping him to pull it up over her head.

A cool draft swept over her. She was completely bare.

His breathing grew ragged as he surveyed her. She tried not to feel embarrassed of her swollen breasts and enlarged belly. It wasn't their first time. Still, she resisted the urge to cover herself with her hands. He desired her. She could see the evidence tenting his trousers. It was proof enough. Desire still licked through her. She throbbed between the legs, still wet and aching, clenching to be filled.

Only a few inches separated them, but he didn't touch her. Not yet. She felt the heat radiating from his stare, from his body, but he didn't lift a finger to touch her.

His gaze tracked hotly over her. He lowered down to the chaise, sitting along the edge. His head dipped until their foreheads touched. "You're so beautiful."

Then he was kissing her. Hot, addicting kisses as he picked her up and carried her to the bed, his big hands clenching her bottom, singeing her skin.

"Hunt," she said against his mouth. "I'm too big . . . too heavy."

"Nonsense."

Pushing away that worry, she wrapped her arms around him, reveling in the sensation of his strength, his power. Even with his garments on, she could feel his flexing flesh quivering under her fingers as he carried her.

He sat down on the bed with her on his lap. His hands moved to her face, broad palms cupping her cheeks, fingers burrowing into her loosened hair as they continued to kiss, their heads angling as if they couldn't taste each other enough.

There was no such thing as too close. He turned, lowering them to their sides on the bed and hauling her as close as her belly between them would allow. Her breasts smashed against his chest and she reveled in the hard strength of him against her.

The pressure of his mouth on hers increased. He nipped her with his teeth and dragged his open mouth down her exposed throat. When he reached where her shoulder and neck met, he bit down, not hard enough to hurt but enough to make her moan.

He closed both hands over her aching breasts. She arched up into his palms. His head descended and his mouth closed over an already aroused nipple, drawing it deep into the wet warmth of his mouth.

"Ohhhh," she cried, burying her hands in his hair and holding him to her. "Don't ever stop. Stay here forever." The moment the words were out, she felt a sharp stab of regret, reminded that they couldn't be true.

His movements became more urgent as he moved to her other breast, his words fanning over her moist nipple. "I'm not going anywhere." *For now.*

He didn't say that last bit, but she heard it. Felt it humming from him. He scooted away from her, shed his clothes. It took only a minute, but it was the longest minute of her life.

A shudder ran through her. He returned to her

side and flipped her fast onto her back. She widened her thighs for him to settle between them, and he did, the faint prickle of hair on his thighs tickling hers.

She rocked, thrusting upward, grinding against him. He felt delicious, hard and insistent against the heat of her, and she ached, her core clenching with need.

She writhed, wiggling desperately up against him. She couldn't take another moment of this. Her fingers dug into his bare back. Incredibly, she felt small and delicate as he rained kisses all over her body. He was so much bigger than her, hard and muscled. She felt fragile. Prized. *Loved*.

His fingers touched her, featherlight, skimming up the inside of her thighs. She arched, clawing the counterpane as his fingers found her and delved inside her heat.

"Hunt," she choked, bewildered as his thumb found that tiny, hidden nub. He pressed down on it, rolling it between his fingers. "Hunt, please."

"Not yet." He slid down her body and put his mouth there. She shrieked and lurched up off the bed. He curved a hand over her belly, cupping and caressing her there as his fingers surrounded that aching nub. He lowered his head and sucked, drawing her into his mouth.

His tongue played against her as he worked her between his lips.

She gasped and shuddered, sensation eddying out from where his mouth worked her to a frenzy. She seized his head, fisting his hair. His hands slid under her, lifting her higher and holding her in place for him like she was some kind of succulent feast.

"Hunt . . . please!"

"Say it." His lips moved against her and this only excited her more. She tugged on his hair, trying to bring him back over her. He continued to toy with her, indulging himself. She released a long moan as he eased one finger deep inside her.

"Say it," he demanded, thrusting in and out of her slowly, tormenting her. He went deeper, pushing, hitting a spot that sent her spiraling. All the while his mouth sucked her harder, only adding to the intensity of the experience.

She was still shaking, pleasure rushing through her when he lifted away from her body.

"Hunt," she moaned his name, squirming for him.

Then his mouth was on hers again.

The hard length of him slid over her needy core, not penetrating, just teasing against her folds. She lifted her hips, her breaths coming in shallow pants.

"Please, Hunt," she begged.

His eyes glinted down at her. "I want tae remember this. You. Like this." Her skin turned to gooseflesh at his raspy words. "Always."

Her nails dug into the skin of his back. "Take me now, Hunt." Was that her voice? She didn't even recognize the low growl. She moistened her lips.

He smiled, slow and wicked, and a shiver rippled through her.

She felt him then. His hardness easing inside her. Her eyes widened at the sensation. Her fingers clenched his biceps, marveling that it was still new. Each time with him felt new and different and wondrous.

He groaned, dropping his head in the crook of her shoulder, his mouth moving against her oversensitive flesh. His hands slid under her back, his fingers curling over her shoulders, anchoring her between his body and the bed, pulling her as close as he could with the swell of her belly between them.

And then he plunged, pushing deep inside her, wrecking the last of her composure as he seated himself to the hilt.

"Oh!" she gasped at the swift invasion. It was too much. She felt stretched, full and complete in a way she had never imagined possible. Her muscles hugged him, throbbed around his hard length.

He lifted his head off her shoulder and smoothed a lock of hair from her forehead. His eyes gleamed down at her with an emotion she did not imagine. Something that looked suspiciously like longing. Like regret.

She shook her head, unable to speak, too busy absorbing everything. Like how he actually seemed to expand inside her. How she clenched around him and that shot sensation to every nerve in her body.

She wiggled, experimenting with what seemed to heighten and intensify her pleasure.

He groaned.

Her hands flew to his backside, encouraging him to increase his movements.

He answered with a harder thrust that made her yelp and arch under him. "Yes!" she cried, delighted that he wasn't treating her like some bit of fragile glass. His hips worked then. She whimpered at the drag of him against her over-sensitive flesh. He went faster. Small, animal-like sounds she didn't even recognize escaped her. The friction drove her wild.

A pressure built at her center, coiling between her legs. She angled her hips, taking more of him inside her, following her instincts, searching for a way to bring him closer, deeper, to assuage that ache that only seemed to grow.

Her body demanded more. Needed more.

"Clara," he choked. "We have tae take care . . . the babe—"

"The baby is fine. And I won't break," she growled.

She lifted her head and sank her teeth down on his shoulder and it was like she set a fire loose in him. It flamed to life.

He moved then. His big hands slid under her, lifting her higher, positioning her in a way that altered everything. He hit that hidden place, that spot that unraveled her.

She came apart in his arms. She cried out his name, dropping back on the bed with a satisfied sigh. His arms wrapped around her, pulling her closer as he finished with a shudder and then stilling. He turned his head to press an open-mouthed kiss to the side of her neck.

She held him close, one hand in his hair, the other smoothing over his back.

He'd stamped himself on her. Permanently. Indelibly. He was in her blood. A part of her soul now.

The sound of their serrated breaths filled the air. They both knew their time together was limited. She didn't want to lose this, didn't want to let it go, didn't want to look at his face and confront the regret she was certain to see in his eyes.

Because longing and regret were there, in every moment of this, in every ragged draw of breath. It was cutting deep and razor sharp between them.

Chapter 23

They stayed a fortnight with her brother and Alyse at Kilmarkie House. It was wonderful being with Marcus and her sister-in-law and cuddling with her new nephew. She and Alyse finally had their long walk along the shoreline, although the dolphins didn't appear for them. No. The dolphins decided to wait and make an appearance when she and Hunt took a late afternoon stroll along the pink-pebbled beach the day before their departure.

It was just the two of them when dozens of dolphins began cresting the surface of the water, their fins like blades cutting through the liquid deep. She gasped when the first one dove into the air in a beautiful arc, its dark body sleek and sinuous in the air. Soon after others followed. She clapped her hands in delight. She felt like she was witnessing something miraculous. It almost felt holy. Certainly God's hand was in this, and it filled her with serenity and the belief that all would be well.

She and Hunt admired the beautiful creatures for long moments before continuing on their stroll, and she couldn't help but think that he had already lived up to the promise he had made to her on that long ago day.

I'm offering you a chance at a new life. Away from boring, oppressive London . . . as my wife, you will have freedom. You can do more . . . experience more . . .

Standing here, she had never felt more alive. More free. True, she would have seen the dolphins eventually. She needn't have married him for that to happen, but it wouldn't have been the same with anyone else. With anyone other than Hunt beside her.

She looked down at the ground. "I've never seen pink stones before. Extraordinary," she murmured, bending down to scoop a small handful of the glossy, water-polished rocks into her gloved hand. Hunt immediately gripped her arm to make sure she kept her balance on the uneven ground.

Straightening, she examined the assortment of stones. They were all shades of pink. Some pale.

Some a deeper rose shade. Some streaked with gray, some with black marbling. But all were undeniably pink.

"Wait until you see what this shoreline looks like lit up on a sunny day." He tilted his head back to look up at the overcast sky. "That won't likely be for months from now. Not until the summer."

In the future. That's what he meant. That's what he was saying even though he had not directly stated it. It was an innocent slip. Not harmless, however. If it were harmless, his words would not have felt like such a blow to the chest—like a dagger to the heart.

Months from now he could be gone. *If the curse is real. If the curse wins.*

She quickly scolded herself. There had been no recent accidents. Hunt was fit and hale. The perfect visage of health. All appeared well. She shouldn't let fear rule her and destroy the happiness that could be hers if she would only seize it—embrace it.

"You should put a few in your pocket. Tae keep," he suggested. "Tae always remember today." A faint smile hugged his well-carved lips.

She looked down at the stones filling her palm. He was right, of course . . . even if his words spoke to the fear that threatened to devour her. She would be back to this place again. Any time she chose, she could come here. Her brother and his family would always live here.

But there was no guarantee she would ever be back here again with *him*. No assurance that she would be standing on this shore beside Hunt. That dreaded fear pumped through her, whispering, taunting that she would never have this perfect moment with him again.

Sucking in a deep breath, she closed her fingers over the assortment of stones and tucked them into the pocket of her cloak. "That's a brilliant idea." She smiled at him brightly, hoping her smile looked more natural than it actually felt.

"Well, I have been known tae have a brilliant notion now and again."

"Indeed?"

"Indeed." He nodded. He was hatless and the wind ruffled his hair. She had to fight back the urge to touch those silky strands. She knew their texture so well by now. "Not everyone appreciates the brilliance of my ideas at the time, but people usually come around." His eyes twinkled with a mischievous light. "Eventually."

"I am quite certain you had a couple of dubious ideas over the course of your life."

"Shall I give you an example of one of my more spectacularly brilliant ideas, lass?"

"Please do." She rested her hand on his arm,

allowing him to escort her along the shoreline. She was vastly enjoying herself. She liked this lighthearted Hunt. She had a flash of him laughing as he brawled in a taproom. He was joy. He was exciting.

He is mine.

"Well," he began with heavy exaggeration. "I met this fetching lass. She is charming, really. She even enjoys taproom brawls."

She snorted. "She *enjoys* them? Really?"

"Aye. She appreciates them as one does fine art . . . or a good whisky. When others flee, she stays and watches. She is truly a female ahead of her time."

She laughed outright, holding her side. "Oh, she sounds marvelous. A female after my own heart."

"She is. She is indeed, and I knew at once. Clearly this was the woman I should wed."

"Clearly," she agreed with gleeful mockery.

"I am glad you agree. It was a verra good idea. One of my best." He shook his head. "So can you believe she refused my suit at first?"

"No!" She feigned astonishment. "Daft girl."

He shook his head with consternation. "Some people haven't the sense tae recognize brilliance."

She tsked. "What a shame."

"Happily for her, she came around tae the idea of me." Smiling seductively, he leaned down and kissed her mouth deeply, leisurely. As though they had all the time in the world. After several moments, he lifted his head, all mockery gone from his eyes. "Happily for me, tae," he amended, his voice whisper-soft.

All at once it occurred to her that he just called marrying her a *happy* thing. Even though it might kill him. Her heart swelled within the sudden tightness of her chest.

He reached between them and took her hand, his gloved fingers lacing with her own. "Let's start back. I'm sure you will want tae rest before dinner and refresh yourself."

They turned and headed back toward the house, their hands locked and swinging between them. Her heart brimmed with emotion at the gift of this day . . . of all these recent days. She couldn't help thinking this was what life was about. What it was meant to be. Good times. The building of memories. Family. *Love.*

Immediately her thoughts jumped to the man she had married and she felt a wave of emotion. She blinked back burning eyes. Goodness. She was so very sentimental lately, prone to tears over the slightest thing. It wasn't just Hunt and what he did to her heart.

Every time she held her nephew, tears sprang to her eyes. She couldn't get enough of little Edward's sweet smell or cooing gurgles or the comforting weight of him in her arms. It made her all the more excited to meet the child growing in her womb . . . until she remembered that quite possibly meant losing Hunt. Then the tears came again with renewed vigor.

They departed for home the next morning, and exchanging good-byes with her family was only another opportunity for her to shed a few tears.

Hunt actually spent some of the journey back home riding with her and Marian inside the carriage. That was a new occurrence and one that did not go unappreciated. He still insisted they travel at a snail's crawl again. She didn't object, though. His concern was endearing. Really. She was too happy spending time with him to protest.

This time they shared a room both nights at the inn. He acquired Marian her own room. Clara wasn't certain what had shifted exactly between them, but something had.

He talked to her now. He shared things with her. He teased her, for goodness' sake, revealing his playful side. Oh, they never discussed the curse. That was not to be spoken. Not allowed. Not ever. No sense in ruining their happy existence, however fleeting it might be.

It was almost dusk as they neared home. Yes, home. She was beginning to think of MacLarin

Keep as her home. As wonderful a place as Kilmarkie House was, she was glad to be returning to her home.

Hunt was riding his mount this last leg of the journey. Every once in a while she would peek out the curtains to spy on him. She had just settled back down in her seat and stuck her tongue out at Marian for her smirk when the driver shouted.

The carriage pulled up hard and jerked to a shuddering stop. Clara grabbed the loop above the door to keep her seat and not end up on the floor.

"What happened?" Marian cried, righting herself on the cushion.

Shaking her head, Clara pushed open the carriage door and clambered down.

"Careful," Marian cried in warning. "Mind that you don't fall."

Once on the ground, Clara peered around, rubbing a hand on her belly as though the motion lent comfort. There was no sight of her husband. Much of the snow had melted, but that didn't mean the road wasn't wet with mud and occasional ice patches.

She stepped forward to address the driver still in his seat. "Why have we stopped? Are we stuck?"

He shook his head and hopped down from his perch, pointing ahead of them. "The laird was riding just ahead of us and suddenly he went down. I dinna see him anymore." He pulled out a pistol from inside his coat and glanced around, as though searching for enemies. "Could be brigands about—"

He didn't even finish the sentence before she was gone. Running as fast as she could, which, given her condition, wasn't very fast at all. Still, she pressed on, desperate to reach him. Desperate to assure herself that he was not injured.

"Clara! Clara!" Marian called. "Have a care. You shouldn't be running in your condition."

The driver shouted after her, too, but she ignored him. Just as she ignored Marian's shout. She had to get to Hunt. She had to reach him. It was her only thought.

She topped a slight incline in the road and stopped, panting and holding her stomach as she scanned the landscape, searching and finally spotting Hunt in a ditch along the side of the road. His mount milled a few yards away, nosing the ground for grass in the barren earth.

"Hunt!" She ran down the sloping road toward him. Lifting her skirts in one hand, she carefully made her way into the ditch, mindful of her footing.

He didn't stir. His eyes were closed, but thankfully his face wasn't submerged in the muddy water. Alarm pierced her heart. She grasped for his arm. "Hunt! Are you hurt?" She cringed. Of course he was hurt. He was unconscious.

Not dead. Not dead. Be not dead.

She slid her arm under his shoulders and carefully lifted him up, pulling him against her. She didn't know the extent of his injuries.

"Clara! Is he alive?"

She looked up to where Marian and the driver hovered, concern writ all over their faces.

"Of course I'm alive," a voice grumbled just below her ear. The familiar gruff brogue sent a wave of goose bumps over her skin. He was alive! He was still with her. She had not lost him—yet.

She looked down into Hunt's wide eyes staring back at her. "Hunt! What happened? Can you move? Are you . . . seriously hurt?"

"Think I just had the wind knocked out of me. Stunned me for a spell."

Her racing heart gradually subsided. He wasn't dead. *Not dead.*

He shook his head and then winced, his hand flying to the back of his head to touch gingerly. "My horse threw me." His voice sounded as astonished as she felt.

"Your horse threw you?" she echoed.

How could that be? Hunt was an excellent horseman. He rode his horse everywhere. Every day. He spent more time atop that animal than with any other living soul. She knew it wasn't impossible, but it seemed unlikely. Very, *very* unlikely.

"Aye," he said slowly, his gaze drifting over to where his horse wandered aimlessly. The beast looked as docile as a lamb. Hunt stared at the beast thoughtfully, his forehead creasing in contemplation.

Her chest clenched tight, the now familiar fear resurfacing. She knew what he was thinking. It was the same thing she was.

"Have you ever been thrown by a horse before?" She nodded her head in the direction of his mount. "By *that* horse?" She tried telling herself that accidents happened all the time. They had nothing to do with curses . . . but the assurance didn't ring true in her mind.

He shook his head rather than answer.

They both released a heavy breath. Words were not needed. They both understood perfectly without them.

The curse had not forgotten them.

Chapter 24

*F*or the next few months they held to their original agreement and did not speak of the future. Nor did they speak of the curse, which, of course, was tangled up in the threads of the future. They both clung to this rule as though it was the only thing keeping their fragile world intact.

They lived for the present. They continued loving, talking, laughing as though it were their mission. They spent all their time together. All their days.

Thoughts, however, were another thing entirely.

Thoughts could not be controlled, sadly. Fear lurked. Hunt often read it in her eyes and that was when he would distract her with a walk or a game—or he would simply make love to her.

As the days passed and winter melted to spring, Hunt watched Clara grow and swell with his child almost in concert with the flowering buds on the trees.

Life was renewing, and he couldn't help wondering what his child would be like, who the babe would grow to be. All thoughts he kept to himself, of course, relying on the assumption that he would not be there for any of it. He would be gone.

He consoled himself with the fact that Clara and his child would live on. They would be well. There would be a period of mourning, but Clara was strong and resilient. She would recover. She had family to support her. Hers and his. Nana would likely never die.

Sitting down to a fine dinner of fresh salmon and roasted pheasant, he admired his wife across from him. Clara picked at her food. Her appetite had been off lately. Nana insisted it was normal—that she didn't have very much room for food in her belly.

Her time was near, and Hunt was still here. Still alive. Even though he shouldn't, hope swelled in his chest. There had been no accidents lately. Perhaps the curse would skip him. Perhaps he had won. Perhaps they both had.

"Are ye no' feeling well this evening?" Nana directed the question to Clara across the table as she was served more wine. Once her cup was refilled, she lifted it to her lips, eyeing Clara with concern. These days, her gaze was always concerned.

Nana had continued to be solicitous. He could not fault her since their late-night conversation. She took special care of Clara, attending to her and looking after her needs. Her expertise when it came to midwifery was very useful. She knew more than any woman around when it came to childbirth. He felt fortunate they had her.

Clara shook her head, lifting her gaze to Hunt. She offered him a wan smile, her eyes tired. She hadn't been sleeping well of late.

He smiled back encouragingly. He knew she had been vastly uncomfortable these last few weeks and he had done everything he could to make her feel better, rubbing her back and feet, bringing her things so she needn't fetch them herself, but there was only so much he could do. Discomfort near the end was the nature of things. He knew that. Everyone assured him of this. But he still hated to see her suffering.

She gasped and her eyes flared wide.

Everyone at the table looked to her.

"Clara? Is something amiss?" Marian asked sharply.

She shook her head, stopped and then nodded. "I—I think my waters have broken." She looked sheepish. Embarrassed even.

Everyone rushed to stand. The dining room became a festival of motion. Hunt swept his wife up into his arms.

"Oh! I'm much too heavy!" Clara swatted him on the shoulder. "Put me down! Put me down at once before you wrench your back."

"Hush now. I'm fine. And you're light as a feather," he lied.

At this she laughed but the sound gave way, broken with another sharp gasp from her.

"Take her upstairs!" Nana admonished.

He obeyed, glancing behind him where she followed. He knew she knew what he was thinking. This was too soon. Clara had another fortnight. Perhaps two. She was just so very large already. Perhaps her body couldn't wait. His grandmother had informed them that MacLarins were always big babies. His wife wasn't particularly small, nor was she large.

She shook her head once at him, signaling what, he wasn't sure.

They all converged in the master chamber. He settled Clara in the bed and then looked to his grandmother expectantly, waiting on instructions. Serving girls arrived with items and Nana began snapping commands. Marian sank down on the bed beside Clara and clasped her hand, rubbing the fingers between her own, lending what comfort she could.

"Nana?" he murmured quietly beside his grandmother. "What should I do?"

She turned on him quickly. "I have been waiting for this moment." She snapped her fingers at a pair of grooms Hunt had not noticed standing nearby. If the room wasn't so busy he would have noticed them. They were big lads and obtrusive as the only other men in the room—in a room they had no place being.

But they were here at the behest of his grandmother.

"Take him," she announced. "Lock him in the storage closet. Remember, no one enters and he's no' tae come out until I come for him."

Hunt looked wildly between his grandmother and the grooms. "Nana! What is the meaning of this?"

She nodded emphatically. "I have given this a great deal of thought. Ye made it this far. I will no' see ye die before this child enters the world. Ye will be safe until that time. Ye will be the one tae break this curse for future generations. It ends here. I'll no' have yer life stolen in these last few hours." Her eyes gleamed with a triumphant light and he knew she really believed that. "I have taken . . . precautions."

"Precautions? I dinna ken what you speak of, but it's no' necessary. Nothing is going tae happen tae me." He motioned to his wife. "She is about tae give birth."

"Aye, and my husband died on his way tae my birthing bed! He fell off his horse and broke his neck. Until then we'd thought he'd escaped the curse, too."

"I promise no' tae go riding—"

"Nay!" She cut a hand angrily through the air. "I will no' risk it. Ye will be locked away in a room where nothing can happen tae ye."

Incredible. She really believed that locking him in the closet for however many hours could save his life.

He looked back to the bed where Clara's face was now flushed in pain, and then he looked back at his grandmother. "I am no' leaving her."

She made a groan of frustration and threw her hands up in the air. "She will be fine. Yer the one I'm worried about."

He sank down on the bed beside Clara. "I will no' abandon her when she is like this. No' when she is in this state. I'm staying right here. Right by her side."

With the woman I love.

With a Gaelic curse, Nana shook her head. "It must be this way. The lads here will see ye tae the closet. 'Tis best fer ye."

Hunt stood abruptly from the bed and leveled a deadly stare on both grooms. "I'm your laird."

They stopped and swapped hesitant looks, then gazed at Nana for help.

"Och! Ignore him. Ye will be saving yer laird's life. He will give thanks later."

"I'll no' thank you," he promised. "You will be looking for a new home when this is all over because you will no' be welcome here. No man in this clan goes against me."

The lads backed down and Nana stomped her foot.

Clara reached for his hand and gave it a squeeze. "Perhaps ye should go. We will all feel comfort knowing you're safe somewhere until this is over . . . until your son is born."

He scowled and dropped down beside her, lifting her hands to press a kiss on them. "I dinna want tae leave you."

"You're not leaving me. Someone will come for you as soon as it's over." She pulled a face, trying to hide how uncomfortable she was. He felt the tension coursing through her body as she fought against the pain—and in that moment, he knew he was a distraction to her. She should not be thinking about him. She should be focused on the work of getting through this and bringing a baby into this world.

He stood. "I'll go and leave you tae it then." He

swept a glare over everyone in the room. "You will send for me if anything . . ." He could not finish the thought. Not in front of Clara.

Nothing would go amiss. Not for her. Not for him.

He had to believe that. He *did* believe that.

With a quick kiss to her lips, he left her. Only he did not lock himself like a coward in some closet, waiting for the storm to pass. No, he had spent enough of his life in hiding. He had quit that. He took to his library and poured himself a drink.

Graham soon joined him and together they waited, minutes sliding into hours, the only sounds in the house the screams of his wife from upstairs.

SOMETHING WAS WRONG.

Clara knew it. She felt it in the pain vibrating through her. A pain so acute it made her teeth ache. There was no part of her unaffected. Something was going to happen. Something bad.

Except she didn't think it was going to happen to her.

The threat was to her husband. Even now. After all this time. After these many months without mishap, something was going to happen to Hunt. She was convinced. Wherever he was, he was not safe.

Nana had taken a position at the foot of the bed,

examining Clara, guiding and instructing her in a soothing voice with knowledgeable words. It was surprising. Who knew at the start of all this that Nana would be the one to provide such comfort?

"Aye. You're close, lass." She patted Clara's sweat-slick knee. "Verra close now."

Clara fell back on the bed with a moan, long past letting such words relieve her. She'd heard them many times. "Thank God. I can't do this much longer. I'm so tired." She panted. "So tired." Her head lolled on the pillow weakly.

"Soon you will be able to sleep," Marian promised, wiping her brow with a damp cloth. Her friend had been diligently at her side through it all.

Clara knew there were others in the room, too. She heard the faint rustling and the soft voices of other maids as they assisted Nana and fetched things for her.

She was out of her head. The pain was too great. Her entire body one tight writhing ball of agony that centered on her drum-tight belly.

Suddenly everything intensified and a sharp stabbing pain shot straight through her center. She arched off the bed with a scream.

The agony ebbed to dull hurt and she dropped back on the bed with a whimper. "Hunt. I need Hunt." The words came softly, just a plaintive whisper, but she released them into the air. She put them out there.

She wanted her husband, the man who had come to mean everything to her, and she needed him right now.

HUNT DID NOT know what it was about that last scream, but it did something to him. He'd heard her cries for hours now, but that scream reached inside him and pulled him up from his chair. Even when it stopped and a hush of silence fell, he felt a call, compelled to move, to go to her.

He flew toward the door.

"Where are ye going?" Graham called.

"I can't sit here anymore." Hunt raced from the library and took to the stairs.

He was only halfway up the steps when his foot hit something slick. Water on a step, probably spilled by a maid. There had been a lot of carrying of water back and forth upstairs for his grandmother. His feet flew out from under him and his body sailed backward down the stairs. He hit the base of the steps with a jar that rocked through his entire body.

For a long moment he could not move. Warm wetness glided along his skull, trickling through his hair. "Clara," he whispered to no one.

He could only lie on his back, his head splintering with pain. He was not even sure if he was alive. His vision darkened at the edges and went black.

Chapter 25

*O*ne more push. Keep going, lass!"

Clara shook her head, more tired than she had ever felt in her life. The pain was constant and the weariness was overwhelming, threatening to pull her under. "No," she moaned. "Too . . . tired."

"Clara." Marian squeezed her hand as though hoping to inject her with strength. "You can keep going. You are the strongest person I know. You can do this."

Clara had thought she could. She had hoped . . . Now she didn't know. Now she was too tired.

"Clara," Nana said severely. "Open yer eyes, lass, ye can sleep later. Now ye have work tae do." Nana clapped her hands with harsh efficiency.

"Understand me? Ye have a child that is waiting tae get out and see this world . . . He wants tae meet his mother *and* his da. Do ye understand me? Ye do this now."

Clara blinked at the hard words, and then she nodded, propping herself up on her elbows on the bed. "Yes. Yes, of course." She nodded once. "I'm ready. Let us do this. One more push."

Nana nodded. "Very good, lass. One more push should do it."

Clara had to do this. There was no choice. No alternative. She would do this for herself. For this child. For the man she loved. Hunt was out there somewhere. Waiting. Every minute she dallied bringing this child into the world was a moment he was at risk. No more. Now was the time.

The door flung open. Slammed against the wall. Even in her state, panting in pain and exhausted, she looked toward the door and gasped at the sight of her husband with blood streaming down his face. "Hunt!" she screamed.

Nana groaned. "'Tis happened! 'Tis the curse!"

With a bellow of rage and pain and frustration, Clara grabbed on to both of her knees and leaned forward; pushing through it all, screaming through her teeth, using everything she had left, she pushed out every emotion.

She pushed out her baby.

HUNT HAD MADE it up the stairs and to his bedchamber.

Blood streamed into his eyes, but he wiped it clear so he could see where he was going. He was alive. He wasn't dead yet. He'd reach Clara . . . and his child.

His presence caused a commotion when he entered the room. A maid rushed at him. He accepted the towel, pressing it against his head wound, and then waved the girl away. It bled like the dickens, but he didn't think it was mortal. At least he told himself it wasn't.

His attention focused on his wife on the bed. She looked like hell. He'd never seen anything more beautiful.

"Hunt!" Nana shouted shrilly. "Come! See your child. Quickly."

He approached and gasped, unsure what he was looking at.

Nana beamed as she held the bundle in her arms. "Twins. Born in the caul."

He shook his head, wondering if his head wound had created this bit of fantastical fiction and what he was seeing wasn't real at all.

"My baby?" Clara demanded, falling back down on the pillows.

"Aye, *babes*. And *they* be fine, lass." Nana turned back to him. "Quickly, Hunt, take them both into your arms before the caul breaks and they take their first breaths. Hold them."

Hunt dropped his bloodied towel and took the sac that contained the two babies, trying to examine them under the bluish membrane. "Twins," he murmured as their weight settled in to his arms. "Twins," he called to Clara, not caring if he was being redundant.

His wife smiled wanly. "Yes." She attempted to prop herself up on her elbows, but too weak, she fell back on the bed. "What are they?" she asked. "Boys? Girls?"

He lowered the sac of babies to the bed and Nana gently tore the membrane. Fluid rushed out and both babies took in a great gulp of air— breaths that soon turned into gasps and then lustful wails.

"Boys!" Nana proclaimed, sniffing back tears. She rubbed Hunt's shoulders happily. "'Tis good luck. A baby born in the caul . . . and ye have two of them. Ye held your sons before their first breath. The curse is broken. The lass did it. She did it!"

His heart swelled with more love than he had ever felt. He scooped both babies up to bring them to their mother . . . and that's when he noticed she wasn't awake.

She was sleeping.

"Clara?"

Instantly, Nana was at her side. "Clara?" She shook his wife, but Clara did not stir.

"Clara!" he raged.

Two maids quickly came forward to relieve him of his sons and he rushed to her side as Nana and another servant examined her below.

"She's bleedin'," Nana proclaimed, fear tight in her voice. "Tae much blood!"

He plucked up Clara's limp hand and pressed his lips to it, understanding. This was the curse. Losing her. It was worse than his own death. This loss he could not overcome.

"Clara, Clara, Clara." Her name rolled from his lips in a desolate litany. "Stay with me. You promised. You said you would stay, damn you! Stay. I love you. Dinna leave me."

STAY. YOU SAID ye would stay . . . I love you . . .

Clara sucked in a pained breath as though someone had given her a great push and demanded she breathe. The air felt like marbles going down, but she dragged it in and filled her lungs.

She opened her eyes to fog. She shut her eyes, waited a moment and then tried again. This time she saw light. Fuzzy shapes. She blinked several times, gradually clearing her vision, focusing on the head resting on her chest. She lifted a hand weakly and ran her fingers through the familiar brown strands.

She knew that hair. *Hunt.*

Her chest felt wet . . . and his head was moving against her like . . . was he crying?

"Hunt?"

His head shot up off her, eyes red-rimmed and tear-filled, blood crusting along his hairline. "Clara! You're . . . alive."

"Of course I am." She frowned and then winced at the sudden pinch of pain between her thighs. She glanced down to see Nana and the other midwife working there.

Nana sent her a reassuring nod. "Everything is going tae be fine, lass. We've stopped the worst of the bleeding. It was a mite scary there for a moment."

"Was it?" she murmured, not remembering anything. Gasping, her hand flew to her stomach. "The baby?"

"Babies," Hunt corrected, grinning widely. Turning, he motioned with his hand and Marian and a maid appeared, each one placing a blue-eyed, cooing infant on either side of Clara. Beautiful blue eyes as remarkable as their father's, but each babe had a shock of dark hair to match her own.

"Your sons," Marian exclaimed, happy tears tracking down her cheeks.

"Sons?" Clara marveled, her heart overflowing as she looked from each perfect little baby to her husband. "Two sons, Hunt?"

"Aye, my love. You did it. Gave me two sons born in the caul. I held them in my arms before their first breaths. We broke the curse. You did. We're no longer cursed. We're blessed." He gave her a lingering kiss. "You did it. You gave me this gift."

"No." She shook her head. "We did it."

Epilogue

Three months later

"Twins," Nana announced—not for the first time since the babies' births months ago. "They run in yer family, I see." She eyed Clara's screeching siblings as they tore across the garden.

It was a beautiful day. One of the last of the summer. Fall was already in the air, a windy nip that hinted at the winter to come.

"Yes," Clara replied cheerfully.

"Fortunate for us." Nana lifted her teacup to her lips. "Perhaps you will have another pair before long."

Clara choked on a laugh and averted her face

so that Nana could not see her roll her eyes. She met Hunt's gaze and they exchanged a conspiratorial grin.

"Nana," Hunt chided. "We are no' speaking of shoes here. The babies are only three months old. Must you already be planning for more? Can we no' simply enjoy our blessings?"

"Aye. I must. The curse is broken and for the first time in five generations we can look tae the future. I intend tae do just that, and that means populating our clan with several of yer bairns."

A happy shriek drew Clara's attention away from Nana.

Mama and Colin had forgotten all about the refreshments and joined the children in their vigorous game of chase about the lawn.

Her mother hardly looked like a grandmother as she lifted her skirts and raced across the grass, exposing her slender ankles to the world. Her dark hair gleamed with vitality, as did her dark eyes. Her cheeks were flushed with fine health and color as she scooped up her son and whirled him in the air.

Mama's handsome husband was treating their daughter similarly, pinning her to the grass and tickling her into fits of laughter.

They'd arrived shortly after Clara gave birth to the babies, staying a few weeks with Clara, and then with her brother and Alyse, and now again with Clara.

Clara was immensely enjoying their visit and in no hurry to see them depart for their home. In addition to a carriage full of gifts, they had come bearing the most delicious news of Clara's former fiancé.

She was not usually one to relish in gossip, but this tittle-tattle was most satisfying. The Earl of Rolland had affianced himself to a very eligible young lady from one of the finest families in England. Clara had snorted at that, immediately pitying the unknown girl. Mama had contin- ued, imparting with glee that shortly after their marriage, Rolland's wife ran away with the local blacksmith to the Continent.

Currently Rolland was holed up at his estate, hiding from Society and the shame of being abandoned. Clara couldn't help feeling inordi- nately pleased that he had no wife to abuse and crush beneath his boot. Things had a way of working out for the best.

"They are . . . noisy," Nana remarked, nodding toward her family.

"Indeed, they are." Clara smiled fondly at her family as she repositioned one of the babies on her shoulder to gently pat his back.

Hunt held their other son, looking utterly besotted with him as he rubbed his small back in smooth circles with his large hand. Of course, that was his customary expression when he held either one of their children.

That besotted expression did not alter much when he looked at her either—except there was a decided amount of lasciviousness when he gazed at her. It did things to her, that look. Heated her blood. Squeezed her heart. Convinced her of love and goodness and all things wonderful. It affirmed the beauty of her life.

Suddenly Marian was there, rushing across the lawn without her usual composure, her face distraught and her voice strained as she called out to Clara.

She frowned. "Marian? Is something amiss?"

Marian held a crumpled bit of parchment in one hand and lifted her skirts up with the other as she hastened over the lawn. Her pretty face looked bloodless, her eyes wide and haunted. Nothing about this sight of her boded well. For once, Clara's usually garrulous friend struggled for words.

Still holding her baby, Clara rose to her feet. "What is it, Marian? What is wrong?"

Marian's slim throat worked as she gulped a breath. "Something has happened. There has been an . . . accident."

Clara quickly transferred her son to Nana's ready arms and turned back to her friend. She reached out to clasp Marian's hands in her own. "What can we do? Tell me. We shall help."

Marian shook her head, a strangled sob breaking free, shattering the last of her composure. "You cannot help. I wish you could. I have to leave. I have to go home. At once. Before it's too late."

The next scintillating novel in Sophie Jordan's
bestselling Rogue Files series, Marian's story,

The Duke's Stolen Bride

goes on sale October 2019!